# PREPARED FOR MURDER

# THE BEELER LARGE PRINT MYSTERY SERIES

Edited by Audrey A. Lesko

# PREPARED FOR MURDER

## CECILE LAMALLE

URBANA FREE LIBRARY

BEELER LARGE PRINT
Hampton Falls, New Hampshire, 2002

**Library of Congress Cataloging-in-Publication Data**

Lamalle, Cecile
  Prepared for Murder / Cecile Lamalle
p.      cm.—(The Beeler Large Print mystery series)
ISBN 1-57490-389-6 (alk. paper)

Library of Congress Cataloging-in-Publication Data was not available at the time of publication.

Libraries should call  (800) 818-7574 and we will fax or mail the CIP Data upon request.

Published in Large Print by arrangement with
Warner Books, Inc.

BEELER LARGE PRINT
is published by
Thomas T. Beeler, Publisher
Post Office Box 659
Hampton Falls, New Hampshire 03844

Typeset in 16 point Times New Roman type.
Printed on acid-free paper, sewn and bound by
Sheridan Books in Chelsea, Michigan.

"I have known more murderers than most people, and in my recollection they have been devoid of the characteristics they are commonly credited with, and quite ordinary individuals such as you or me. So ordinarily, indeed, that sometimes when I have watched them going to execution I have been inspired to echo the famous words uttered on a similar occasion by the sixteenth-century divine, John Bradford, and say, 'But for the grace of God there goes Sydney Smith.' "

from *Mostly Murder* by Sir Sydney Smith,
Emeritus Professor of Forensic Medicine,
Edinburgh University

# PREPARED FOR MURDER

# PROLOGUE

(from a newspaper article, date unknown.)

### FORMER FDA INSPECTOR SENTENCED IN
### SEAFOOD SCANDAL

*PERTH AMBOY, N.J.—A FORMER INSPECTOR FOR THE U.S. Food and Drug Administration was sentenced to six years in prison for bribing FDA workers to allow tons of contaminated and rotten seafood into the country. Arthur Arpati was ordered to pay a fine of $15,000 by U.S. District Judge Robert M. Smith, who said that Arpati's crimes put the public's health at risk and denigrated the reputation of a government agency. Arpati was also convicted of accepting bribes and illegally reimporting 200 cartons of seafood that had been condemned because of high bacterial content. Instead of being destroyed, the cartons were shipped to Mexico where they were disinfected, then repacked and labeled "Product of Mexico." FDA officials said they had initiated safeguards to prevent such crimes from happening again. In an interview Judge Robert M. Smith said, "This is but the tip of the iceberg. We know that Arpati was not working alone."*

# CHARLY DETECTS A PATCH OF NETTLES

CHARLY POISSON, CHEF AND OWNER OF LA FERMETTE, the finest French restaurant in Van Buren County, (well, the *only* French restaurant in the upstate New York county) loved prowling his fields on an early May morning. Seven o'clock, the air was crisp, the sun already high, a thousand birds sang, and the scent of elderflower and wild cherry was strong in his nose. He tramped through wild garlic-mustard, dandelions, milkweed, buttercups, dozens of other wild plants, on his way to a stand of young nettles, the finest spring tonic one could ask for.

Bruno, of course, ran ahead. Dogs did that. Charly, well-bundled up against *les courants d'air,* the drafts that French people know cause illness, swung his canvas shopping bag as he strode through the weeds in heavy rubber boots. In his bag were a paring knife—in case any morels were about—scissors, plastic bags, rubber gloves. Even young nettles gave a nasty sting. But steamed in their washing water and chopped with butter, sea salt, and freshly ground pepper, they were sublime. Every year, Charly waited for the nettles.

*Maybe if there are enough, I make a nice soup with shallots,* Charly mused, stroking his pencil mustache. *Good filling for an omelette, too. And good on top of baked potato. The liquid I will drink, for it purifies the blood and aids in the circulation.*

Charly came from solid French peasant stock, and the peasant set great store by the nettle. Rolling naked in a bed of nettles was meant to increase men's virility and

2

alleviate rheumatism. This, Charly felt, was going too far.

Charly was happy. He sang. That is, he hummed, and said "la-la-la" when he couldn't remember the words. A song of his father's, back in the Jura Mountains in France, something about "*au temps des cerises.*" Well, it was cherry blossom time, so the song was appropriate.

"Not too fast now, Bruno," Charly called. "*Pas si vite.*" Bruno, a hundred-pound cross between a black Labrador and a Bernese mountain dog, had become bilingual since joining Charly's four-cat household last February, and a strong bond had formed between dog and new master. Bruno stopped, panting happily, waited for Charly to catch up, then took off again.

"Bruno, *viens ici*" Charly called. Bruno turned and trotted back. "Sit, *s'il vous plait.*" Bruno sat. Charly had just spied a small patch of nettles. He put on his rubber gloves, cut the shoots, and placed them in a plastic bag.

Soon they set off again. Charly detoured into a copse of old apple trees, many fallen and turning to the rich humus that was so good for Charly's garden. He peered around and sighed. No morels. Once he'd found fifty-one morels in this very spot, but the elusive fungi never returned.

*Ah, voilà.* The big patch of nettles that he remembered from years past. A magnificent stand. Charly pulled down his jacket sleeves to cover his wrists and pulled on the rubber gloves once again. Nettles stung as badly as bees, and though fresh dock leaves, rubbed on the stings, were meant to help, they were never around. *Urtica Urens,* homeopathic extract of nettle, was also an antidote, but by the time Charly got home and unearthed the bottle, the pains were unbearable. The microscopic hairs got into your skin

3

and itched furiously. No wonder people rolled in nettle beds for their rheumatism. The pain of the nettles was so great that you forgot about your other pains.

Charly snipped and snipped. One bag filled, then another, and yet another. The shoots were pale green and tender, and scissors released their perfume, like no other scent on earth, except, possibly, the old Balmain perfume Vent Vert that French ladies used to dab behind their ears. In another week the nettles would be too tough for steaming. Then, Charly would cut them for drying, to make nettle tea, which was good for arthritis, clearing mucus from the lungs, cleansing the bladder. Being alkaline, the nettle aids in the removal of uric acid. Charly also threw nettles on his compost heap, to enrich it, and set nettle plants among his culinary herbs, which increased their volatile oils. No wonder Maurice Messegué, the great French herbalist, called nettles one of the most valuable of plants.

"Come, Bruno, I have *une surprise.*" Charly had worn his rubber boots because he'd planned to take Bruno swimming in the little pond near County Route 16. The pond, fed by a natural spring, was deep enough for a dog to paddle in. Bruno hurried to the edge of the water.

The dog stood at the edge of the pond and froze. He refused to enter the water. The hairs on his back stood on end, and he growled. *Perhaps the water is too cold?* Charly wondered. Bruno was trembling, pointing his nose, and staring at an old bundle of clothing at the edge of the water.

*Now, isn't that disgusting,* Charly thought. People throwing their garbage in the water. A piece of meat was floating near the clothes. Charly bent down and peered, then jumped back as he got hit in the face with a violent stench. The meat looked like a gnawed, rotted

4

human hand. The pile of old clothing, he now saw, was a body. As Bruno churned the water at the edge of the pond with his paws the body shifted, turned slightly, and Charly stared down at the putrefied remains of a head.

The head was grey, spongy, and partially shredded and gnawed. It certainly didn't look human. There was no nose, only a knob of cartilage, and the eyes were long gone, the sockets filled with mud. Bruno kept up a steady growling as he backed away from the corpse. Charly retreated, too, feeling faint and nauseated.

"Come, Bruno. We go home, now."

Charly's first thought was, *Stark will not believe . . .* because Charly had a knack for finding bodies. He'd found one in his downstairs freezer last winter, and he'd found the body of a woman very near here, last fall. Several years ago he'd found the body of a hunter in his fields. He almost smiled as he thought of his friend John Stark, the chief of police of Klover, New York. "Good Lord, Charly, not another one," Stark would undoubtedly say.

*Is special gift that I have,* thought Charly. Perhaps he'd been an executioner in a previous incarnation, and his victims were returning to haunt him. Anything in this strange, cruel, and unpredictable world was possible.

# SATURDAY LUNCH AT LA FERMETTE

"GOOD LORD, CHARLY, NOT ANOTHER ONE," CHIEF OF Police John Stark said.

"But yes, is true." Charly replied. He'd telephoned the police station as soon as he'd returned home.

5

"I'll be out there in a few minutes. You'll wait for me at your house?"

"In the restaurant kitchen, if you please," Charly said. Stark's "few minutes" were sometimes a few hours. The Klover Police Station was perennially understaffed and overworked.

Charly sat at his kitchen counter and finished his chamomile tea laced with Dr. Bach's Rescue Remedy—for emotional stress. Charly didn't trust doctors, but he was a great believer in the gentle homeopathic medications, and kept a full supply on hand. The body had shocked him badly. He'd stashed the nettles in his refrigerator, to prepare at a later time. He called Bruno, checked on his cats, Frère, Marcelle, Tin-Tin and Suzanne, (all outside, normal for a spring morning) and walked the two hundred yards to the kitchen of La Fermette.

Benny Perkins, Charly's young sous-chef, was washing leeks and Joe Okun, Charly's dishwasher, was changing the oil in the deep fat fryer. "Morning, Charly," both men called as they heard the back door slam shut. Bruno hurried over to Joe. "Morning, Bruno," Joe said. "Hey, Charly, the dog's looking funny. What happened?" Joe, part Passamaquoddy Indian, originally from Maine, claimed that he could communicate with animals. This might be true. Bruno certainly adored him.

"We're running out of leeks, onions, carrots." Benny told Charly. Then he looked down at the dog. "Hey, Bruno, fella. You okay? Joe's right, Charly. Dog's got his tail down, and he's got a funny look on his face." Joe was teaching Benny the secrets of animal behavior.

Charly nodded. "No, Bruno is not himself. We walk through my fields this morning, looking for *les orties,*

6

the nettle, and we find a body in the pond. Chief Stark will be here soon, I call him."

Benny put down his knife and stared, openmouthed, at his boss. Joe Okun wiped his hands on his apron, and said, "Oh, boy. Here we go."

"Benny, close your mouth," Charly said. "Flies will go in. Is true. We find a body. Is old body, and it smell bad. I take Bruno for a swim, but he will not go in the water. At first, I think I see a pile of old clothes. But"— Charly shrugged—"is not old clothes. Is body."

Joe said, "You think you been put on this earth to find dead bodies? You sure got the knack."

"Is possible," Charly replied. "I think the body was left there months ago, before winter when the pond freeze over. Whoever dump the body think it will sink into the mud and be lost forever. They do not know this pond dry up in summer. But the body is old, very old."

"Body's been there over the winter, I'm pretty sure," Stark said sometime later. He, Charly, and Will Hackett, the young officer who had replaced the retired Clem Hughes, stood at the edge of the pond. "Doc Bingham's coming over. We'll get the body to the morgue, so there's no need for you to stick around, Charly. I know you're busy. This'll take a while."

For once, Charly took the hint. "I go now, Chief Stark."

Stark watched the little man step carefully over the rough ground of the field. "Damn fella, finds bodies everywhere," he told Hackett.

"It's his land?" the young officer asked.

"Owns all this side of the road, and then some. Has over a hundred acres." Stark looked across the field, where Charly was making his way back to the restaurant. "I think

7

he's got a lot of cash stashed away, but he's a nice guy, not like most rich folks. He was real good to Mick Hitchens, his old dishwasher, adopted Mick's dog. The old man died of heart failure last winter. He's good to all his help. Good restaurant, you been there?"

"Only for lunch," Hackett told his chief. "You said he's found other bodies? Like, recent?"

Stark told the young officer about the woman last fall, and about the body in Charly's refrigerator. "There was another case last winter," Stark continued. "The bodies of two men, looked like they'd had a shoot-out, man named Kendell and another one called Winlove. Funny scene—looked staged. I always thought Charly had a hand in that business."

"You mean," Hackett said, "you think Charly shot them?"

"No. He's not a shooter. But—I don't know. Hey, he's a businessman. I think he did something to protect one of his customers, a gangster from across the river. We had the bloodstains tested, there was Winlove's blood and two other blood types, not the other guy at the scene, Kendell. Kendell was shot after he died, it turned out, and he died a natural death, from heart failure. Doc Soames, the cardiologist, said his heart was real bad. We never found out who the other blood belonged to."

"You bring Charly in?"

"Nope," Stark said. "Never said anything, either. But Bob McKinnon, you know, chief across the river, says that the man, Buonsarde, his two bodyguards went missing, and he's got two new ones. And Winlove bought antiques for this guy, and I'll bet he tried to cheat 'em. So, you put two and two together, but what're you going to do about it?"

"Why go looking for trouble, right, Chief?"

"That's right, son," Stark told the young cop. "You see a lotta stuff, you take note, and then you turn your back. Everything works out sooner or later. You know the biggest thing you gotta have on this job?"

"Courage?"

"Well, I suppose. But I was going to say, patience. You know a man's guilty, you know he did it, but you have no proof. So you wait, and sooner or later, he'll shoot himself in the foot. I tell you, it never fails. Sooner or later."

Will Hackett scratched his head. "But the waitin'. Doesn't that bug you? Knowing some creep's walking around free, and he should be in jail?"

"You don't have time to think about it," Stark said. "This job'll run you ragged, one incident after another, you don't have time to sit and analyze. Just be patient. We'll find out who this poor sucker is, and why he was killed. It will all come out. Sooner or later."

The young cop shook his head. "Sooner or later," he muttered. Maybe he could go to the morgue, the basement of the local hospital, watch Doc Bingham go through the man's pockets. Maybe he could identify the man. Boy, wouldn't that be something. "Good job, son," Chief Stark would say.

The Saturday lunch crowd in the barroom at La Fermette was different from the weekday customers. During the week the restaurant catered to the electricians, plumbers, construction men, as well as the few doctors and lawyers and office workers who had time to drive the three miles out to Klover from the city of Hogton. They came on the dot of noon, ate quickly, and were out like a shot. But Saturday brought a more diverse, leisurely group—more women, businessmen freed from their offices, weekenders from New York, more local cops and state police, who knew Charly gave a substantial discount to law-enforcement personnel.

Today's specials were local shad roes with bacon on sourdough bread, roast-beef hash, creamed chicken on penne pasta. When the orders were all out in the dining room and customers were eating dessert Charly wandered out into the barroom to greet his friends.

"I hope," said Win Crozier, sipping his coffee, "that you're catering Honoria's cocktail party, this evening." Win and his companion, Morty Cohen, owned the Paint Barrel, in Hogton, which sold paint, wallpaper, and supplies needed in interior decoration.

"*Oui, certainement.* Max and Fred and Patty work all morning on the party, and will work all afternoon. Very nice food."

Charly smiled at Win and Morty, and nodded to their guest, a tall, thin, aristocratic-looking stranger with salt-and-pepper hair and a frightened-rabbit look about him. In his thirties, Charly guessed, with prematurely greying hair. Win performed introductions. "Everston Pilchard, Charly Poisson." Charly bowed, Everston gave a watery smile. His voice was soft, with the hint of an English accent: "Very decent corned beef hash, sir. I look forward to the food at Honoria's."

"It is rosbif hash, *Une specialté de la maison,*" Charly said. "Are you a visitor in these parts?" Who could confuse corned beef hash with Charly's celebrated roast-beef hash? Charly pursed his lips.

"Everston lives near the Massachusetts border, about half an hour's drive, just beyond Highdale," Morty said. "He teaches English at The Brooke School. He's here for the day. We'll all go to Honoria's together."

"You know Madame Wells a long time?" Charly

10

questioned. He liked to place people, and he hadn't quite gotten Pilchard's wavelength. A nice-looking man, properly dressed in a good, worn tweed jacket, but he wore a furtive air. Charly decided that he didn't like Mr. Pilchard. Imagine confusing Charly's world-class roast-beef hash with corned beef, an inferior meat. Win and Morty were certainly *sympathique,* and they paid proper homage to Charly's fine cuisine, but they did have peculiar friends.

"Honoria and my mother went to school together," Pilchard said.

"Ah, friend of family."

"Precisely," Everston said in his clipped and slightly prissy voice.

Charly offered herbal infusions and desserts on the house to two of his most loyal customers and their friend. As he left their table, he overheard Morty say, "Don't be so afraid, Evvie. Everything will work out."

Back in the kitchen Julius was eating the remains of the roast-beef hash and Benny's nose was in a bowl of penne topped with parsley, chopped garlic, and olive oil. Fred Deering and Max Helder were working with Patty Perkins, Charly's dessert chef and recently promoted catering manager (and Benny's mother) in the dessert room, and Joe Okun was loading the dishwasher. Julius, a stockbroker who'd wanted to gain experience in running a country inn, was a wealthy man, but he wore his affluence modestly. He loved working in Charly's kitchen.

"You tell everyone about the body you found?" Julius asked Charly.

"*Non.* It would do no good to La Fermette, for me to

11

always find the body. We say nothing, eh? Benny, Max, Fred, Joe, you hear? Nothing."

"You got it, Charly, yeah, sure, nothing." Everyone agreed.

"No more playing detective, it is infantile," Charly said.

# MAURICE BALEINE ARRIVES WITH NEWS

THERE WAS A RAP AT LA FERMETTE'S KITCHEN DOOR and Maurice Baleine strode in. In his well-tailored tweed jacket, smelling of designer aftershave, with his beautiful teeth, plump Maurice looked the picture of prosperity. Charly had inherited Maurice when his partner, the senior Maurice, died and left his shares in the New York restaurant to his son. When Charly moved La Fermette to Van Buren County, Maurice dragged along as well, complaining that country life was too uncivilized for a Princeton man. But he'd married well. Barbara De Groot came from a good family and enjoyed a prosperous career as an interior decorator. La Fermette was one of her designing successes.

Last February Charly bought Maurice's restaurant shares. Maurice had done nothing for years but drink the restaurant's liquor, yet he expected half the profits. And yet . . . Maurice could have been a wonderful partner. He was cheerful, he made a good impression, and he could discuss the finer points of French cuisine in a way that whetted your appetite. In short, he could have been a real partner. Sadly, his ego, his snobbishness, and his liking for liquor had gotten in the way. Charly still hoped that one day Maurice might change. It hadn't happened yet, but there was always hope.

"Allo, Maurice, 'ow are you?" Charly said, not cordially.

"Ah, Charles, my friend, I have a marvelous proposition for you." Maurice ignored the rest of the kitchen staff, though he nodded to Julius.

Maurice was wary of Julius, not knowing exactly what social class Julius belonged to, very important for a Princeton man like Maurice to know. Julius had a rich aunt, Honoria Wells, he'd been a stockbroker, but where had he gone to college? (Julius, refusing to tell, said that he'd been educated in the school of life.)

"Excellent, Maurice." Last winter Maurice had lost most of his savings investing in a dodgy company. Charly waited for the magic words. They came.

"It's the investment of a lifetime," Maurice said, right on cue.

"*Sans aucune doute.* And it will make my fortune, eh?"

"Listen, Charly, this is a serious business."

"Tell me." Charly looked dubiously at his former partner.

"Fabulous Foods. I'm sure you've heard of it."

"No, Maurice, I have not."

"They're the most exclusive prepared-food company in the country."

"*Tiens.* Imagine that. What do they make?"

"Mainly seafood entrées. Shrimp dishes, fish fillets stuffed with crabmeat, oh, I can't remember. They'd been operating out of a factory in New Jersey, but they wanted to expand. So they bought some property north of here and turned it into a food-preparation facility. They've been up there for three months. Absolutely gorgeous. State-of-the-art."

"Ah. Staidoff Hart. I am impress." Charly had heard the words "state-of-the-art" many times but he always assumed it was the name of a company, Staidoff Hart. Whenever anyone wanted to *epater les bourgeois,* impress the good burghers, they called something Staidoff Hart. Charly took care never to use the noxious phrase. "And they are looking for investors, am I correct?"

Maurice drew himself up, puffing out his chest importantly. "They want to invite you to become a shareholder."

"I am flattered," Charly said. "Give me the names of the principals."

"I'll give you more than that," Maurice said proudly, and, with a flourish, he presented Charly with a heavy, cream-colored envelope. Charly opened the envelope and withdrew a card:

*Fabulous Foods requests the pleasure of your company at a reception and food tasting at their state-of-the-art-facility on May 11, from three to six P.M. Route 33, Sharpsville, New York.*

"Look, Julius, Benny, you see this?" Charly held out the card. "Beautiful paper," he said. "But, Maurice, it does not answer my question. Who are the owners of this company?"

"The owners are Martin Scungilli and Richard Zampone."

"I see," Charly said. The names, for some reason, sounded vaguely familiar. "And where do you meet these gentlemen?"

"Oh, contacts," Maurice said airily. "I met them in New York, and we got to talking. They used to know someone in Klover, I don't know who."

Maurice knew a few dubious characters. Charly

could imagine the scene. Maurice, showing off as usual, pretending to be a millionaire, bragging about his "estate" in the country, impressing the wrong people.

"Who do they sell to?" Charly asked.

"Here's some merchandising stuff," Maurice said, ignoring Charly's question. He presented tearsheets showing vividly colored entrées. Each sheet was emblazoned with the logo, Fabulous Foods.

"Maurice, who do they sell to?"

"Oh, clubs and hotels and cruise lines, I imagine."

"And you think that I, Charles Poisson, want to mix myself with *produits congelés,* the prepared food from the freezer?"

Julius and Benny strolled over. Julius plucked a sheet from Charly's hand. "Look, Benny. Creamed shrimp and a tomato rose. And a little lobster tail topped with a fluted mushroom. Isn't that elegant."

"Yeah, I guess," Benny said. "Wonder what it tastes like?"

"Not bad at all," Maurice said. "Why don't you all come up and see? It's day after tomorrow and the restaurant is closed. Besides"—Maurice paused, obviously pulling out his trump card—"the owners have dined here at La Fermette. They think you're the best chef in the world, Charly."

"Are you certain of this fact, Maurice? When do they come?"

"I haven't the least idea."

"Are you investing money in this operation, Maurice?"

"Yes, Charly, I am. Barbara said she might put in some money, too."

"I see," Charly said. "And it is in Sharpsville, just up

15

the road. Well, perhaps we go up, just to see. Julius, Benny, are you interested?"

Julius and Benny said sure, why not?

"And Joe? You want to come, see Staidoff Hart kitchen?"

Maurice winced, but he needn't have worried at having a mere dishwasher as guest.

"I 'spect not," Joe Okun said. "I don't mess with no sharpies from Sharpsville."

# HONORIA WELLS GIVES A PARTY

"SON OF A GUN," JULIUS CROWED AS THE BACK DOOR slammed shut. "Maurice has done it again. Going to lose the money he's got left."

"*Mais bien sûr*" Charly sighed. "That is Maurice's role in life, just like his poor father. Always making the bad investment. One fine day he will go too far, I promise you. To invest in an unknown company— stupid, stupid."

"You're not putting any money in, are you, Charly?" Benny asked anxiously. Charly clapped his sous-chef on the shoulder.

"*Non,* of course not, Benny. But we will go up on Monday. I am curious. Are you not? Perhaps you can recognize the men who ate here."

Patty appeared from the door of the dessert room. "I heard that. Maybe I'll come, too. But, listen, Max and Fred are ready to load the van for Honoria's. Are you going to check things off, Charly?"

"*Oui.* Let me get my list from the office."

La Fermette did a good business in private parties, and now that Patty Perkins was catering manager they were busy almost every weekend. Fred Deering and Max Helder, Benny's sparring partners at Tae Kwon Do, the martial-arts classes that Charly paid for, were lunchtime cooks at a nearby private day school and had become part of the permanent staff. They prepared the extra dishes that Charly sold, fresh and frozen, as takeout, and on weekends they prepared the food for cocktail and dinner parties.

Max Helder was short and muscular, built like a wrestler, with shiny, straight black hair. Fred Deering had the tall, supple body of a dancer, with shoulder-length hair so blond it was almost white. Max and Fred shared an apartment in Hogton, and Charly assumed they were a gay couple, but with his French reticence he did not pry.

Charly stood at the entrance to the dessert room, list in hand. "Hokay. Asparagus, herb mayonnaise. The asparagus, she is crisp?" Charly reached over and took a stalk, which he bit into. "Excellent." He dipped a finger into the bowl of mayonnaise and tasted. "Perfect." He continued to sample the remainder of the menu, the salmon roses with sorrel cream; seafood terrine; miniature meatballs with spicy tomato sauce; pâté de campagne with Riviera toast; shrimp with dill sauce. "Not bad at all," Charly concluded.

"None of the really fancy stuff," Fred pointed out. "The caviar and the filet mignon. Remember Walter Maxwell and his kilos of caviar?"

"Madame Wells is careful with her money, and I approve of that," Charly said. "Besides, she has had money all her life, so she has no need to show off. She has plenty of food for forty people, and it is good food, too."

"She hire that party firm to serve?" Max asked.

"They cost too much," Julius said from the doorway. "She'll have Juanito and Estrella, her maid and butler, and Tiger Cavett. She's promoted him to farm manager. And Patty's staying in the kitchen."

"Harry Clark has never been seen again?" Charly asked. Honoria's dalliance with her former farm manager had ended badly, to say the least.

"I hear he left town," Julius said. "And good riddance."

*"Alors, en route,"* Charly cried, and they all carried containers out to Charly's little red van. Charly was certain that the party would go well, but he always worried and, being superstitious, he hoped finding the dead body was not an omen of bad things to come. He couldn't stop thinking about that mass of rags and decayed flesh. What a horrible ending to a life.

Honoria Wells's ancestors, textile mill owners, had lived in Van Buren County since 1830, and Honoria was accepted by the population as being "one of us" despite her money and her wild ways. She was generous. She'd built a day-care facility, helped found the unwed mothers' center, refurbished a home for battered women, sent checks to families whose houses had burned—in short, she was a respected and generous presence in the town.

So it was a monstrous travesty of justice—one of those miscarriages on which the American judicial system appears to flourish—when Harry Clark had been declared "not guilty" of trying to murder his former employer.

Harry Clark had been Honoria's farm manager and twenty-five years her junior. Last year she'd formed an alliance with him (or, more bluntly, she'd bedded him). Harry tried to kill Honoria by bashing her on the head

18

and then throwing her over a waterfall into the pond below, believing, rightly, that Honoria had left him some money in a will which she was about to change, as the relationship soured.

Harry's clever lawyer made much of Honoria's wealth and her previous affairs with younger men. He also had Harry appear in court in a black suit, Bible in hand, claiming that Jesus had saved him from a lecherous old sinner who'd tried to get him drunk, then fallen, besotted by liquor herself, into the woodland pool and hurt her head on the rocks.

"She never should have lost her temper in front of the judge and called Harry and his lawyer lowlife white trash," Julius, who had sat in on the trial, told Charly. "Trust my aunt to shoot herself in the foot. Some local folks on the jury identified with Harry. He said Satan tempted him to crawl into an old woman's bed but Jesus pulled him out. Most revolting thing you've ever seen. Took them a half hour to declare Harry not guilty."

"Harry will be punished, *le bon Dieu* will see to that," Charly had replied, a prophetic utterance as it turned out.

Now, at five o'clock Saturday evening, guests due soon, Honoria stood in her front hall, an older woman dressed in a floor-length beige-silk crepe dress, (a little Armani number, very simple), jonquil blond hair pulled back in a tasteful chignon. She was as skinny as a teenager, with a long, horsy, handsome face suspiciously unwrinkled. At her neck were several strands of chunky turquoise nuggets, and she wore a bulky silk knit cardigan, sleeves rolled up, which matched her dress and gave her a sporty air.

"Charly, everything looks smashing," she said.

19

"Tastes good too, I tried everything." Honoria could have passed for forty in a dark room.

Charly bowed. "I hope so, madame." He and Julius smiled at Honoria.

"You'll come back for the party, Charly?"

"If I can," Charly promised. "It is a quiet evening. Max and Fred will help Benny, and Julius, he will not stay here all evening."

"Julius hates cocktail parties, I'll bet he stays fifteen minutes, no longer," Honoria said. "I just want him to meet everyone, that's all. He's the only family I have left and"—poking Julius in the ribs—"I'm proud of this baby."

"Hey, for calling me a baby, I'll stay all night," Julius joked. His frizzy golden hair was receding more and more: he looked like an aging archangel. He put his arms around Honoria and hugged her. "My Tante Miel," he said, "*miel*" being the French word for honey, and Honoria's nickname was "Honny." "You're the only family I have left too, so you'd better behave."

"No one to misbehave with," Honoria pointed out glumly. Charly noted, sadly, that Honoria was indeed beginning to fade. The Harry Clark affair had taken a lot out of her, and, worst of all, she'd felt betrayed by the townspeople she'd supported all these years.

Back in La Fermette's kitchen, hardly state-of-the-art but plain, orderly, and scrupulously clean, Charly, Fred, Max, and Benny continued the preparations for dinner. The twenty reservations indicated a modest group. Many of Charly's Saturday night regulars would be at Honoria's party. Tommy Glade, the barman, would take Patty's job as host and seat the customers, and now, half past five, he dashed into the kitchen to grab a sandwich. Charly had had his doubts about hiring Tommy, a recent graduate of

20

Alcoholics Anonymous, but Tommy stuck to his resolution and proved a versatile employee, being barman, waiter, host, and even, on one or two occasions, bouncer.

"Party look okay, Charly?"

"Yes, beautiful as always with Madame Honoria. But, Tommy, she is not happy. She is still frightened that Harry Clark will return, I am convince."

"Oh, he's long gone, Charly. He won his case, but no one would have anything to do with him; even his buddies turned against him. And I hear he never finished paying his lawyer, who was smart and got most of his money up front. Most, but not all."

Julius came in. "Why don't you go on over, Charly," he said.

"I will, Julius, as soon as the first group of customer are seated. Now, everything is in order, yes? The roast duckling with the new peas, the asparagus mousseline, the pasta with asparagus and morel, the filet en croûte, the salmon with new potatoes and dill, the steak Marchand de Vin." As he spoke, Charly opened ovens and warmers and checked ingredients. "And there is enough new potatoes to offer them as another vegetarian entree, with asparagus and wild mushroom, just like the pasta," he noted. More and more customers were asking for vegetable entrées.

"Yes, yes, Charly, everything's okay, I promise you," Julius said. "When you do get to Honoria's be sure to greet Billy and Midge Warburton. They asked about you, especially."

"They rarely come to La Fermette to dine. They used to come with Walter Maxwell."

"Well, I was talking to them, and they're awfully nice people. I think they just don't like to eat out. They were saying how badly Honoria's trial had gone. Harry Clark used to work for them, you know."

21

"Why did he leave?" Charly asked, ever curious.

"Oh, I'm sure they fired him for doing something awful."

Charly went to his office and removed his white jacket and apron. He put on his blue blazer, and adjusted his spring-weight beret on his head. He took down his bottle of Dr. Bach's remedies and dropped some in his mouth, so that he would appear composed. He strolled back into the kitchen.

"They're awfully worried about their old cat," Julius told Charly.

"Who is worried about what old cat?"

"The Warburtons," Julius said. "Remember, I was telling you to be sure and greet them? They heard, possibly from Walter Maxwell, about your homeopathic pills, and how you dose your animals with them. Maybe you can give them some tips."

"Animals respond very well to homeopathic treatment," said Charly. "But not even homeopathy can keep an old person, or an old cat, from dying. We live, and then we die. Is what happens."

# CHARLY MAKES NEW FRIENDS

CHARLY DROVE TO WELLS FARM. HE PASSED THE stone gatehouse that Honoria had given Julius Prendergast, her nephew, noting that the wooden window frames were newly painted and the slate roof mended. Farther along, more than two dozen cars were parked at the sides of the wide gravel driveway. In the sprawling, grey-shingle-and-stone house, built by Honoria's grandparents, every window was lit. Charly had always thought the house ungainly, with its boxy additions and clumsy proportions, but tonight it looked graceful and welcoming in the soft May dusk.

The yellow front door was opened by Estrella, Honoria's maid, who wished Charly *"Buenas tardes, señor,"* and ushered him into the living room roiling with people. Charly could smell Honoria's "Cypres" Rigaud candles above the cigarette smoke and the aromas of food. He stood in the doorway, a small, compact man in nondescript clothing, peering intently at the crowd. There were the Vanns, Dinah and Peter, trying (and failing) to look like landed gentry. Why must Dinah wear so many rubies? She looked like a Tiffany Christmas tree. Tweedy Emelie and Michael Crisp, loyal customers of La Fermette, were deep in conversation with old Mrs. Collins, who drank straight bourbon and never missed a party; Billy and Midge Warburton, the people with the horse farm who'd asked Julius to have Charly speak to them, were picking delicately at almost-empty plates. They were both so thin, they looked like they rarely ate anything at all. The lawyer Jonathan Murray was chatting with Jimmy Houghton, the investment adviser, and old Evelyn Holmes, Jimmy's office manager, who looked like a benevolent praying mantis, was aglow in emerald silk. Everyone was smiling and chatting, sipping and nibbling. Honoria stood laughing with Father Evangelista; old Doc Ross, white hair carefully brushed back, sat at a side table, eating from a plate piled high with meatballs. Win Crozier, Morty Cohen and the Pilchard fellow were talking to Maurice and Barbara Baleine who stood, arms entwined, like the happiest of married people. Tiger Cavett, Honoria's newest farm manager, came up to Charly. "The food's great, Charly."

"Ah, Monsieur Tigre. The party, it flourish, yes?"

"Oh, absolutely. Everyone came, and they're having a great time. Here, let me get you a drink, I'm the barman tonight."

"A simple juice of tomato, no ice, please."

Tiger poured the tomato juice into a tall glass, wrapping the bottom of the glass in a paper napkin. He handed it to Charly, and smiled.

"Here you are, Charly. Oh, the Warburtons were asking for you."

"Thank you, Tiger. Ah, Monsieur Vann, good to see you," as Peter Vann materialized at the table.

"Hi, Charly. Good party. Beefeater martini, Tiger, you know the prop—prop—portions. Stirred, not shaken, eh?"

"Right you are, Mr. Vann," Tiger said, chuckling. Tiger had worked for the Vanns but he'd quit when Dinah wanted him to wash out her silk underwear. He'd then gone to Charly, who had suggested Honoria Wells.

Peter Vann poked Charly's chest. "Taught this youngster to make . . . proper martini," he said. "What do these kids know? They all drink Budweiser. Martini's a man's drink."

"Yessir, Mr. Vann," said Tiger, handing over a brimming glass.

As Peter Vann lurched off, Charly went in search of the Warburtons. They were not steady customers of La Fermette, dining there perhaps once a year. When Walter Maxwell had been alive they'd come as his guests, but since Walter's death Charly had quite forgotten about them.

Ah, there they were. "Madame Warburton, monsieur. Allow me to wish you a good evening. You are enjoying?"

"Very much so, Charly," said Midge.

"Your food's wonderful, Charly," said Billy.

Both the Warburtons spoke in such low voices that Charly had to strain to hear them over the din. "You have a cat who is ill, Julius tells me?"

"Socrates," said Midge. "Very old. A stray."

"He is lucky that you found him," said Charly.

"We're the lucky ones," Billy Warburton said. "He's fading. And he's suddenly desperate to prove his manhood. Stays out all night, comes in all bitten up." Billy smiled wryly.

"Our children are gone, and we treat this beast like our child."

"He is our child," Midge whispered. "Julius said you used homeopathic medications on your animals. Can you suggest something?"

Charly thought for a bit. "Perhaps ignatia for grieving, since he is lamenting his lost youth, and Rescue Remedy. Then the Bach flower remedy elm, for feelings of inadequacy, and gentian, for people who are discouraged. Gorse, because he is losing hope, and olive, for exhaustion. Honeysuckle, for living in the past, and star of Bethlehem, for grief. I will write them down."

Midge Warburton chuckled. "Maybe we should take them, too."

Charly smiled. "I take the Bach remedies every day." He hadn't known the Warburtons had children. In fact, he knew nothing at all about the couple. "I will give you the number of my Bach flower counselor, Mrs. Whaley. She is a professional. I am but a novice."

"Walter Maxwell said you were the world's best cook, and now you prove to have other talents." Billy Warburton smiled.

"Ah, Maxwell," Charly said darkly. "Good customer,

but not a nice man. He tried to kill me, you know."

"No!" said the Warburtons together. "We thought you were the best of friends, and as we didn't like him, we avoided La Fermette. Of course, because of our businesses, we had to socialize a bit." Walter Maxwell had raised Black Angus cattle, and the Warburtons, horses for breeding: vastly rich, it was rumored. Now, they'd retired. He must get to know them better. They loved animals, they must be honorable. They were certainly compassionate.

"Let me know how the remedies turn out," Charly said, as Honoria hurried up with some other people.

"Wonderful food, Charly," said Win Crozier. "I wish I could learn to make those smoked-salmon roses." Win lowered his voice. "What do you know about a company called Fabulous Foods?"

"Maurice Baleine is buying stock in their company. They prepare frozen food for restaurants, but I know nothing about the company."

"Evvie, you know, Everston Pilchard, the man who came to lunch with us, has accepted a summer job with Fabulous Foods as their driver. The Brooke School closes for the summer soon."

"That sound hokay," said Charly, wondering why Win was evincing such a paternalistic interest in this Mr. Pilchard.

"In fact, he's already started driving for them in his spare time," Win continued. "Evvie says the owners are thugs from New Jersey."

Charly smiled. "Many people are thugs, monsieur. *Hélas*, many of my customers are thugs. But as long as they pay their bills, I do not pry." This was hardly true, as Charly had an insatiable curiosity about people. Still, his French propriety kept him from questioning Win

26

further about Everston. So Charly merely said, "I trust that Monsieur Pilchard is enjoying his evening."

"Evvie's parents were close friends, then they died," Win told Charly. "I feel that I must watch out for Evvie. He's—uh—well, he's not entirely stable. Intelligent, and a wonderful teacher, I'm told. He's also a gifted landscape gardener, he's doing over our backyard, and he's done work for Honoria, as well. But, well, he can't seem to quite make a go of anything."

"Ah." Charly began to feel great uneasiness. Was Win leading up to a proposal that Charly should offer this misfit a job? At La Fermette?

But perhaps not. Charly was relieved when Win merely said, "I'd hoped you knew something about Fabulous Foods, so we could counsel Evvie. He's been trying to get landscaping jobs, but it's hard."

"I am going to the grand opening of Fabulous Foods on Monday," Charly told Win. "I will call you, monsieur, and give you my opinion." Charly suddenly felt so affable toward Mr. Pilchard, the misfit, that he said, "And perhaps I ask around to see if anyone would like a landscape gardener."

"That would be nice, Charly. Evvie's got a real eye for color and a wonderful sense of mass. Of course, you, uh, have to keep an eye on him, but isn't that true of most people?" Win chuckled, a bit nervously.

*What in the world is "a sense of mass"?* thought Charly.

# NETTLE SOUP

## Yield: 4-6 servings

4 tablespoons butter
3 large shallots, peeled and chopped
4 quarts young nettle tops
1 quart water
Salt and pepper to taste
Additional butter as needed

Melt butter and soften shallots in nonreactive pot. Pick and wash young nettle tops with gloves on. Add to shallots along with the water. Bring to a boil, lower heat and simmer 15 minutes. Cool. Puree if desired. Serve piping hot topped with 1 Tablespoon butter per serving.

# CHILLED POTAGE CRESSONIERE

## Yield: 6-8 servings

1 quart de-fatted rich chicken stock
3 bunches watercress
1 large boiled potato, chunked
1 cup heavy cream, or as needed
Salt and white pepper to taste

Bring chicken stock to a boil in a large nonreactive pot and add watercress and potato. When soup returns to the boil turn off and cool, uncovered. Puree in blender and add heavy cream, salt and white pepper as needed. Chill overnight.

# SUNDAY DINNER AT LA FERMETTE

WHILE MOST OF HONORIA WELLS'S COCKTAIL PARTY guests were sound asleep early Sunday morning Charly was breakfasting, feeding his cats and Bruno, preparing for a busy day. The cats would spend the day stalking prey in nearby fields while Charly's customers feasted on La Fermette's fine cuisine.

On Sundays the restaurant was open from noon to six. A wave of customers arrived at noon, and another group arrived around three. Charly had had his bath, and now he made mental lists of restaurant chores.

Now that Julius lived nearby, and Max Helder and Fred Deering and Patty Perkins handled the catering, Charly had more free time. Tomorrow, Monday, the restaurant was closed, and, until afternoon when he had to go up to the Fabulous Foods reception, Charly would work in his garden.

Charly's Sunday specials were always roast prime rib of beef and roast range-run chicken. He'd also made a big pot of oxtail stew, mainly for himself, since this delicacy wasn't considered upscale restaurant fare. But it took a great deal of work, so Charly was delighted when his favorite customer, Ugo Buonsarde, dining with his bodyguards late in the day, sent word to the kitchen that he was in the mood for something hearty.

"Tell him, Elton, no, better yet, I will tell him myself."

Ugo clasped Charly's hand. "Ah, my good friend Charly. I woke this morning thinking of my mother's cooking. I am in a nostalgic mood, I yearn for a plain and simple stew. Can you suggest something?"

"Oxtail stew." Charly smiled. "May I bring you a bowl?"

Ugo's two bodyguards looked stricken. Like tigers, they appeared to exist solely on rare meat. Charly quickly reassured them.

"I will bring also two large and juicy portions of my prime rib."

The afternoon diners were beginning to drift out. It would be closing time soon, and it had been a busy mealtime.

Charly, Benny, and Julius had sauteed veal, grilled salmon, carved roasts, garnished plates with nasturtium flowers or sprigs of rosemary. Charly inspected each portion. He knew that his customers paid for more than food. They wanted a dining experience.

A police car drew up outside the back door, and John Stark stepped out. A moment later, he entered the kitchen. Charly sat with the chief.

Stark asked, "Remember Honoria Wells and Harry Clark?"

"Ah, la la," Charly remembered all too well. "And Mr. Clark is freed when the jury say he did not try to kill Madame Wells. Such lies."

"Well, somebody got to him. That's his body you found, Charly."

Charly gasped, but tried to appear nonchalant before the chief of police.

"I am not surprise," he gulped.

Benny, Julius, and Joe Okun clustered around the table. "It was just a question of time," Charly added. "How do you know it was Clark, Chief?"

"His wallet was in his back pocket. So whoever did it wanted him identified. Might be a revenge killing, huh?

Like someone he once harmed put him away?" Stark was careful not to mention names.

"Not Madame Wells," Charly said, intuiting Stark's thought.

Stark pretended to ignore this. "I've got some of my men asking around: when he was last seen, where he lived after he left Wells Farm. We have nothing on him. In fact, apart from the Wells thing, I'd never heard of Harry."

Charly said, "I have never met the man, Chief Stark."

After Stark left Charly spoke to his crew. "Mr. Clark, he is stupid. If he commit one crime, we may be sure he has done many others. And Chief Stark think that Madame Wells has killed him."

Julius disagreed. "I can't believe that. Stark's smart, he can't really believe my aunt had any part in Harry's death."

"Even dead, Mr. Clark still makes trouble. Of course Madame Wells did not kill him. So now, we must find out who did kill him."

Julius pointed out, "Charly, you were going to stick to your cooking."

"Not true when my customer are involved."

"Oh, boy," said Benny Perkins. "Here we go."

"I must," Charly continued, "find out more about this Harry Clark."

Julius looked up from the potatoes he was cutting into balls. "Look, Charly, I'll get the employment record he filled out for my aunt. I'd like to know where else he worked, too."

"Good idea," said Charly happily.

Patty Perkins stuck her head in the kitchen door. "It's Maurice with two other men. Should I seat them? It's pretty late."

"Seat them if you please, Patty," Charly said. "I am curious."

***

Charly hurried over to Ugo's table. "The oxtail, did it please you?"

Ugo put his hand to his heart. "If I have tears in my eyes, my friend, it is because of this dish. It reminded me of my dear mother. It was . . . superb. I shall dream about it tonight. These are the simple dishes of my childhood, they are the foods which bring warmth to the heart and clarity to the brain." Buonsarde's eyes were shining.

"I will give you a container to take home," Charly said.

Suddenly Ugo glanced across the room and made a choking sound. Charly looked over. "It is my former partner Maurice and two of his friends."

"I know exactly who those men are," Ugo hissed.

"Do you know about the company, Fabulous Foods?"

"No," Ugo said. "Some sort of food company, but I don't know what."

"It is precooked food for the restaurant industry," Charly said.

"I didn't know there were such companies."

Charly, the authority, spoke. "America is filled with such companies. A good chef is hard to find, and much too expensive for many restaurants, so they buy their foods already cooked. Value added, they are called. Fish stuffed with crabmeat; fried fish; soups and stews and pies and cakes. One company in Wisconsin makes nothing but appetizers, already coated with batter: onion rings, battered cheese sticks, stuffed jalapeno peppers, other battered vegetables, nearly a hundred items."

"My friend, you amaze me."

"Fish products are especially lucrative since many cooks cannot prepare fish so that it tastes good. So,

33

signor, this is what Fabulous Foods does. It prepares fish dishes for restaurants."

"I can't believe Maurice is involved with such . . . such . . . vile creatures," Ugo sputtered.

"Maurice is no longer my partner. I do not know his friends or what he does." Charly wanted to disassociate himself from his former partner.

Ugo's face looked like a thundercloud. "This will end badly. You do not turn your back on such people. Maurice is a very foolish man."

And with that, Ugo and his two bodyguards swept out of La Fermette, forgetting to wait for Charly's container of oxtail stew.

# CHARLY CHATS WITH HIS FAN CLUB

"WELCOME, GENTLEMEN." WITH FALSE BONHOMIE, Charly greeted Maurice and two men who looked vaguely familiar. Charly was sorry his visit with Ugo Buonsarde had ended on a sour note, but enemies often met in Charly's dining room. So far, there had been no bloodshed.

"Charly, I'm sure you remember Richard Zampone and Martin Scungilli," Maurice said jovially. "They're the men who love your cooking. They've dined here before. They're the owners of Fabulous Foods."

Charly peered at the two men. Both were plump, with an oily sheen to their faces. One had curly black hair flecked with grey; the other man was almost bald, and the few strands of grey hair that he possessed were combed back from his dome in a stiff helmet that suggested hair spray. Two pairs of fat hands rested on

34

the table, four pinkie rings glittered with diamonds.

"Ah, Fabulous Foods," Charly said. "I am honored that you send me an invitation to your tasting tomorrow. Of course I will be there. Staidoff Hart kitchen, Maurice tell me."

"Gorgeous place," Maurice said smugly.

"Monsoor Poisson," said the curly-haired one in a gravelly voice. "We dined here some time ago with Big Wal—I mean, with Walter Maxwell, and you gave us a fabulous repast. Wonderful shrimp with garlic, then lobster, then steak with the most fantastic sauce I've ever tasted."

"Great meal, great meal," agreed Mr. Hairspray, smoothing down his helmet and baring his teeth in a sharklike smile.

Charly clapped his hands together, feigning delight. "But of course I recall you. You were guests of poor Walter Maxwell."

Before arriving at La Fermette that night Walter had killed someone, though Charly had not known it at the time. "His appetite was poor that evening, may he rest in peace."

"May he rest in peace," the two men intoned, solemnly making the sign of the cross. Zampone and Scungilli had been brought up from New Jersey by Maxwell to murder Charly, which they'd declined to do. They'd decided that to kill such a creative chef was out of the question. Charly knew none of this, though he would have been immensely flattered.

"But let us return to our muttons," Charly said. "You are here to eat, though it is very late and many of our Sunday specials are off the menu. But I can offer you some of our famous Shrimps Charly with your drinks, a *saucisson en croûte*, garlic sausage in a pastry crust, with some fresh asparagus. With that I bring little sauce, a mousseline. After that . . ." Charly racked his brain, trying to remember what was left in the kitchen. "Le rosbif is especially delicious today; or a roast of pork, rich and succulent, with roast potatoes that will crackle in your mouth. Or duckling, served simply roasted with currant-and-red-wine sauce."

Choices were made (ducklings for three), and Charly retired to the kitchen. "Do not worry," Charly assured his crew, "we will have them out in an hour. We will not be late. They are drinking only Coca-Cola."

"Even Maurice?" Julius made an unbelieving face.

"Even Maurice," Charly said. "He has been seriously following the good doctor's *régime*." Some months ago Maurice had succumbed to cirrhosis, not surprising in an alcoholic. The doctors at the rehabilitation center had convinced him that to stay alive, he had to give up alcohol. Apart from a few slips Maurice had stuck to this, though he'd gained much weight.

"Who're those guys with Maurice?" Tommy Glade asked. He was filling in as waiter today. "They're eatin' like crazy—three baskets of bread, two crocks of mushroom spread. Ate every bit of that sausage plate."

"Friend of Maurice," Charly said. "And owner of the frozen-food place up the road. I find out who they are: they dine here long time ago with Walter Maxwell."

"Well, they look like thugs," Tommy said, chewing on a nicely charred end of roast beef. "And not godfathers, like your buddy across the river."

"Ugo Buonsarde is not a godfather," Charly chided. "An uncle, perhaps, or an adviser, merely. Anyway, Ugo does not consort with such raffraff."

Tommy snorted. "Well, they're *raffraff* all right." He took up the heavy tray and hoisted it to his shoulder.

At the end of the meal Charly came out into the dining room and offered infusion of chamomile or brandy to Maurice and his guests. He thought the one with the curly hair was Richard Zampone, which made the other one Martin Scungilli. At any rate, these were the men who were going to help Maurice part with his money—not an unusual event.

"Another terrific meal, Monsoor," Zampone said. "As soon's my wife Bernice moves up here, we'll be dinin' *chez vous* regular."

"An honor, sir." Charly winced. "And when will that be?"

"Well, we've only just opened up here, and we're keepin' the Jersey house, so it'll be sorta part-time for a while. I haven't found us an upstate residence yet. But first, we gotta help the chef hire a first-rate team, and old Morrie here, he's gonna help us. Really knows his way around, this fella."

Charly looked at Maurice to see how he liked being called "old Morrie." Maurice smiled widely. "Millions, Charly, we'll be making millions before you know it. Fabulous Foods will put Van Buren County on the map."

That was what Charly feared: that the county would become synonymous with criminals. "I do not doubt that for a moment, Maurice."

Where did Maurice find these awful people? Perhaps now was the time to do some investigating. He turned to Zampone. "You already have a gentleman from these parts working for you, yes? I am referring to one of your drivers, Everston Pilchard."

"Who?" Both men looked blank.

"Everston Pilchard," Charly repeated, enunciating clearly.

"Well, if he's a driver, then our chef Arthur Arpati must have hired him," said the man named Richard Zampone. "Arthur takes care of the kitchen help, the drivers, like that."

"Pilchard? Name don't ring no bells," continued Zampone. "Maybe it's someone Harry recommended, before he left." And to Charly. "We had a driver before, first guy our chef hired, when we was first bringing the stuff up from New Jersey. But he disappeared."

Charly tried to appear casual. "Harry? Harry who?"

"What was his last name, Marty?"

"I think his name was Harry Clark," said Martin Scungilli.

Charly swallowed hard. He thought furiously. "Harry Clark? That name, I have heard before. What was he like, this Harry Clark?"

Scungilli and Zampone furrowed their brows and gave themselves over to deep thought. Finally, Martin said, "I hardly knew the guy, but I heard he was a flake, right, Richard? Always braggin' about his, uh, ladies."

"Yeah, not a serious worker. Arthur said he'd phone in sick, or not show up at all, and wasn't there something about sticky fingers? Didn't Arthur say some of his knives went missing?"

"Not someone you'd want as a friend," was Martin's assessment to Charly. "Guy was a blowhard, lots of big talk about all the important people he knew. Not true, none of it. Couldn't depend on him."

Charly's head was reeling, but he felt he should remain silent for the moment. Wiliness and craft were needed, and this required serious thought. So he didn't stay in the dining room for further chats. But Tommy Glade came back to the kitchen to report.

"Something fuckin' peculiar's going on, Charly.

38

Those two thugs are treating Maurice like some long-lost cousin. Maurice's lapping it up. He's saying some amazing stuff, too. He said, 'Well, I'm the owner here, so there's no question Charly will be carrying your food, I guarantee it.' "

Julius said, "Tommy, Maurice is crazy. You know that, don't you? He's on some insane ego trip. Those guys are out to skin him alive, and he doesn't even know it. He thinks he's in on the deal of the century."

Benny came up to Charly. "Charly, please don't get mixed up with Maurice and those crooks."

"Ta-ta-ta, my dear Benny, you must calm yourself. I will have nothing to do with Maurice or his friends."

But even as he said it, Charly knew that this was not the truth. He also knew, he felt certain, who had laid Harry Clark to rest in his pond.

## MONDAY MORNING—BARBARA BALEINE VISITS CHARLY

CHARLY WOKE EARLY MONDAY MORNING AND THOUGHT about today, Monday, his free day. It was always pleasant to lie abed after a busy weekend and spend the day doing nothing in particular, though "nothing in particular" was a relative term. So was "lying abed." It was only five minutes to five—far too early to get up, but already Charly's four cats, sensing movement, were alert, ears up, prowling the mattress and sharpening their claws on the little Oriental prayer rug as a means of getting Charly's attention. Bruno, lying on the floor by the side of the bed, stirred and grunted. The red, illuminated numerals on the little electric clock moved to 4:56. Charly turned over, closed his eyes and feigned sleep.

When Charly opened his eyes again it was 5:43. Now it really was time to get up. Charly swung his feet over the edge of the bed. He grasped the little bottle of Bach flower remedies, *to give you peace of mind,* and squeezed four drops onto his tongue, noticing that the bottle was almost empty. He'd have to make up a new batch. He kept bottles by his bed, in his restaurant office, and down in his home kitchen. He got up, slipped on his woolen bathrobe, toed into his sheepskin slippers. Peered outside. Very dark and humid. Today would be overcast, perhaps rainy. His back was stiff, he felt creaky and achy. *I am better than the weather forecasters,* he thought.

Downstairs, Charly let the cats and Bruno out and filled his little stainless-steel saucepan with water for coffee. It was sulfur water, very healthy, and gave a rich, if strange, taste to Charly's strong Puerto Rican brew. He opened his basket of homeopathic remedies and chose Rhus Tox, for rheumatism. Then he went out onto his back porch and sniffed the air. Definitely rain. Felt very damp. No wonder his back was giving him trouble. But May rain was always welcome, seeping into the earth that was putting forth many plants. Many *healing* plants, Charly emended, thinking of his nettles. This morning he would wash and steam the nettles and have a big bowl for breakfast. He needed something nourishing, for he suspected that today would be a busy day.

He regretted, now, that he'd accepted Maurice's invitation to drive up to Sharpsville, to visit that frozen-food company. Why get involved? He was neither going to use the foods nor invest in the company. Maurice, "*ce coco,*" that crazy, telling men that he still owned La Fermette. How could he lie so? And could Tommy possibly be right, that Maurice had told the men that he, Charly, would be using their products in his restaurant? Maurice had never dwelt in the palace of truth, but now a fantasy scenario seemed to be taking possession of his mind. What did he hope to gain, by telling these vulgar men that he owned La Fermette? They'd find out soon enough that this wasn't true, and who wanted to be caught in a lie?

After his bath, Charly, now dressed for the day in sensibly warm corduroy trousers, a cotton turtleneck and a light woolen shirt, wrapped his big white apron around his middle and got the nettles out of the refrigerator. He put on his rubber gloves and ran tepid water in the sink. He soaked the nettles, shaking them to remove any loose dirt, then he placed them on the wooden cutting board. With his #10 chef's knife he sliced them into pieces, which he threw into a stainless-steel pot. He drizzled olive oil, sea salt, and water over the greens, covered them, and turned the heat to HIGH. In less than a minute they were done. Charly lifted the lid and inhaled the sweet wild aroma of steamed nettles.

It was nine o'clock and Charly was halfheartedly dusting his living room (flicking a clean rag over his furniture, books, and bibelots) when Barbara Baleine, Maurice's wife, telephoned, asking if she could pop in for a few minutes. Charly liked Barbara very much. She appeared to be a young woman very much in charge of herself. She owned and operated a successful interior-design firm, initially helped along by her mother, the socially prominent antiques dealer, Martha De Groot. Now, Barbara was so busy that she could afford the luxury of turning down clients.

"It's a business, not a religion," she'd often say. She'd turned La Fermette into a showplace, and since people go to a stylishly decorated restaurant much more eagerly than to a plain one, Charly felt that Barbara was responsible for much of his business. He had no illusions about the palates of his customers. Raised on TV dinners and frozen vegetables, their palates dulled by Coca-Cola and chemicals, his customers didn't know good food when they saw it, but they demanded a "dining experience." And with Barbara's beautiful rooms and Charly's high prices, customers felt safe in proclaiming that Charly's food was the best in the world.

"Charly, I'm at the end of my rope." Barbara sat at Charly's kitchen counter dressed in a sand-colored silk ensemble chosen, Charly was sure, to match her sand-colored Cadillac. Tall and broad-shouldered, Barbara was a big woman, not fat, but robust. "Junoesque," she called herself. Charly sniffed. She smelled wonderful, as always, an expensive scent that reminded him of those discreet and tiny restaurants in Paris, windows camouflaged by billowing white batiste curtains, where only the most choice foods, superbly cooked, are offered to loyal patrons.

"My dear Barbara."

"Maurice is driving me mad, Charly. You know those dreadful Fabulous Foods thugs?"

"Maurice is not himself these days."

"Maurice," Barbara sniffed, "*is* himself. I'm the one who's changed. I was such a naive little country bumpkin when I married. I thought him so worldly, all that talk of Paris. I married him for his Givenchy aftershave."

"You marry the illusion, no?"

"Absolutely. And the illusion turned into a disillusion."

"Ah, la la. He cannot get at your money?"

"No, thank God, Mummy's got it all tied up in trust funds. Poor Maurice, I still love him, but I can't bear him. All that self-importance."

"He tell me you are thinking of investing in Fabulous Foods."

"There you are," said Barbara. "Another illusion. Not for anything in this world would I do such a thing. He told me *you* were putting money in."

"*Jamais de la vie.* Never. But this afternoon I will drive up there, I am curious. Perhaps Benny and Julius will come with me."

"Take my advice, Charly, and stay away. Maurice is crazed. He's even thinking of putting our house on the market; the bank won't give him a second mortgage. Well"—Barbara shook her head—"it's his house, and it's in his name. He can do what he wants with it. I'll manage."

"Not a divorce?" Charly whispered. "That would kill Maurice."

Barbara shrugged. "Probably not. I'm still fond of him, don't ask me why. He has so much potential. There's so much he could do with his life. If only he'd get serious and stop trying to make a million dollars without working for it. He's crazed by greed, Charly. I hope it's a temporary madness."

Charly felt this line was unproductive. He, too, hoped that Maurice would change, but as the years scrolled by, it became more and more unlikely.

"Your perfume, it is wonderful."

"Amazone from Hermès. Thanks for listening, Charly, I really didn't mean to take up so much of your time complaining about Maurice. I have to run to Old Chatham, soon, so let's talk about your plans. You want to redecorate during the last two weeks in August, right?

When the restaurant's closed? I've got it blocked out in my calendar, and I've alerted the painters and the upholsterers, they're reserving the time. We'll have to work like lightning. Two weeks is nothing. I've been thinking about the colors."

"I am getting tired of this *abricot*. It is too pink and like *crème glacée,* ice cream. I want something that make us think of the woods and the fields. Green, perhaps? Or the grey of the little mouse?"

"A good choice," decreed Barbara. "People are getting interested in saving our natural resources, so we want to show them we're ecologically minded. We want earth colors." Her eyes lit up. "Moss," she said, patting her imposing bosom. "Let us think moss."

"One more thing before you go, my dear Barbara. What do you know of the Warburtons in Highdale? They used to breed horses."

"Oh, Charly, the nicest people in the world. Even Mummy's impressed by Billy and Midge. They're very rich, but very quiet about it. She was Marjorie Haybridge from Philadelphia. Their son was trampled to death by one of their horses, and their daughter died of some horrible disease."

"They are most compassionate," Charly pointed out.

"They are people who have known tragedy," said Barbara simply.

# A VISIT TO FABULOUS FOODS

THEY WENT IN JULIUS'S CAR. CHARLY, IN A SOBER PIN-striped suit, sat in the passenger seat next to Julius, the driver, and Benny and his mother Patty Perkins sat in the back. While it was true that Charly's driving left much to be desired, Julius got around this in his usual diplomatic fashion.

"My car may be old, but it's trustworthy, I have it serviced regularly," Julius said of his ancient white BMW, "and, Charly, your van just isn't comfortable for four people. Besides, we'd have to find the backseats; they're probably stored down in the cellar and very dusty."

Charly grunted. He was, he felt, not only an excellent driver, but cautious to boot, whereas Julius put his foot to the gas pedal in an alarming way. Still, what Julius said about the seats was true.

Fabulous Foods was easy to find: a group of cinder-block brick-faced, one-story buildings just off the road, with a loading dock at the back, along with refrigeration and freezing units and generators. It had an industrial look: like a Fernand Léger painting brought to life. Julius turned into the drive, by the ugly metal sign that said FABULOUS FOODS. Charly sniffed.

"Roasting and frying, I smell."

"Well, they do make food," Patty said. "Smells good, doesn't it? I didn't have much lunch. I'm starved."

The buildings were haphazardly landscaped with privet and boxy yew, both poisonous plants, Charly was happy to point out.

"Boy, Charly, you really don't like those guys," Benny said. "And if they're anything like Maurice, I won't, either."

"They are far worse than Maurice," Charly said. "Maurice is but a fool. These men are not fools."

"I bet this is another fly-by-night operation," Julius said. "It fits the pattern. This complex has been empty for over two years. The previous company moved its operations to China. The crooks move in when people

45

are desperate for jobs, and Van Buren County's hurting. Big companies are moving their operations to the Far East because labor's cheaper. That leaves the little people hanging. And the big companies pay almost no taxes, either."

"Of course they pay no taxes," Charly agreed. "The government should prohibit big companies from moving out of the country. It is always the little people who suffer in a so-called democracy when money is king."

"Maybe I should move to Tibet," Benny said. He was currently reading about Tibetan Buddhism. "But that's overrun by the Chinese Communists. You can't win. I wish I knew the answer."

"There are no answers, because there are no questions. At least, no questions that have answers," Charly said.

On this inscrutable note Julius parked his car in the vast parking lot, and, Charly leading the way, the group walked up to the double glass doors inscribed in gold block letters, FABULOUS FOODS.

The spacious room, filled with couches and occasional chairs and low cocktail tables, was already populated by at least fifty people, all helping themselves to food from a long buffet table. There was the hum of conversation and a pleasing aroma hung in the air. Charly could see Maurice in a corner chatting with some men. He recognized a number of area restaurateurs and nodded to them. He wandered over to the buffet table. The food looked extremely appetizing, rosy shrimp in tomato sauce lying on beds of angel hair pasta; crabmeat in cream sauce on yellow rice; brochettes of swordfish and peppers; cubed fish fillets swimming in cream sauce.

Beside each platter were stacks of colorful tearsheets

describing the product: crab cakes to use as appetizers, entrées, in sandwiches; lobster tails in cream to serve plain or atop pasta or rice; mounds of fried shrimp, clams, oysters, fish strips. Charly's mouth watered, and his nose quivered pleasantly.

He strolled over to Patty, who was filling her plate. He took a batter-fried shrimp in his fingers and cautiously nibbled it. It had a fresh, clean taste. He then took a plate, and spooned onto it small portions of tasty-looking food. Then he moved over to a couch, where Patty was sitting and eating.

"This is delicious, Charly, not at all what I expected. You think this really is the food they're selling? It doesn't taste frozen at all."

"The fish fillet is fresh," Charly noted, chewing. "The shrimp is frozen, all shrimp is, but it is of good quality. The fried clams are sweet."

"So," Patty said, chewing. "You're telling me that this isn't the food they'll be selling, it's prepared specially for this tasting."

"I am certain of that," Charly agreed. "This is fresh food nicely prepared with butter, white wine, madeira, good ingredients. It does not have the taste of frozen food at all."

"Monsoor Poisson, the greatest chef in America," said a voice nearby.

Charly looked up and saw one of the men Maurice had brought to La Fermette for dinner. "Ah, sir," not recalling the man's name, "we are enjoying your excellent food."

"Richard Zampone, sir, at your service." The fat man bowed. "Isn't the food great? We have a first-class chef."

"The food is very good, sir," Charly said. "But I cannot believe that it has been frozen."

"Oh, but it has been. A special process, all very new. It's a secret technique involving flash-freezing at very low temperatures, which preserves the taste and the texture. And of course we only use first-class ingredients, nothing but the best."

"*Tiens*. Frozen, all frozen. I would not have thought it. I would very much like to know how the food is processed."

Zampone looked smug. "It's top secret."

"Sure, sure, everything in prepared-food business is top secret. Then an employee leaves, and sells the secret to another company, and it is no longer top secret. Then the new company improves on the original top secret method and it is again top secret. And the dance continues . . ."

"That's why we wish to remain a small operation," Zampone told Charly. "Only three of us know the secret. Arpati, me, and Martin. The workers, senior citizens and Mexicans, mostly, work in another room. They have no idea what's going on."

"And your drivers? A man like Everston Pilchard, who is a schoolteacher, could he not figure out what is going on?"

"Our drivers don't know anything about food," Zampone said shortly.

Charly had probed enough. "Then you have nothing to worry about."

"Absolutely right, Monsoor."

Charly, deep in speculation on which of the men, Zampone, Scungilli, or chef Arpati, had dispatched Harry Clark, snapped to attention as Zampone continued, "I understand your owner, Mr. Baleine, is going to stock La Fermette with many of our products. That is good news, sir."

Charly had had enough of Maurice's charades. "*My owner?* I do not understand, sir. I am the owner of La Fermette. Maurice Baleine was my partner until a few months ago, when I bought him out. He has no affiliation with my restaurant at present. Unless . . ." Charly smiled craftily. "Ah, I understand. Maurice has bought a restaurant of his own, and it is this place he will stock with your food. But not my restaurant. I am the chef of La Fermette, all food is freshly made daily by me and my crew."

Now it was Zampone's turn to look puzzled. "I thought old Morrie said he owned La Fermette."

"Poor Maurice is little bit forgetful," Charly answered, tapping the side of his head significantly. "And sometimes he imagine thing."

"Ah," Zampone said. "And perhaps Maurice is telling us a fib?"

Charly's face was inscrutable. "His father was my partner in the New York restaurant. Naturally I cannot, out of loyalty, speak against the son."

"Naturally, sir," said Zampone. "Loyalty is a beautiful thing. We will speak no more on this matter."

"*Merci, monsieur,*" said Charly. "I wish you the good luck on your frozen-food business." But Zampone didn't hear Charly as he had drifted away, a pensive look on his face.

"Well, Charly, isn't it every bit as good as I said?" Maurice, smiling, was at Charly's elbow, exuding clouds of expensive aftershave.

"What we taste," Charly said cautiously, "is very good."

"Would you like a tour of the facility? Martin and Richard are taking people around the factory in small groups."

Charly motioned Patty to stand up. "Come, Patty, we see Staidoff Hart kitchens. You can finish your *petit casse croûte,* your snack, later."

## AN EVENING ON THE TELEPHONE

"THE KITCHENS WERE INDEED BEAUTIFUL," CHARLY SAID as he, Benny, Patty, and Julius drove home. "Were they not?"

"Sure were," Julius agreed. "They looked like a stage set, all stainless steel, brand-new. Must have cost a fortune."

Charly agreed. "I ask if the kitchens are designed by a local firm, Monsieur Scungilli say all the equipment brought up from New Jersey. Architect, contractors, laborers, everyone. I wonder why they move north?"

Patty said, "Something's weird about that place. They whisked you through the kitchens so fast, I didn't have time to notice a thing. I tried to examine one of those big tilting kettles, and they pushed me away."

Julius said, "Did you notice chef Arpati? He looked nervous."

Bruno and the cats were pleased to see Charly when he arrived home. It was, after all, past their dinnertime. Charly spooned their food into bowls. They were emptied with gusto. The animals rushed outside, and Charly washed the bowls and thought how nice it was to feed animals, they rarely criticized. Then he thought about his afternoon.

The food that he'd tasted was freshly prepared. The state-of-the-art kitchens were expensively gotten up— stainless-steel stoves and refrigerators, white-tile walls,

50

brown-tile floors, wooden duckboards by the sinks, all first quality. Charly would have enjoyed seeing chef Arpati at work, though by tour time all remains of food prep had been cleared away, and even the garbage cans—a source of discovery, always—were empty. Charly had peeked.

Charly had looked around for his friend Rex Cingale, who had also received an invitation, but Rex hadn't arrived by the time Charly left.

It was late afternoon and time for Bruno's walk. The dog, leading Charly, walked up the little dirt road behind the restaurant. They were just on the point of turning left, for a nice tramp over Charly's fields, when Charly sensed the presence of a car. Turning, he saw Barbara Baleine's big Cadillac slowing to a stop. The driver's window buzzed down.

"How was the food factory, Charly?"

"Ah, my dear Barbara. They make a nice presentation, but I do not believe the food they serve us is the frozen food they sell to restaurant."

"Well, natch. Maurice even admitted it."

"*Tiens*. He tell you that?"

"This morning he said he had to go up early, see if the chef needed to get extra food from the distributor's or the supermarket. I took it to mean that all of the foods at the party were prepared from scratch."

"Trust Maurice to always let the bird out of the cage. And how was your meeting, Barbara?"

"Tiring but profitable, Charly. A huge house with guest cottage and pool house, all to be redone. If this keeps up, I'll have to hire more staff."

"Perhaps owners are new customer for La Fermette?" Charly mused.

Barbara made a face. "Possibly, Charly. I'll tell you

51

one thing about Van Buren County. The poor stay poor, but there's lots of money moving in. The county is changing, fast. Perhaps not for the better, either. These are all show-off rich, want you to know they've got cash."

Charly remembered what he'd been meaning to ask Barbara. "Do you know Everston Pilchard?"

"Nutty Evvie? I've used him as a landscaper. You have to watch him, but he's good. He has a real understanding of color and mass."

*Mass.* There it was again. Charly asked, "What is this mass?"

"I mean he knows how to mass plants together to create great effect," Barbara explained. "You know how most gardeners, they'll have a little clump of zinnias and a little clump of marigolds and a little clump of delphinium, and it all looks small and messy?"

"Well . . ." This was exactly what Charly's flower bed looked like, and he thought it most attractive.

"Evvie'll take a flower bed and plant it all in blue and white flowers, and not too many varieties. A huge mass of blue delphinium and a huge mass of white asters and a huge mass of baby's breath, that sort of thing. Not a zillion little poopy groupings."

"I see," Charly said sadly. Poopy groupings. He thought his flowers so pretty and bright. Now he discovered they were nothing more than poopy groupings, in the eyes of the professional decorator.

"But he's kind of spacy," Barbara continued. "He gets carried away. Listen, Charly, talk to you later, okay? I've got calls to make."

Charly and Bruno walked to the end of the second field. Charly was pleased to see that the milkweed was growing in profusion, since milkweed flowers were, he had heard, the sole food of the monarch butterfly. Before Charly had bought the fields, they had been drenched in herbicides, which had killed off many native growths. But now, all of the wonderful wild plants that Charly prized, the St. John's wort, the milkweed, the goldenrod, the wild garlic and thistles, were growing in profusion. The balance of nature was being restored. Charly, of course, used no pesticides on his land, which was posted with big orange signs to discourage hunters.

Back in his kitchen, Charly decided to make up some more of his Bach flower remedies. He assembled three one-ounce dropper bottles, rinsed them, and filled them three-quarters with spring water. He added several drops of rum to each bottle as a preservative and opened his tin box of Bach bottles. He added two drops each of the following flower extracts: beech (for criticism); chestnut bud (for making the same mistake over and over, that is, getting involved with criminals); crabapple (for detoxification, necessary when confronting unsavory characters); honeysuckle (for mourning the past, his wife Claudine and his son, dead now over thirty years). One fine day the chestnut bud would take effect and Charly would stop getting involved with the criminal element. It hadn't happened yet.

After he put the bottles away, Charly called Fred Deering and Max Helder. He apologized for calling them at home, asked if they knew any people at The Brooke School. He wanted to inform himself about a man called Everston Pilchard.

"Our school, Wilson, isn't far from Brooke, and we know the cooks," Fred said. "We'll ask them about this guy. Everston Pilchard?"

"Yes, please. It would be of great help to me."

Fred asked, "Is this man one of your suspects?"

"Perhaps. He lunch at the restaurant the other day. He say my famous roast-beef hash is corned beef hash. Can you imagine?"

"Hey, Charly, anyone who makes that mistake has got to be a murderer, right?" Fred laughed. "I guess he killed that guy you found."

"Ah, you make the joke, Fred."

"Listen, Charly, we'll find out about him, okay? It shouldn't be hard."

"Thank you, Fred. My best regard to you and to Max.

Next, Charly called Julius Prendergast. "Little favor to ask, Julius."

"I know exactly what it is," Julius said. "And the answer, Charly, is no. You want me to find out about the owners of Fabulous Foods, right?"

"Is true." Charly didn't ask how Julius knew. But it was, after all, the next logical step. "But why is the answer no?"

"The answer is 'no,' Charly, because it takes time to check people out, and those guys have 'crook' written all over them. It costs big bucks to investigate people, and I can't ask my friend to keep doing it for free. I've already called in most of my markers. Call your buddy Buonsarde."

"Only as last resort," Charly said. "Signor Buonsarde is not a 'buddy.' He is a valued customer." Ugo, too, might be considered a less-than-honest businessman, but Ugo was a gentleman, as well as being president of Charly's fan club. It made a difference.

Charly had just put down the telephone when it rang. It was Rex Cingale, who wondered why he'd missed Charly at the Fabulous Foods tasting. "You taste that food, Charly? Fucking great. I'm gonna order some."

54

"I think you make the mistake, Rex."

"You kiddin', Charly?"

"It was very good, Rex, but I am convince it wasn't the frozen food they sell. It was fresh food, cooked especially for the tasting."

"Aw, Charly. You sure about that? Listen, come over, we'll have a little food at my place, instead of going out. I ate a lot, so I'm not too hungry."

Most Monday nights Charly and Rex Cingale dined at a local restaurant, to see what the competition was up to. They also enjoyed each other's company.

# CHARLY TALKS WITH REX CINGALE

CHARLY PARKED HIS RED VAN AND MOUNTED THE steps to the sprawling pseudo-log cabin that was home to the finest steaks in Van Buren County. Steak Heaven was called Snake Heaven by Tommy Glade and Trash Heaven by Julius Prendergast and "that awful place" by Patty Perkins, none of whom felt that Charly Poisson, distinguished restaurateur and chef, should associate with the likes of Rex Cingale and his lowlife steak joint.

Charly, of course, felt differently. Rex, he claimed, added color to his life, spice to his thoughts, and only occasional indigestion. Rex, in addition, was a walking encyclopedia of Van Buren County gossip, very much needed if you were a pretender to the throne of Sherlock Holmes, as Charly was.

"Charly!" Rex boomed, his voice extra loud because the bar was three deep in noisy customers drinking beer with Kahlua chasers. Rex was sitting just inside his dining room at a deuce. Now he rose and beckoned

Charly over to a larger table in a corner of the nearly empty room.

"Wasn't this afternoon fuckin' great?" As usual, Rex was dressed in a shiny navy blue sharkskin suit, white shirt, white-on-white polyester necktie. His thick, curly black hair was well brushed, and he looked freshly shaved. He exuded an air of prosperity. He was drinking, Charly knew, plain seltzer. Later on in the evening, a single slug of anisette would be added. "I already ordered us steaks, and your wine's coming."

"So, Rex, you enjoy this afternoon? The beautiful kitchen? The good food? The nice company? I look for you, then I leave."

"Hey, Charly, that was fuckin' class. Loved it. I didn't get up there till after four. But they still had food left, and it was good. I got to talk to the owners, Scungilli and Zampone. Nice guys. You know Zampone's family, in the old country, lived right near where my grandparents lived? Near Bari? Whaddaya think of that? Small world, huh?"

"Small world," Charly agreed.

"Richard says they can turn my dining room around. They'll come down, have a look. Free consulting service if you buy from them. I said my dining room, you could shoot a gun down it Mondays, Tuesdays, Wednesdays, never hit nothing. Thank God for the bar, uh? I said I'd get those guys into The Italian Heritage Club down here, maybe they can make some contacts."

"Very interesting," said Charly. He realized that no amount of bad-mouthing on his part would change Rex's mind about Fabulous Foods, so he didn't try. "Their food, it is expensive? I did not see a price list."

Rex waggled his hand to indicate not so bad. He leaned over the table to whisper. "You sign on for six months, like a club, and the first order's free. And during that six months you can change your order any way you like, to fit in with what your customers like. No, Charly, it isn't expensive when you consider the quality. I'd have to charge less than a fancy restaurant of course, so I'd have a food cost of about sixty percent, maybe more." A normal restaurant food cost was forty percent, and if you cooked from scratch, you might get it down to twenty percent, if you didn't offer steaks or seafood and went heavy on the pasta. Charly's food cost was around thirty-five percent, pretty low considering the high quality of his food, but of course there was a lot of labor involved in his soups, stews, pâtés, roulades, and fresh vegetables.

"You sign on like a club?" Charly echoed. "In all of my years in business, this is something I have never heard of. What if your customer do not like the food, what if the food change quality, you have sign the paper, you cannot get out of the contract?"

Rex laughed loud and deep. "Oh, Charly, I love ya. Just like my Uncle Mario. He'd say the same thing. But, Charly, you gotta move with the times. People want fancy, these days. All that Novel Kwezeen shit. Angelo and Ricky, they're the best broilermen in the business, and now they make the vegetables and the french fries too, but, ya know, Shrimp Romano, or crab with brandy and cream—they couldn't do it to save their asses."

Charly sipped Rex's sour red wine, knowing that he'd have to take several homeopathic charcoal tablets before going to bed. "It sound like a strange way to do business."

"Oh, I dunno," Rex said defensively. "They come in, really examine things, your menu, your prices, put in a

57

lotta time. They're professionals. That's built into the cost of the food. Oh, here we are."

"Hot plates, don't touch," said Sal the waiter. "Done just the way you like, Mr. Charly. Black on the outside, blue inside."

"Delicious, Rex," said Charly, as he chewed.

"Best meat you can buy," said Rex. "Now that, I won't change."

Charly decided not to say any more about Fabulous Foods, but when he was midway through his meal he couldn't resist one more shot. "About Fabulous Foods, Rex, I have the funny feeling."

"Uncle Mario, he used to get funny feelings, too," Rex said. "And I gotta admit, he was usually right."

"So am I," Charly said. "And do not forget, our Maurice is putting money in the operation. That should tell you something."

"Maurice the asshole." Rex snorted. "But this time, Charly, I think that dumb snob is right on the money."

Bobby Matucci appeared at the table. "Takin' a break, Uncle Rex. Wanted to tell Charly about that body he found."

"It is good to see you looking so well, Bobby," Charly said. After a serious incident across the river last winter, Bobby now claimed that his gambling days were over. He was hanging out at the gym, and it showed.

"Fitness, that's where it's at," Bobby said, flexing his right arm. "And no more junk food. You know what Benny told me? Said eatin' vegetables increases your stamina. Vince and me, we're shovin' down the broccoli." Vince, Bobby's brother, was a cop, and a good one. He was the source of Bobby's news, as always.

"The body I found," Charly said. "Is Harry Clark, I hear."

"Yeah, Harry Clark," Bobby said, disappointed that Charly knew. "Killed by blows to the head, hadn't been dead as long as they thought, maybe five, six months, Doc thinks. They could even analyze the food in his stomach. His last meal was a burger, fries, some greenery, they even found some a' them little hot peppers we serve at the bar. So we think his last meal was here, since none of the other bars serve them peppers."

"Pepperoncini," Rex said. "Got a nice bite to 'em. Hey, you want some, Charly, with your steak?"

"Perhaps not," Charly said, thinking of the decayed peppers in Harry Clark's very dead stomach. "And what else does Vince tell you?"

"Not much," Bobby said. "Vince asked if I remembered Harry coming in here on his last night on earth. 'Course I couldn't. Tried to ignore him. The men didn't like Harry, always braggin', tellin' you how much testosterone he had coursin' through his veins."

Charly asked, "Did Harry Clark mention that he'd gotten a driving job?"

Bobby, standing, did a good imitation of Rodin's *Thinker,* chin on fist, right elbow held up by left. He frowned. Finally, he said, "No."

"Do you know what work he did before he disappeared?"

"No. He almost never talked about his job. Just bragged about the broads he shacked up with. He was full of, whatddaya call it, *sexual innuendo*—he's playin' grab-ass with this one, that one. No one believed him, much."

"You helping Stark look for Harry's killer?" Rex

asked. "My guess is, some hubby comes home early one night, there's his wife gettin' it on with old Harry, husband takes a hammer or whatever's at hand, and *ba-boom*."

"Husband gets Harry out of the house, follows him to his car, then he lets him have it," said Bobby. "That's what Vinnie thinks. And Chief Stark."

Charly said, "They do not suspect Madame Wells anymore?"

"Naw. Chief decided that's not her style. She's got a history of screwing young guys, it's a game with her. She's not a killer."

# SIGNS AND PORTENTS

TUESDAY MORNING WHEN CHARLY WENT DOWNSTAIRS he found an ominous sight in front of the refrigerator: drops of blood. He counted: one two three four small drops of blood, now turning dark as they dried. Evidently his cats had encountered a mouse last night.

"*Ah, la la, la pauvre souris*," he thought. Though why the mouse hadn't died sooner was a mystery. How could a house with four cats and one large dog harbor a mouse? The mouse had lived under the refrigerator since last fall and Charly fed it, pushing crackers and occasionally bits of cheese under the grating at the front. He'd always been charmed by the tiny rodents.

"It is a portent," Charly thought gloomily. He was fond of portents, signs, omens. He knew that a full moon meant disturbances at the restaurant, customers drinking too much and arguing; he knew that a bird in the house meant death; and that his cats could predict storms better than the weather bureau: when the cats all

60

came inside on a pleasant summer's night, he knew there would be rain before morning. Now, these drops of blood presaged, as sure as anything, that someone he knew would die soon. (Since Charly, as a well-known restaurateur, heard about the death of an acquaintance or customer practically every month, this wasn't a difficult prediction to make.)

So it was in a slightly glum mood that Charly and Bruno made their way to the restaurant kitchen at half past seven Tuesday morning. Today there would be lunch but no dinner—it would be a short day.

It didn't occur to Charly that his negative mood might be due to the heavy meal he'd enjoyed with Rex Cingale last night, nor to the fact that he'd forgotten to take his charcoal pills to ward off the ill effects of Rex's sour wine. All he knew was that he felt depressed, and not in tune with the world. The weather abetted Charly's mood: the air was cold with a chill wind, lumpy clouds scudded across a grey sky, and summer seemed very far away. Rain began to fall as Charly and Bruno entered the kitchen door of La Fermette.

The sight of his beautiful, tidy, clean kitchen lifted Charly's spirits a bit. The metal racks were filled with shiny copper pots, and the stainless-steel stoves, cupboards, salamander, and refrigerator gleamed. Charly first turned on the ovens and checked the refrigerator and the walk-ins. His policy was to discard—either throw away or give away—most prepared foods on Sunday night, so that Tuesday mornings they would start afresh. He went to his office, where Bruno was already lying on the rug. Charly removed his jacket, but not his beret, and sat at his desk.

He made lists of menu specials, and telephoned purveyors until eight o'clock. Orders for Elmo

61

Richards, at Richards Diary and Produce; Southwind Farm for poultry; beef and pork from an Albany supplier; veal from a farm in Virginia which raised calves in a humane way; fish and shellfish, bread, liquor and wine, soft drinks and fruit juices.

He heard Joe Okun and Benny come into the kitchen, then Julius. Recognized their footsteps, and by the way that Bruno raised his head: an alert pointing of the head for Joe and Benny, and much tail wagging; merely a twitching nose for Julius, saluting the fact that a friend had appeared, but a friend who wasn't a dog person.

Charly called out, as usual, "I am in my office." He heard Julius and Benny discuss the tasks: the chicken stock to make; the soups; the sandwich meats to cut; the ground beef to form into patties, as soon as it arrived; the egg pies to make and now, an addition because there had been so many requests for meatless items, Benny's variation on Charly's now-famous sausage and egg pies, Veggie Wedges, a melange of vegetables and cheese bound together with beaten egg. Benny had thought up the name.

"The men at lunch want meat," Charly had argued.

"The customers you have now ask for meat, because that's all you have," Benny reasoned. "But just as you've had to increase your meatless items at night, I think you'll find that if you offer meatless items at lunch, you'll get new customers." As a new vegetarian, Benny foresaw a new veggie brotherhood emerging. Max and Fred bore him up.

They made mushroom-and-barley soup with vegetable broth; tomato and mozzarella grilled sandwiches; eggplant melts and now, the latest, Veggie Wedges. Charly was surprised and pleased to find that new customers did appear, asking for the meatless dishes. At first they were Benny's friends from Tae Kwon Do, but the friends told other friends. "I am behind the time," Charly told Benny, Max, and Fred, as they sat in the kitchen one afternoon eating baked potatoes topped with spicy vegetarian chili.

"It's the only way to eat," Fred said, tossing his ponytail of white-blond hair. "Meat not only clogs your arteries, it clogs your brain. Makes you slow and sluggish." He stood up, positioned his feet and executed a spin-kick.

"Hum, hum," said Charly. It was true that whenever he felt under the weather, a few days on a grain-and-vegetable diet soon put him right. "We shall see," he said enigmatically. "The world, it is changing fast."

"We're moving forwards by moving backwards," Max said. "Back when men were monkeys, this is the way they ate. Veggies, fruit, and nuts."

Charly thought of the men connected with Fabulous Foods: man-eating gorillas, and what they were up to was, he feared, far worse than monkey business. He looked up at Julius, who stood in the doorway.

"Changed my mind, Charly. I'm going to find out a few things for you."

"*Tiens.* That is nice, Julius."

"I contacted my buddy in Connecticut who does investigative services. We use him at my old firm. They do screenings for prospective employees and for companies we might want to do business with, you know, mergers, buyouts, various investment services. Before we recommend a company to our investors, we check them out pretty thoroughly. I asked him to find out what he could about Fabulous Foods."

"I will certainly pay for what you find out."

"Okay, I'll tell him that. This is a college classmate of

63

mine," Julius went on. "And he still owes me a few favors. My company gave him an exclusive on all their investigations when he was starting up."

"What is his background?"

"Well," Julius grinned, "he tells everyone he was in law enforcement, but *entre nous,* he was really with the CIA, and he learned a lot of dirty tricks. I mean, this guy knows it all."

"And you are happy with him? Your company uses him still?"

"Using him as we speak," Julius said. "As you know I'm still consulting for my company, and we're running a few background checks. I'm working on a couple of companies right now."

"Will it take long? To investigate Fabulous Foods, I mean?"

"No. You'd be surprised what a couple of phone calls will get you."

Charly thought of the Gestapo but decided not to voice the thought. How else could you fight fire, except with fire? "Julius, the methods of your friend, are they lawful?"

"Some of them are awful and few of them are lawful," Julius joked. "That's why I'm not telling you his name."

"Just as well," said Charly.

"I can tell you one thing right off the bat," Julius continued. "Fabulous Foods is listed nowhere, not in Dunn & Bradstreet, not on any of the stock exchanges, nor are they registered with the SEC. Any so-called stocks that they're selling, they're doing it without benefit of any regulatory agency. In other words, they're phonies."

"So once you give them your money . . ." Charly said.

64

Julius waved his arms. "It's over the hills and far away."

"And don't forget you were going to get information from your aunt about Harry Clark," Charly reminded Julius.

"I did forget, Charly. I'll do it soon."

It was three o'clock, and Joe Okun was mopping the floor of La Fermette's kitchen. Benny had gone to his martial-arts practice, Patty Perkins had looked in to get Charly's list of what desserts to prepare for the week and to deliver her white chocolate chip and walnut cookies and three cakes, and Max and Fred were due in to prepare three stews and two soups for takeout. Charly was again making lists and paying bills in his office, and Julius had driven off to collect shad roes, smoked shad, and boned shad from the Hudson River fisherman who supplied the restaurant with much of his catch.

"Hello, Charly," called Max and Fred, as they opened the kitchen door. They came into the office.

"We've got some news about Everston Pilchard," said Fred.

"Tell me, *s'il vous plait*."

"He comes from a rich family, but his father, a drunk, lost most of the money. Everston has a tiny private income. He teaches, and in the summer he works as a landscape gardener. He's been at the school for six years, and he's generally disliked: by the students because he's a stickler for rules and is always punishing them, and by the faculty because he's such a snob. He thinks he's better than they are and shows it at every opportunity."

Fred continued. "He took a leave of absence a while back and everyone said it was because he went crazy

65

and had to be locked up. I think he had a temper tantrum in a classroom, and threw a chair at someone."

"*Mon Dieu*. How did you learn that?"

"Oh, we asked around," Fred said vaguely. "You know how it is, people talk." Charly nodded. He knew exactly how it was.

"Hello?" called Julius. He'd just come in the door. "I've got some news for you, Charly. It's no-news, really, I just had a talk with my buddy on my car phone. You know, the one with the information service."

"Yes?"

"My friend made a few phone calls, and he can't find out a single thing about Fabulous Foods. They're not listed by Cole, Lexis-Nexis, local banks, they have no credit history, no credit cards. The only telephone listing was a number in Sharpsville for Fabulous Foods. Nothing for Scungilli nor Zampone. As a company, they—in theory—don't exist."

# WHITE CHOCOLATE CHIP AND WALNUT COOKIES

### Yield: 20-24 cookies

1 stick (4 ounces) butter
½ cup sugar
1 egg, beaten
1 teaspoon almond essence
1 cup flour
½ teaspoon baking soda
1 cup white chocolate chips
1 cup walnut meats

Preheat oven to 350°. Cream butter and sugar; beat in egg and almond essence. Add flour and baking soda, white chocolate chips and walnuts. Drop by tablespoon onto ungreased cookie sheet and bake 10–12 minutes or until just turning golden. Cool.

# A MORNING AT FABULOUS FOODS

ARTHUR ARPATI, THE EXECUTIVE CHEF (THE ONLY CHEF) at Fabulous Foods, stood on the loading platform with his clipboard, checking in the most recent shipment from Splendid Shrimp in New Jersey.

Same old, same old. Wasn't the world sick of shrimp? No. People were eating more of the expensive seafood. And, as is always the case when demand exceeds legitimate supply, some pretty strange shrimp were entering the market place, shrimp that should have received the last rites long ago and been turned into fertilizer.

He was certain Fabulous Foods had a great future: more and more restaurants were opening, and customers demanded a large menu. There weren't enough first-class chefs to go around, and who was going to cook all that fancy stuff? The answer was simple: restaurants bought ready-cooked, or "value-added" foods. It was already prepared, just heat and serve. In many restaurants 90 percent of the menu was value-added, which meant a much lower payroll. All you needed in the kitchen were a couple of low-priced cooks.

Fabulous Foods was starting out small, but would grow larger as the orders came in. Arthur was doing a lot of recipe development. He was thankful for his knowledge of chemistry. Much of his work consisted in masking the chemical taste of these products. The swordfish brochettes, for example, developed a salty, metallic taste upon reheating—possibly from the MSG, or maybe from the excess tripoly (trisodium polyphosphate, used to keep fish plump by retaining

68

water in the flesh). Some of the shrimp tasted rubbery, but meat tenderizer might help. Crabmeat had problems, too. Caramelized sugar, flavored salt, and other less innocuous products like sodium nitrite and nitrate masked a lot of sins.

Arthur had already developed some great product: Swordfish Genovese; Shrimp Milano; Crabmeat Palermo; Shrimp Romano; Flounder Capri; Shrimp alla Napoli. He needed a dozen, for starters. Later on, he'd hire some sous-chefs and maybe even a food scientist or two. Then they'd branch out into meat, poultry, maybe wild game, as well.

Arthur Arpati, ex-FDA inspector, was an old hand at the food business. He considered himself a professional. True, there had been some setbacks: like being sentenced to six years in the slammer for importing bad fish but actually serving only eighteen months; like selling shrimp infected with the bacterium *Clostridium perfringens* to a cruise ship, which had to return to port when everyone on board became ill. That sort of thing, nothing major.

What really turned Arthur on was the idea of becoming a world-class chef. He was fascinated by food, but more than that he was intrigued by the general public's fascination with "Gourmet Fare." Those suckers would pay two hundred, four hundred bucks for a meal at one of those fancy restaurants in New York City. Arthur had eaten at some of those palaces. Food was generally edible, rarely great. So, what the hell was it? The snob appeal? Or being seen with the celebs? Or did the jokers really love the timbale of parsnips and arugula, the flan of crayfish and truffles, the risotto of sea urchin roe and foie gras? Who the hell knew?

And yet . . . food could be wonderful. Some of those

chefs really delivered, using beautiful ingredients cooked perfectly. But how many of the dumb yuppies could tell? Both good and bad restaurants seemed to flourish, and the public couldn't tell the difference between the two. Prepared foods had a great future. True, they were loaded with chemicals, but the restaurant-going public appeared to be unaware of this. Fabulous Foods was only one of hundreds of prepared-foods companies in the United States. But, Arthur vowed, it would be the best.

This was an interim period in Arthur's life. Fabulous Foods was but a grimy way station in his ascent up the food-service ladder. At the top was his own restaurant. Chez Arturo. Casa Arpati. Arpati's Place. Whatever. He'd get there, never fear. But not tomorrow. Arthur was a philosopher. It took time.

For the moment, Fabulous Foods was Arthur's life. The licenses and documents needed for operating a food-preparation company, and the recent health department inspector's certificate (not one violation, kitchen was squeaky-clean) were hanging in his office. Certainly it was a beautiful environment: state-of-the-art, indeed. A good place to hone your culinary skills. If Arthur's sauces, stuffings, marinades, and flavored butters made these awful raw ingredients taste good, think of how they would taste when paired with really first-class foodstuffs. At Casa Arturo.

The owners had agreed with Arthur that for the product to taste really great it had to be made in small batches, no more than a hundred portions. Once made, packed, rapid-cooled and flash-frozen, the product would be stored in the second building's freezer room and shipped out in containers packed with dry ice. Fabulous Foods was a boutique operation—for now.

Scungilli and Zampone made their legal profits in the importation of thousands of pounds of raw ingredients to brokers and other wholesalers across America. Fabulous Foods was merely an offshoot of this venture. Scungilli and Zampone's illegal profits were in heroin. The drug money was laundered at Fabulous Foods. It paid the help's salaries—all in cash, of course—and it bought all of the raw ingredients. The profits from Fabulous Foods, thus cleansed, would be sent to the bank.

Because the New York–New Jersey area was having a crackdown on crime, the old Splendid Shrimp company was closing down, given a new name, and moving upstate, away from those crazed Colombians for whom murder was merely a daily exercise to keep their trigger fingers nimble.

There was a quick rat-a-tat on the door, and Zampone and Scungilli entered the kitchen. Arthur disliked his bosses; they were ruthless and had no class. Still he was paid two thousand dollars a week, not bad for a job he considered merely an apprenticeship. They also paid his rent, car lease, and other expenditures, not out of altruism but because they wanted to keep Arthur Arpati under their thumbs.

"Reception on Monday went great, huh?" Ricky Zampone said.

"I gather," Arthur replied. "I was back here, so I didn't see much, but the amount of food they ate—double what we'd planned. Good thing you got that Morrie guy to get extra. They picked the table clean. Fuckin' locusts."

"Morrie's been real useful getting us introductions," Scungilli said. "He's the one, insisted we invite that Italian guy owns a steakhouse near Klover. Cingale's

71

gonna get us into The Italian Heritage Club, he says every Italian restaurateur in the Hudson Valley's a member. Yeah, Morrie's okay."

"You believe he went to Princeton?" Arthur asked. "Not too swift, if you ask me. Saying he owns that French restaurant."

"He's okay," Scungilli said, "but it's like talking to a kid. Wants us to notice how smart he is. And he lies. You catch someone in one fib," Scungilli moralized, "and everything else the fucker says, you know that's a fib, too."

"Sure it is," Ricky agreed. "And listen, that guy Charly? The one who really owns La Fermette? We should stay away from him. I don't trust him. I saw him looking at the shrimp very carefully."

"That's my advice too, stay away," Martin Scungilli said. "Charly knows too much about food. I don't want that guy near our operation."

"I agree, too," said Arthur. He didn't know what guy they were talking about, but he agreed with everything they said. Healthier that way.

"So, Arthur," said Ricky Zampone, "What you working on today?"

"The swordfish brochettes," Arthur said. "We gotta hide that metallic taste. Then I'm going to work on the Shrimp Milano, the sauce separates, and then I'll deal with the Shrimp alla Napoli, they're too rubbery."

"Yeah," said Zampone. "I'll tell you one thing I learned yesterday. The people up here, they don't like nothing new. It's a spaghetti-and-meatballs crowd."

Arthur could picture the people who would be eating his food. Overweight, wheezing with asthma, lots of varicose veins and heart murmurs, on every sort of medication known to the drug industry. The kind who would eat a bag of fake-fat potato chips, devour some bologna, then a strawberry sundae, then reach for the Maalox. A few more chemicals wouldn't hurt them.

"So, carry on, Arturo," Scungilli said, waddling out, followed by Zampone. "We got a meeting with Morrie."

Maurice Baleine parked his dark blue Mercedes SL 200 in the visitors' slot at Fabulous Foods. He slid from the leather interior. He knew that this small company was taking luxury foods into an entirely new dimension. Most value-added product was pedestrian: meat loaf, beef roulades; battered cheese sticks, vegetables and fish; soups and stews; chicken and tuna salads. Fabulous Foods was upscale. Fabulous Foods was, well, fabulous.

He walked up to the entrance and rang the buzzer. Scungilli unlocked the doors, smiling at Maurice.

"Right on time, Morrie."

"Ah, my good Martin. It's a pleasure to be here," Maurice said in his supercilious way. "Beautiful countryside, reminds me of Princeton. I hope I'll have a chance to talk with chef Arpati?"

"Sure, sure," Scungilli said affably, ignoring the remark about the countryside. "C'mon back, we'll sign the papers in the conference room. Then you can meet with chef Arpati."

Zampone, Scungilli, and Baleine sat at the long blond table sipping espresso. Maurice was poring over thirty pages of documentation so abstruse in its legalese that he could only pretend to understand what the arcane language meant. The upshot was, the owners told Maurice, that though Fabulous Foods was not a public company yet, it was applying to the SEC

73

and hoped to be selling stock within two years. By getting in on the ground floor Maurice, by virtue of his twenty-five thousand dollars, would receive shares of stock that would be legal tender as soon as the SEC cleared them.

It was a shaky concept and Charly Poisson—or more precisely Charly's investment adviser Jimmy Houghton—would have ripped up the thirty pages on the spot, since the intricate wording really said that *if* the stock became legal (and Jimmy would have said that Fabulous Foods hadn't a chance in hell of ever becoming legal) Maurice would receive stock.

"What it really says," Scungilli told Maurice, bypassing the stock issue, "is that by investing twenty-five thousand dollars you have become a limited partner in our operation."

Zampone added, "A very basic document, really." He didn't understand the prospectus, either. "You become a subsidiary partner. Not a major partner, you unnerstand, there are only two of us. But we'll have ten subsidiary partners. You'll have limited input into the workings of the company, but your input will be very valuable." And very limited, Scungilli and Zampone neglected to point out.

"Yes, yes," said Maurice eagerly, seeing himself seated behind a large desk, speaking into a telephone while two other calls awaited his attention; piles of documentation on the desk needing his signature; a secretary lurking nearby ready to take rapid-fire dictation.

His dreams of glory soared, and Maurice envisioned the future: a *pied à terre* in Paris; a studio in Greenwich Village, large enough to entertain clients to caviar and smoked-salmon.

Richard Zampone interrupted his reverie. "Wanna sign here, Morrie? Then we'll go, talk to Arthur. I know he's been waitin' for your input."

Maurice uncapped his Mont Blanc pen, shot his cuffs importantly, and signed with a flourish.

# MAURICE AT FABULOUS FOODS

THE TWENTY-FIVE-THOUSAND-DOLLAR CHECK DISappeared into Scungilli's pocket, and Maurice's contract with Fabulous Foods disappeared into a folder.

"It's a wonnerful company, Morrie, you'll be a millionaire soon."

"Great food," Zampone echoed. He'd sampled it once, a very small bite. "You're a lucky fella, Morrie. C'mon, let's go to the kitchen."

Three more subsidiary partners were arriving in an hour: a luncheonette owner; the owner of a company which sold preowned vehicles; and a mortician. They were investing ten thousand dollars each. It wasn't easy to find people willing to pour twenty-five big ones into Fabulous Foods. All three, former classmates at the local community college, considered themselves gourmets, and were anxious to participate in such an exciting venture. No troubles anticipated, there.

Zampone knocked briefly, then opened the door to the kitchen, where Arthur Arpati was standing by the stove, stirring shrimp in a red sauce. Another saucepan held shrimp in a cream sauce. A crackling under the salamander indicated that brochettes were grilling. Arthur frowned.

"I don't like people in my kitchen when I'm running

tests, you know that, Richard." Arpati wiped his hands on his apron and glared at his visitors.

"Yeah, yeah, Arthur, we won't be long. I wanted to introduce you to Morrie Baleine, our newest—uh—subsidiary partner."

"I've met him," Arthur said, and turned back to his pots.

"I was hoping we could sit down and discuss the product," Maurice said. He'd quickly learned that you didn't call food "food" in the professional world. It was "the product." Just like a restaurant was "the store."

"*Discuss the product?*" Arpati echoed. "What's to discuss?"

Maurice smiled urbanely: the epicure giving the kitchen help advice. "I thought we could discuss the seasonings. That shrimp in tomato sauce, yesterday, I thought it had a shade too much oregano. Maybe you could halve the oregano, add some saffron . . ."

" '*Add some saffron*'? At five hundred dollars for less than you can hold in your fist? You nuts or something?"

"Well, maybe not saffron," Maurice conceded. "I'd like to sit down and discuss it. I've had"—Maurice coughed—"a bit of experience in the kitchen."

"Yeah?" Arpati turned his back on the two men and picked up one of the sauté pans, which he agitated. The creamy mess, he stirred with a wooden spoon. He turned the brochettes under the salamander, pulled one out to inspect it, smelled it, then pulled the other two out, laid them on the counter next to the stove. "We got rid of that smell," he announced. "Look, Mr. Uh, I'm busy, now. You mind? Listen, thanks for getting all that food, yesterday, I appreciate it. I don't mean to sound rude, but I don't have time to talk, now."

76

"Of course." Maurice smiled. "The chef is creating. I understand, sir. It's a beautiful occupation, is it not? Concocting celestial dishes, going home to a simple meal—you know that Escoffier's favorite meal was scrambled eggs, and that he neither smoked nor drank alcohol. I have much respect for the creative genius. You have so much to teach the rest of us."

Arthur looked like he'd bitten into a particular fiery habañero pepper, all 300,000 Scoville Units hitting his palate at once.

"Zampon-n-ne . . ." Arthur said. "Some other time, huh?"

"Right, Arthur," Zampone said. "Morrie, we'll leave now. You can visit another time. Come on, I'll show you the desk you'll be usin' when you come up to check things out."

Maurice and Zampone walked out of the kitchen, and down the corridor to an empty office. The grey wall-to-wall was new, as was the small metal desk and the Levolor blinds at the windows. A large plastic ficus tree stood in the corner. A kitchen chair stood behind the desk, another in front of windows that overlooked the parking lot.

"This's it," Richard sang.

"My office?" It was big enough, Maurice thought, but not very imposing. Maybe he could get Barbara to add a few touches. He noted that there was no telephone, and that the fluorescent lighting was weak.

"Well, uh," Richard said. *Oh, hell, the papers are signed, who cares?* "It's the office for all the subsidiary partners. Of course you won't all be here at once. I doubt if you'll come in once a month, any one of you."

Maurice gulped. He laughed, a loud bray indicating

that this was a petty misunderstanding. Ah, the food world. They simply didn't understand the way businessmen worked, all of these culinary geniuses.

"I don't think you understand, Richard, the way financiers work. I plan to be here every day, overseeing the operation."

A choking sound, which might have been a cough, came from Zampone. "Every day?" he said faintly. His stomach was gurgling, too.

"Well, I am a partner," Maurice said. "A limited partner."

"Well, yeah. Listen, Morrie, I gotta run. Why don't you sit in your new office, look things over, hey, make a list of improvements we could make in the public area, huh?" Zampone fled. He was dying of hunger, and he had been craving a Burger King.

An hour later when Zampone returned to Fabulous Foods, the limited partners' office was empty, Maurice's Mercedes was gone, and the three new limited partners-to-be were sitting in the conference room with Martin Scungilli, drinking espresso and eating cannoli brought by Buddy Maris, the owner of Vintage Vehicles, Preowned Cars for the Discerning Driver.

They'd toured the plant, visited the kitchen, and declared themselves delighted with Fabulous Foods. Zampone sighed happily. These were his kind of men. He could relate to these guys.

"Hey, fellas, ready to sign on the dotted line?" He smiled, belching up a small portion of Double Whopper.

Everyone nodded happily. They signed, handed over their checks, "not rubber, like some of the food I serve," Billy Herman, the owner of the Happy Farmer Luncheonette cracked. Then they looked at their watches and said they had things to do.

"You don't want to see the limited partners' office, where you can sit when you come to visit?" Zampone prayed, *Please Christ, let Morrie be the only one who wants to make this his lifetime career.*

"You kidding?" said Joe Scapece, the co-owner of Sardowski, Stein, and Scapece, morticians. "I got a garden to plant, when I'm not layin' out stiffs, and I got a customer arriving soon. Which reminds me, there's a funny smell in the big freezer room. Smells just like my embalming fluid."

"We're havin' trouble with one of our refrigeration units," said Scungilli smoothly. "Must be that."

"Yeah, I guess."

When the three limited partners had left, Scungilli and Zampone sat and sipped their espresso. "It's coming along," Ricky said. "New Jersey tell you about the shipment comin' in this afternoon?"

"Shipment?" Scungilli asked. "No more of that stinking shrimp."

"Nah," Ricky said. "The money. We'll store it in a freezer."

There was a knock on the door, and two workmen appeared in overalls. "Scungilli and Zampone?" they asked.

"Yeah, that's us. You coming up from where?"

"Shipment from Splendid Shrimp," one of the men said. "Four cases."

"Yeah, yeah," Ricky Zampone said. "We know all about it."

With Zampone and Scungilli leading the way, the grey, nondescript van inched toward the big corrugated-iron building that housed the main freezer units. Zampone unlocked the big overhead door and the van slid inside. Zampone pressed a button and the door closed automatically. Fluorescent lights snapped on, bathing the cavernous room in a ghostly blue light.

The two drivers opened the back of the van and slid out four canvas cases. Using the relay system, one driver handed the suitcase to the other driver, who handed it to Scungilli, who passed it along to Zampone.

"You want we should sign?" Zampone asked.

"You betcha. It's our heads if you don't."

"A week's worth, right?"

"No, a month's. Until that plant is up and running in Pennsylvania, you'll be handling the bulk of it."

# LA FERMETTE SERVES REAL FOOD

WEDNESDAY NIGHT'S DINNER AT LA FERMETTE WOULD include: shad roes with asparagus; broiled shad with sorrel sauce; roast chicken with herb and sausage stuffing; mustard-crusted pork. There were also meat loaf and pasta dishes. La Fermette catered to every size purse.

After the lunch dishes were put away, Charly poached the shad roes and placed them on a tray to chill off in the cooler. Tonight, they'd be dusted with flour and, as the orders came in, quickly sautéed in butter. The finished roes would be lifted out of the pan and the butter allowed to darken; the sauce would be finished with a dash of balsamic vinegar, then the roes were plated and sprinkled with Oriental garlic chives from Charly's garden, and capers. Benny was preparing the pork, and Julius was mixing bread crumbs, parsley, onion, sage, and sausage for the chicken stuffing.

"Everything is set for tonight?" Charly asked.

"Yeah, don't worry about it, Charly," Julius said.

"I'm going home for a while, but we'll all be back at four. How many reservations you got?"

"Only ten," Charly shrugged. "But thirty, maybe forty people, a table for six. I think Bruno and I will take a little ride."

Julius said, "I've been thinking about those characters at Fabulous Foods. They've arrived up here at the very time Maurice has extra money from his restaurant shares. It's as if Divine Providence arranged the mysterious coincidence, so that Maurice could lose his shirt."

Charly smiled, a shark's grimace. "Remember, my dear Julius. In life, there are no coincidences. Only lessons that we must learn. *Le bon Dieu* has a plan for Maurice. Of that I am convinced. It will be revealed to us in time. In fact, here is Maurice now, at the door."

The kitchen door opened, and Maurice stuck his head around the door.

"Ah, the chefs are busy creating, I see."

"We rest after a busy lunch. What can we do for you, Maurice?" Charly's voice was more resigned than cordial.

"I just wanted to say hello. I've just been conferring with Arthur Arpati at Fabulous Foods. He's the head chef. Now that I'm a partner, I said I'd give him some cooking tips. I'll be going up every day," Maurice smiled smugly.

"Uh," Charly grunted.

"I'm sure I can help chef Arpati a lot," Maurice continued. "And for that I have you to thank, Charly. Working with you all these years, I've learned so much about food."

Charly was dumbfounded. "Working with me, Maurice? But you have rarely set foot in the kitchen."

Maurice bestowed a superior smile. "I don't chop

onions or parsley, Charly, but I've absorbed the philosophy of the creative chef."

"Have you helped the chef yet?" Julius asked.

Maurice smiled condescendingly. "Of course. Charming chap. And Arpati agrees that my input will be very valuable. All my food experience."

"All your food experience," Charly echoed. "But tell me, Maurice, is it true that you tell them that we will serve their foods here at La Fermette? And did you tell them, Maurice, that you owned this restaurant?"

Maurice smiled patiently. "I said I'd talk to you, Charly, about serving their dishes. I told them I used to be co-owner." Maurice put his hands in his pockets, jiggled some coins, and rocked back on his heels. Charly knew that this was a characteristic pose when Maurice was lying.

"So you are saying that your new partners are telling the lies?"

"Telephone for you, Julius," Benny said, interrupting the confrontation.

Maurice smiled. "Lying, lying, I don't think they were lying. I think they misunderstood. They misunderstand a lot, I've noticed, they're so involved. Creativity, you know. Always thinking of their delicious food."

"I see," Charly said. "And they are happy that you will go up to their factory every day, to give them the benefit of your investment expertise?"

"Gastronomic, Charly, gastronomic expertise."

Julius returned. He was grinning. Ignoring Maurice, he said to Charly, "They've got sheets, both of them. Sheets as long as your arm. Richard Zampone, 'Little Ricky,' is the son of Big Ricky Zampone, the three-hundred-pound gorilla who was gunned down in a

82

Newark bar back in the seventies. Big Ricky and his son were friends of Walter Maxwell."

"But of course," Charly said. "We speak of Maxwell when Maurice bring them Sunday night."

Although Charly was ostensibly speaking with Julius, he observed Maurice out of the corner of his eye. Maurice had puffed up his chest, his face was red, and his eyes were bugging out. "Jailbirds? Scungilli and Zampone? Ridiculous, Charly." Maurice wagged his index finger in Charly's face. "Your jealousy knows no bounds. And you, Julius, you're just as bad. Remarks like that are actionable. I shall speak with my attorney."

"If you're smart, Maurice, you'll shut up about this little conversation," Julius cautioned. "Little Ricky Zampone and Marty Scungilli are connected. You'd better keep very, very quiet."

Maurice stalked out, slamming the door so hard that the pans rattled.

At the Klover Police Station, not two miles from La Fermette, Chief of Police John Stark was sitting at his desk talking to two of his key men, Vince Matucci and Abe Reynolds, about Harry Clark.

"So," Stark said, "he eats a burger and fries at your Uncle Rex's place, Vince, all those little peppers in his stomach . . ."

"Pepperoncini," Vince said.

"Right," Stark continued, "and then he goes out, meets someone, and bang, gets hit on the head. Now, what was Harry Clark up to, right before he died? That angry husband scenario is too easy, too obvious."

Matucci and Reynolds shook their heads. "We've been asking in the bars," Abe said, "And no one wants to remember a thing. 'Jeez, Harry Clark, huh, Officer? I

dunno, I never knew him that well, just to say hello to' . . .
and like that." Abe Reynolds was slow-moving,
overweight, with half-closed, piggy brown eyes, but he
knew how to talk to people. To look at Abe, you'd think he
was the dumbest cop in the world. Big mistake. In between
yawns and belches and scratching and generally looking
stupid, Abe often got folks to talk, say things they
wouldn't say to, well, John Stark.

"Okay, Chief, I'll hit the bars again, talk to the guys
some more."

"Make a list of the ones you talk to," Stark said.

Abe fished around in his pocket. He pulled out a thick
black notebook. "List's right here," he said, waving the
book. "Trouble is, he hung around with such scum, any
one of 'em coulda popped him."

Back in his house, Charly had a sudden thought: He
should telephone the Warburtons and find out if his
remedies were helping their old cat. Midge answered
and Charly identified himself.

"Oh, Charly, how lovely of you to call. We haven't
gotten the medications yet, but we will. Socrates sees
that we're taking an interest in him, and he's pleased.
Animals notice so much, don't they?"

"Madame Warburton, I will be in your neighborhood
this afternoon, I will mix up two bottles of Bach flowers
and drop them by."

"Lovely, Charly. See you in, what, about an hour?"

Charly had suddenly remembered a nursery in the
Highdale area that specialized in geraniums. This way,
he could kill two birds with one stone: get the flowers
for his window box on the front stoop of his house, and
investigate people he'd always thought of as "the
mystery couple." He'd always been reticent about the

84

Warburtons, believing, as they'd dined at La Fermette with Walter Maxwell, that they belonged to Walter's high-rolling set. Now, he felt that he'd wronged a noble, animal-loving couple.

Warburton Farm was a big sprawling stone house set in the midst of fields. Midge and Billy Warburton looked as if they'd stepped out of the eighteenth-century portraits in their front hall. They were dressed in dark clothing, with the high cheekbones and thin lips of old English aristocracy—or so Charly had always pictured these personages.

Charly stood in the entrance hall (antique walnut sideboard, a charming small Degas sculpture of a ballerina) and felt the age of the house: it was like stepping back in time. The centuries-old furniture smelled of beeswax polish. An urn holding irises and mock orange stood on the antique sideboard. Charly held out the small paper bag. "Four times a day Socrates must have the drops," he admonished. "I admire your Degas ballerina."

The statue shimmered with life. Too bad the head was slightly dented—someone must have dropped her. Still, Charly felt, it added to her charm. She was smaller than life but so vibrant, he wouldn't have been surprised to see her execute a *pas de deux*. He could imagine her stumbling, hitting her head. His heart fluttered as he gazed at the beautiful sculpture.

"She's like our child," Midge said. "We bought her in Paris years ago."

Charly felt movement by his trouser leg. An enormous yellow cat was looking up at him with dark, aware eyes.

"My dear Socrate, this is medicine for you," Charly spoke respectfully. "Would you like some, now?" To the Warburtons he mouthed 'may I?'

The couple nodded. Charly bent down with the dropper, and to his surprise the cat opened his mouth, willing to take the unknown medicine.

"*Incroyable,*" Charly exclaimed. "This, I have never seen."

"He's an incredible cat," said Billy Warburton. "He senses that you are a good person and that the medicine will help him."

Charly smiled. "When a person says you are a good person, he usually wants something from you. When a cat says you are a good person, that really means something."

Driving home, Charly spoke to Bruno, who had been waiting for him in the car. "Socrates is a splendid cat, and I think the Warburtons are very kind people."

# BROILED SHAD WITH SORREL SAUCE

### Yield: 4 servings

2 shad fillets, enough for four servings
Butter, melted, as needed

Sauce:
1 quart young sorrel leaves, washed
1 stick butter, melted
1 cup heavy cream stiffly beaten, as needed
Salt and pepper to taste

To prepare shad brush both sides with melted butter and lay skin side down in broiler pan. Broil 6–8 minutes or until fish flakes easily with a fork. Halve each fillet.

To make sauce, finely shred the sorrel and steam in a few drops of water, in a non-reactive pan, until wilted. Drain. Melt butter and stir in cooked, drained sorrel. Beat in whipped cream to taste and add salt and pepper as needed.

# TWO CONTRASTING DINNERS

"FOR YOU, I MAKE SPECIAL, MADAME," CHARLY SAID. He'd been called from the kitchen for a culinary consultation in his dining room with Honoria Wells, who was eating, this evening, with her farm manager Tiger Cavett. Just a quiet little dinner for two. Honoria, bored with her grains-and-greens diet (to keep her looking trim, animal protein aged you so) told Charly she wanted him to thrill her with a gastronomic masterpiece.

"I give you everything you have forbidden yourself," Charly promised. "Will be a meal to remember. Shad filet, very small, in sorrel cream sauce. That is to begin. Then fresh asparagus vinaigrette, with finely sliced shallot, to clear the palate."

"Whatever Ms. Wells is having, I'm having too," said Tiger Cavett.

A year ago Tiger had come to Charly looking for work, and Charly, who'd taken a liking to the young man, had recommended Honoria. Tiger was young and handsome, but, Charly sensed, he wouldn't become amorously involved with his boss.

"Maybe he's gay, maybe he's not," Julius had speculated. "He plays his personal life close to the vest. But whatever he is, he's good for my aunt. She's been a lot more cheerful since he arrived, and it's 'I'll have to check with Tiger,' all the time. He's a no-nonsense person."

Charly agreed. "Monsieur Cavett is old beyond his years. And he is suspicious of everyone. An admirable trait."

It was a trait of Charly's, too, of course.

"And after the asparagus?" Honoria prompted.

"One of my range-run chickens from Southwind Farm," Charly decided. "Simply roasted, served with small new potato. The skins of bird and potato crackling with sea salt. Nothing more. One entire chicken for the two of you and you will eat every bite and lick your forgers. After that, *une salade* of baby lettuces, and then, I propose Pouligny Saint-Pierre, a French goat cheese, and with that a glass of Chateau Chalon. It is a *vin de paille,* the grapes are picked late in the season, then laid on beds of straw to dry, and then they are pressed. It is sweet, but with a taste of the nut."

"It sounds celestial, Charly," Honoria said. "To change the subject, what do you know about that food company Maurice was talking about at my party the other night?"

Charly shrugged his shoulders. "They are not, I believe, nice people. I would not invest in this company."

"Julius told Honoria they were crooks," Tiger agreed.

"You know who was talking about the company?" Honoria went on. "Everston Pilchard. I think he does part-time food deliveries for them. I hope you're not getting involved, Charly. I'm sure they're not honest."

"But madame," Charly smiled, "my entire world is filled with crooked people. I am fascinated by them, their self-importance, the risks they take, thinking people too stupid to notice, the fact that they are always caught in the end." Charly held up an index finger, giving Honoria and Tiger a lesson in human behavior. "Because, you see, other people are not so stupid."

Tiger had the last word: "Curiosity gets people killed, Charly."

✳✳✳

Another little dinner party was going on at the same time that Honoria Wells and Tiger Cavett were enjoying their simple but splendid meal at La Fermette, in a modern ranch house near Sharpsville, New York.

Before leaving the Fabulous Foods plant Joe Scapece had taken Arthur Arpati aside and pushed a twenty-dollar bill into his hands. "Lemme have some of that shrimp in tomato sauce," Joe whispered. "My wife didn't come to the tasting and it'll knock her on her ass. I promised her I'd get some."

Arthur, who was wondering what the hell he was going to do with dozens of boxes of the old-style Shrimp Milano (whose shrimp were tough and stringy) was happy to oblige. He should really throw it out. But twenty bucks was twenty bucks, right?

Arthur pocketed the bill and slid six boxes of Shrimp Milano straight from the freezer into a big plastic carrier bag, and muttered, "Don't let the bosses see this, hear? We're not supposed to let the product out, yet."

"I'll be as quiet as one of my fuckin' stiffs," said Joe the mortician.

So Billy Herman, owner of the Happy Farmer Luncheonette and his wife Mary; Bud Maris, owner of Vintage Vehicles and his wife Susie; and Joe Scapece and his wife Teresa, were enjoying, in the Scapece dining room, a delightful little meal: spaghettini tossed with olive oil, garlic, and parsley topped with Shrimp Milano; iceberg lettuce salad drenched in bottled Italian dressing with raw tomatoes and scallions; and Italian pastries for dessert. They were all drinking Coca-Cola and talking animatedly.

"They're serioso, them fellas," said Joe. "Stuff's

90

terrific. Pretty soon it's going to be all over America. Fabulous Foods. And, getting in on the ground floor as we're doing, we're gonna make nothing but money."

"It's a beautiful little plant," said Bud Maris. "I had a word with Scungilli, he says they're gonna need extra cars for themselves and their salesmen. They're leasing now. I showed him on paper how owning my vehicles made a lot better sense than leasing. He agreed. Dollars-and-cents-wise, there are no flies on that guy."

"Well, it's good stuff but too fancy for the Happy Farmer," corpulent Billy Herman said after his first generous helping. "But I might open up a little place, dinners only, in that new shopping mall, and serve these guys' food. Couple cooks, get 'em cheap, all you do is reheat. Keeps your payroll costs way down. Mary's sister Ethel works for that big carpet company in Albany, she could get me wall-to-wall practically at cost." He wheezed and coughed. "Too many cigarettes. And you met Morrie Baleine, one of the other partners? Scungilli tells me his wife's a decorator. Maybe I could get her at a discount, too. Give the dining room some class, chandeliers, flocked wallpaper, whatever. Pass the pasta again, Teresa, I'm a pig, but that sauce's terrific."

"Great grub," said Joe Scapece heartily, though he only had one small helping. He could still smell it, that formaldehyde-like odor, and the shrimp were rubbery. It made him feel queasy just to look at the dish.

"Whassa matta, Josie, you eating like a bird," said Bud Maris, who had polished off three helpings and unbuttoned his trousers. He felt curiously hot suddenly, and perspiration was beading his forehead. He tossed down half a glass of Coke. "Boy, what's that spice they put in. Pretty hot, huh?"

"It's great, but I'm just not that hungry," said Joe Scapece listlessly.

Buddy Maris hastily pushed back his chair and headed toward the powder room at top speed. When he returned, his face was ashen and he appeared shaky. "I got an early day tomorrow," he croaked, "so, if you'll excuse us, it's the call of the wild almighty buck."

Soon after the Marises departed Mary Herman said she was getting a headache and would Joe and Teresa excuse them.

As they were loading the dishwasher, Teresa said, "Something's wrong with that shrimp, Joe, you notice it? A metallic taste."

"I smelled something like embalming fluid in their freezer," Joe said. "One of the owners said they were having trouble with the refrigeration, but if that's so, why does the shrimp taste like that?"

"I wouldn't say anything," said Teresa. "You know how it is. One or two packages defrost by accident, then they're refrozen and you get stomach trouble. Remember Marsha at Tony's reception? She was going at both ends."

"Aggh, don't talk about it," said Joe. "My stomach's feeling awful."

"You notice Buddy's face when he came back from the john? He looked terrible. Here, why don't we both take some Alka-Seltzer?"

The next morning Susie Maris called Teresa Scapece and Teresa called Mary Herman. Susie had felt fine, but Buddy had had diarrhea all night and a headache, besides. He wasn't going to the showroom, this morning. Teresa didn't tell Susie what Joe had said about the shrimp, but admitted that they'd taken an

92

Alka-Seltzer and slept well. Next, Mary Herman told Teresa that Billy had been up all night with stomach cramps, diarrhea, vomiting, and a headache. Mary herself felt fine, though she'd only picked at the shrimp sauce. They all agreed to say nothing to the owners of Fabulous Foods. Accidents happened, right? Besides, this was the company that was going to make their fortunes. They didn't want any hurt feelings.

# A BUSY TIME FOR EVERSTON

CHARLY WAS SITTING IN THE RESTAURANT OFFICE Thursday morning, with Bruno at his feet, making up a list of dinner specials. This was another night of locals. The big weekend spenders didn't arrive until Friday. At the low end would be steakburgers Parisienne with mushroom sauce and beer-basted spare ribs with mashed potatoes; and at the high end was half a range-run chicken in wine sauce, and sautéed salmon with hollandaise and asparagus. Charly heard the back door slam and a voice called out, "Charly?"

Julius appeared in the doorway, waving an envelope. "I've got that employment sheet on Harry Clark from my aunt. I'm surprised the cops didn't ask her for it."

"Let us see what it say. Do not be critical of the police, Julius, they have many cases to work on and few officers. Stark is a good man, and he does the best that he can."

Together Julius and Charly read the sheet, which had been filled out in a large, childish script. Name, d.o.b., education (he'd attended a local community college, obtaining a degree in accounting); jobs: a stable in Massachusetts; manager at Warburton Farm; manager for Walter Maxwell; assistant produce manager at the Sav-Mor Supermarket in Highdale.

Charly looked up a number, then dialed and asked to speak with the produce manager of the Sav-Mor Supermarket. But employee turnover was so rapid that no one had been there five years before when Harry Clark had worked there, and the manager didn't have the time to hunt up old records.

"Call the Warburtons," Julius suggested.

"Yes, of course." Charly dialed. "Ah, Mr. Warburton? I am calling about a former employee of yours, Harry Clark. Out of curiosity, merely, since the police are handling the case. I suppose you read in the newspaper that his body was found. Yes, poor Mr. Clark. Was Mr. Clark a satisfactory employee? And when did he work there?"

The conversation soon ended. Charly was disappointed.

"Mr. Warburton say that Harry Clark was a satisfactory employee. He left because of ill health, only worked there a few weeks. He does not remember what year, but will check his records. What do you think of that?"

"I don't know what to think, Charly. See, Harry didn't put dates down for Maxwell or the Warburtons, or the Massachusetts stable, only the supermarket. I doubt if my aunt checked. Harry sold her a bill of goods."

The back door opened: Joe Okun; Benny Perkins; Patty. Bruno roused himself and trotted out to greet his friends.

" 'Allo," Charly called. And then, to Julius: "Harry was out for money, I am convince. Mr. Clark is killed because he approach the wrong person."

94

"Hey," Julius teased, "maybe Clark was gay, and there's some kind of gay blackmail ring going on? Why not pursue that for a while?"

"Julius, you make the joke." Charly frowned. "All of these American preoccupation with sex. It is sex, sex, sex, all the time. It is your religious heritage, those vicious people in Massachusetts, killing the poor witch. The Puritans, they have much to answer for."

"The French don't like sex?"

"The French," Charly lectured, "feel that sexual relations between people are private. Gay, not gay, does not matter. In American army, gays are killed; in French army, nobody knows, or cares. Not something to make the joke about, since sex is not funny. Only in America is sex funny."

"So, what do the French make jokes about?" Benny asked. He and Joe Okun and Patty were standing in the doorway.

Charly scratched his head of suspiciously black hair. "Hmmm. The French laugh at fat ladies, rare in France, unlike here. Ladies who are . . ." Charly gesticulated, indicating roundness. "They are amusing. Ladies who have big derrières, and big *boites a lait,* the breasts. What else? Ah, how do you say it in a polite way? The passing of gas. That is considered funny."

"I think it's called 'breaking wind' in polite society, Charly," said Patty.

"Yes, yes, the breaking of the wind. Called fart. In French, called *péter.* A fart is a *pét.* There are little snuffle fritters sprinkled with fine sugar, they are called *péts de nonne,* the fart of the nun. They are delicious. You can serve them plain, or filled with jam or *crème patissiere.* Very delicate, because nuns are meant to be dainty, so of course their *péts* would be, too. And there

95

is a story of an old lady on her deathbed (my father, he love this story,) and she is about to draw her last breath. The family is standing around the bed crying, all waiting for her money, of course, as people always are in French deathbed jokes. Suddenly she make the giant *pét,* and she look up and say, '*Dame qui pette n'est pas morte,*' a lady who break wind, she is not dead yet."

Patty, Julius, Benny, and even Joe Okun were laughing heartily at the picture Charly conjured up.

"It is much nicer," Charly admonished, having, of course, to put a moral on every tale, "to laugh about fat ladies and *péts,* than to laugh about sexual matters which are so private, and can be so beautiful. The mind of the Puritan"—Charly frowned—"it is an ugly, ugly thing."

*A dead and stinking lobster,* thought Everston Pilchard, *is an ugly, ugly thing.* True, they weren't stinking horribly, but there was a definite smell. He was picking up frozen lobsters for Fabulous Foods at a warehouse nearby, he was off from school this Thursday morning. He put the crates in the trunk of his car, a well-kept elderly Volvo.

As he sped toward Sharpsville, Everston thought about his new job. Not bad, good pay, but the owners were . . . definitely not Social Register. He chuckled: "Dilatory Domiciles: Greenhaven Prison; Raiford; Yardville." They were a trio, Scungilli, Arpati, Zampone. Crooks, of course. He suspected they were into far more than fish. Who knew what he'd discover? Maybe he'd be carrying stuff away from Fabulous Foods, as well as making deliveries. Those dreary men, thought patrician Everston (whose sticky fingers had gotten him into trouble before), they had no idea who, sorry, *whom*, they were dealing with. Everston Pilchard had the IQ of a genius.

He drove quickly. Speed was of the essence, as he didn't want the smell lingering in his car. Also, he had homework papers to correct when he got home. Now, at Route 9, he turned right. And here was Sharpsville. There was the big complex of warehouses on the left.

Everston drove to the rear of the building. Honked, as instructed, and the tall black-haired man, Arpati, appeared.

"You got the lobsters, Ev?"

"Yes," Everston said.

Everston got out of the car and opened the trunk. The crates had leaked water, and there was a smell of the sea, not a fresh smell, but a musty, slightly rotten smell. A smell of dead seafood, not surprisingly.

Everston and Arpati carried the crates into the little building and set them on a long, steel-topped table. Behind the table was a tub filled with liquid. Arthur took a clawhammer, opened the four crates, and dumped the bright orange lobster bodies into the chemical solution.

"Not too bad, I've seen worse. They're precooked, which makes all the difference."

"Huh," Everston said primly.

"I wonder how long these bozos have been defrosting? That warehouse just across the Mass border, they're kinda iffy. They get the shipments from Maine, from the big hatcheries, lobsters too weak or too small to make the trip to the fancy markets. So they're parboiled and frozen up there. But believe me, when we're finished with these babies, they'll be just fine."

"Just fine?" Everston said. "But they smell bad. If they don't kill you, they'll make you sick, at the very least."

"Not really. We give them a couple of baths, then we boil the suckers again, and the pickers'll be here tomorrow. We use everything, the lobster meat and the shells, use them to make lobster bisque."

Everston had never been inside a food plant before. In fact, he'd rarely thought much about the food that he ate. He'd naturally assumed that the foods were processed according to strict government regulations, that it was safe, hygenic, even nutritious. Was this possibly not true?

"We haven't killed anyone yet," Arpati said, intuiting Everston's thoughts. "At least, not that I know of. Hey, we're no worse than anyone else. You ever been inside a chicken battery? Filthiest places in the world. Chicken shit's waist high, dead chickens all over the floor, most disgusting thing you'd ever want to see. One guy, I said to him, 'You ever clean this place out?' You know what he said? 'When the shit gets so high you hit your head coming in, then we clean it out.' "

After Everston left, Arthur decided to move the Shrimp Milano from the test kitchen out to the warehouse. He'd need the extra space for lobster meat. He piled the boxes of shrimp on a handcart and secured them with a bungee cord. He trundled the load over to the big building.

He unlocked one of the big freezers, but found the bottom, where he'd planned to put the boxes of shrimp, crowded with four big canvas suitcases. What were those suckers—more shrimp? He prodded the canvas cases and felt little packets—ah, the money had arrived. Well, wasn't that nice.

Arthur had plans for some of that money, plans that wouldn't come to fruition for a while. Naturally, he'd pretended not to know anything about the shipments of hundred-dollar bills, and the partners never discussed the money with him. He was the cook, the hired help. But he knew.

The partners gave Arthur a set of keys: first of all because he was the chef and had to get the food out, and secondly, because it was thought that Arthur was too frightened of the partners even to consider stealing the money. A correct assumption: Arthur wouldn't steal a paper clip from these men, at least while he was employed there. But one fine day Arthur and some of that cash would disappear. Together.

But for now—what was he going to do with the suitcases? He didn't want to put the shrimp into the other freezer, it went on and off sporadically. If these suckers defrosted one more time, they'd be done for. He wondered why the partners hadn't thought of that.

Arthur transferred the suitcases to the defective freezer and moved his product into the bottom of the good freezer. That done, he returned to his prep area, drained the lobsters, rinsed them well to remove all chemical residues, and steamed them in his big steam-jacketed kettle.

Arthur made a notation on his desk to mention the suitcases he'd moved to one of the partners the first thing tomorrow morning. He'd just say, "the suitcases full of product," not admitting that he knew anything about the money. If they frowned, or looked menacing, he'd simply say, "Hey, it's product, right? Don't get your bowels in an uproar."

# MAURICE HAS A COOKING LESSON

"STILL FEELING PUNK, HUH?" MARY HERMAN SAID TO her husband Billy, who was lying in bed looking like death. He'd vomited so much that his stomach was sore. He felt like he was coming down with the flu: sweating, shivering, aching muscles, headache. The skin on his face sagged, and his eyes were listless. Mary had put towels on Billy's pillow since he was still retching. She'd also put towels under his bottom, since yellow diarrhea still trickled out. The washing machine had been going all morning.

Mary's worry turned to terror when Billy, coughing up phlegm, started gasping. His yellow-tinged face turned blue as he fought to get his breath. Mary hauled Billy into an upright position and did the Heimlich maneuver, which every restaurateur and his family knew, and the violent motion caused gobbets of yellow phlegm to spurt out of Billy's mouth. He stopped gasping and resumed coughing. His lungs sounded awful, his cough spongy.

"That's it," Mary said. "I'm callin' 911 for an ambulance."

In the kitchen of La Fermette Charly, Benny, Julius, and Joe Okun were hard at work preparing for an almost-full house: quite unusual for a Thursday night. The specials would be scallops Provençal; London broil with tarragon sauce; mussels with saffron; and pork chops *charcutière,* with a white wine, mustard, and cornichon sauce.

"Hey, Charly?" Julius called. Charly was standing at a prep station, gazing out the window, his thoughts obviously far away.

"Ah, Julius, I am filled with distractions."

"So I see. The pork chops aren't as thick as they usually are."

"I did not even notice."

"Your customers will notice," Benny said. "Why don't you stuff them, Julius? Charly's been in another world all day."

"Yes, yes, stuff them," Charly repeated distractedly.

"What's bothering you now," Julius asked. "Harry Clark, or the Warburtons' sick cat, or Maurice and his Fabulous Foods connections?"

Charly sighed. "Maurice. The police will discover who killed Harry Clark *eventuellement,* and the Warburton cat will either live or die, but I promise old Maurice that I will look after his son. And I have not."

"God knows, we've all tried," called Patty from the dessert room. "But right from the beginning, he's let us know he's better than us."

"Treats me like I was a know-nothing," Benny muttered.

"He can't place me socially because I won't tell him where I went to college." Julius laughed. "As if that mattered."

"Where did you go to college?" Benny asked.

"Yale, majored in English Lit, but that was so long ago I've forgotten everything," Julius said. "I didn't enjoy college. Too many Maurices."

"I will call Maurice. Ask if he would like to help us prepare dinner," Charly decided. "Perhaps in his new role of food consultant, he will not be so snooty." He spoke for a few minutes, then returned to the kitchen. "Maurice is coming," he declared.

✳✳✳

Maurice, dressed in a pin-striped blue suit with a light blue shirt and a tie with regimental stripes, appeared at La Fermette's kitchen some fifteen minutes later. "Charly, this is a great idea, I'll tell Richard and Martin that I've been consulting with you."

Charly smiled bleakly. Maybe this wasn't such a good idea, after all. Maurice would now begin calling himself Charly's consultant. He was dressed for Wall Street, not for a restaurant kitchen.

"You are not here to consult, Maurice, you are here to cook. Take off your jacket, put on an apron, wash your hands, we will put you to work. You can make the stuffing for the pork chops."

Although Maurice passed Joe Okun on his way to the washroom, his nose was in the air; nor did he condescend to speak to Julius, Benny, or Patty. Charly immediately regretted his good deed.

"I've never made a stuffing for pork chops," Maurice said, implying that he'd made many other kinds of stuffing.

"We will show you," Charly replied. "First, you read the recipe. Then, assemble your *mise en place,* the ingredients. Can you do that?"

"Of course. When Dad ran the restaurant, I was often in the kitchen."

"I do not recall ever seeing you there," Charly murmured. "But no matter. Here is the recipe card. You will need a quart of toasted bread crumbs, a cup each of chopped shallots and chopped parsley, four ounces butter."

"That's easy enough."

"Yes," Charly said. "It is easy, but you must follow the recipe. First, you make your bread crumbs and toast them in the oven. Then, you chop your shallots and your parsley . . ." Charly stopped as Maurice's brow furrowed.

"Is something the matter, Maurice?"

"How do you make bread crumbs?"

It took Charly and Maurice an hour to make the stuffing. Charly did the work and Maurice stood by, exclaiming, "Oh, is that how you do it?" Charly demonstrated how to toast bread crumbs, how to peel and chop shallots, how to trim and chop parsley. Even the weighing of butter appeared to be beyond Maurice's ken.

"Now you taste, Maurice."

"Why on earth would I want to do that?"

"Because now you must add salt and pepper, and you want to estimate how much you will need."

Maurice, ignoring this, dipped a small ladle in the bin of salt and started to add it to the stuffing mix.

"Stop!" Charly screamed. He leaned on the counter and put his head in his hands. "Maurice, I will take over from here and stuff the pork chops. Thank you very much, but I cannot take any more of this. Please leave the kitchen. My nerves have collapsed."

"Well thanks, Charly, this has been most instructive. I'm sure it will help me a lot in my work consulting with Fabulous Foods."

After Maurice left the kitchen no one spoke until Julius finally said, "You did your best, Charly."

Charly lifted his eyes to the ceiling. "Maurice, wherever you are, I did my best for your son. I try and I try. Now, I give up."

Thursday afternoon Betty Stark made a big pot of beef stew with carrots, parsnips and dumplings, as well as mashed potatoes, garlic bread, beet-and-onion salad, all of John's favorites. They were alone since Rebecca and Elizabeth had cheerleader practice.

Stark was weary. He hadn't slept well last night. He'd doze off, then he'd hear his son's footsteps, tippytoeing up the hall. Late again. Stark would have to give him what-for in the morning. Then Stark would come fully awake, knowing this was all a dream because Johnnie had been dead six years. Killed in a car crash the night of his senior prom. Then he'd sink back into a troubled sleep and the footsteps would start up again.

When he'd told Betty this morning, she said, "Full moon. You always do that. Hear Johnnie's footsteps. When are you going to stop this, John? You've got to let go of Johnnie. You've just got to."

Stark said he was doing the best that he could. But he knew that he'd never let go. Johnnie, his beloved son, would never go away.

So now, pretty beat, Stark planned to have three helpings of everything, watch TV for an hour, then hit the sack.

"You think you'll ever find out who killed that Harry Clark?" Betty asked. "After what he did to Honoria Wells, whoever killed him did the world a favor."

"It's not that I have no suspects, I have too many suspects," Stark told his wife. "I checked out some of the guys who knew him, most of them have sheets. I called his former employers, found a résumé in his desk drawer."

"That must have taken time," Betty said. "Nobody's in, you have to leave messages . . ."

"The Warburtons said they fired him because things went missing, and he'd never show up on time, called in sick a lot, he lasted less than a month with them. Harry worked for that supermarket in Highdale, and the manager went back in his files and discovered that Clark had been fired for stealing."

"I wonder if Charly's been snooping around?" Betty mused.

"Of course he has. Warburton said Charly called, but he told Charly Harry left because of ill health. He told me Charly's been real kind about their cat, but he doesn't approve of people nosing around."

"Charly's just trying to help, John."

"Yeah, right. I figure every place he went, Clark made enemies. You mind if I finish the potatoes?"

"There's more in the kitchen," Betty said. "The girls'll want a snack when they get home, so I made plenty."

The telephone rang and Betty Stark said she'd get it. Stretching the cord, she passed the receiver to John at the table.

"Nothin' for you to come out for, Chief," said Abe Reynolds, "but I wanted you to know. Billy Herman, owned the Happy Farmer Luncheonette in Sharpsville, died at the hospital, something to do with his heart, I think."

"I didn't even know he was sick," Stark said. "Poor guy, he was way too fat. I liked Billy Herman." Putting his hand over the mouthpiece, Stark mouthed to Betty, 'Billy Herman died.'

Stark said, "Nothing the police should know about, is it, Abe?"

Abe said no, he guessed not. "Oh, and, Chief? On that Harry Clark thing, couple barflies told me Harry was talking big one night, said he had a list of people he was 'going to get', whatever that meant. My two hombres could only recall a few names, Miz Wells, the Warburtons, Peter Vann, and a farmer named Jim

105

Halloran. Seems they all done him wrong at some point."

"Uh-huh. Think any of them could have killed him?"

"I doubt it, but anything's possible."

Stark hung up.

"I'll call Brad Greenpeace, find out what arrangements are being made," Betty said. "Poor Mary. They're just about our age, too. Boy, it's scary, isn't it? We could go too, just like that."

# SEA SCALLOPS WITH SAUCE PROVENÇAL

**Yield: 4 servings**

1 ½ pounds sea scallops
¼ cup olive oil, heated to smoking

Sauce:
2 cloves garlic finely chopped
2 shallots, finely chopped
2 large tomatoes, peeled, seeded and chopped
1 cup tiny Niçoise olives
½ cup dry white wine
½ cup fresh basil, chopped, plus extra leaves for garnish

Wash and dry scallops and sear in hot olive oil. Remove scallops from pan and reserve, leaving juices in pan. Add all sauce ingredients (except whole basil leaves) to pan and cook uncovered over high heat for 5 minutes. Add scallops to sauce and cook 1 minute longer to heat through. Serve scallops and sauce in serving bowl garnished with basil leaves.

# MAURICE ENCOUNTERS OBSTACLES

MAURICE BALEINE, IN A GOOD MOOD THIS FRIDAY morning, made little humming noises as he stood in front of the wide, mirrored guest-room closet (he and Barbara had separate bedrooms) and tried to decide what a food consultant would wear when visiting one of his factories.

Nothing as serious as the pin-striped suit he had on yesterday. Would chinos be too casual? No, they'd be perfect. He'd wear his newest chinos, with a pale blue Brooks Brothers oxford shirt, and his navy linen blazer. Gave him an air of casual authority. The slumming Princetonian.

Finally dressed, Maurice admired himself. He didn't look forty-eight. Didn't look 220, either, though at five-foot-ten he could carry it. He looked . . . important. A man of substance. A cosmopolite who felt at home in London, Paris, Rome. Maurice smiled, admiring his beautiful white teeth, his straight nose, his penetrating eyes, a sign of astuteness and intelligence.

Maurice wanted to make his office at Fabulous Foods a more distinguished-looking place. He decided to carry up the Chagall lithograph from his home office, the dark Kazak rug in front of his desk, and the George III mahogany armchair from the back room. The chair was Barbara's, but she wouldn't mind. Later, he could carry up other objects, but right now, this was all that would fit into the backseat and trunk of his car.

Methodically, Maurice first backed his navy blue Mercedes—newly washed and waxed—out of the garage and brought it around to the front of the house.

He carried out the rug, then the lithograph wrapped in an old bedspread, which he placed in the trunk. The chair just fit in the backseat, lying sideways. Maurice went back to his office, got extra cash, and made sure his credit cards were in his wallet—he might invite the chef to lunch. He pulled the front door shut and set off for Sharpsville.

It was nearly eleven o'clock when Maurice pulled up to the front doors of Fabulous Foods. Funny, there were no cars in the side parking lot, the place looked deserted. Everybody should be here by now. He rang the buzzer by the front door, waited, then rang again, but there was no answering buzz to unlock the doors. After waiting a few more minutes Maurice walked back to his car. He drove around to the back, to the big building with the massive freezer rooms and free-standing freezer units. There, at least, were some cars. He parked by the kitchen, went up, and peered through the windows.

Arthur Arpati, in his whites, was standing by the stove stirring something in a large pot. Two men and two women, quite elderly, were sitting at the big center table with piles of boiled red lobsters in front of them, industriously picking the meat from the shells. Maurice knocked on the window, at first softly, then louder.

Arpati and the senior citizens looked up, then the oldsters went back to their work. Arpati, recognizing Maurice, went to the door and unlocked it.

"Yeah? What do you want?"

Maurice prided himself on his diplomacy. Again, he had disturbed the artist at his work. He knew better than to ask if he could come in. "Chef Arpati, I'm sorry to disturb you, but I have come to work in my office in the front building, and it's locked. No one's around. Can you let me in?"

"Yeah, yeah," Arthur said impatiently. "I don't know where they are, I don't keep track, they're in and out so much." Arthur unsnapped a key ring from his belt and stood facing Maurice, jiggling the key chain in his hands.

"Are they often away?" Maurice asked. "Because I plan on being in my office up here every day. Perhaps you could lend me your key, I'll have a copy made, so I can come and go at will."

Arthur decided that Maurice was either nuts, or so innocent he didn't know who he was dealing with, so he spoke gently to this simpleton.

"No, no, Mr. Uh,"—Arthur could never remember the guy's name, some kind of fish, Mr. Goldfish? No, that didn't sound right "The bosses are real particular about who has keys. You want keys, you gotta ask them."

Maurice made the mistake of pulling rank. "I'm a partner, you know. I'm going to be here every day, making sure everything's running as it should be. Of course they'll give me the keys." He glared at Arthur, speaking in the supercilious tone that worked so well with headwaiters.

Something clicked in Arpati's mind. "You're a partner? No fucking way. There's two partners, Scungilli and Zampone. You're no partner."

"I'm an investor in the company, and I am a limited partner."

"They got about a dozen investors, like silent partners, and none of 'em has an office here, so you don't, either." Arthur grabbed back his key and squinted at this fat jerk with his piggy little stupid eyes. "I only let people in on orders from Marty or Ricky. And they didn't tell me nothing about letting you in. Sorry." Arthur slammed the door in Maurice's face.

Maurice penned a note on the back of his calling card and wedged it into the glass front door. "Richard and Martin: Meet me at seven at La Fermette, tonight, you can taste some of my cooking. Maurice." Then he got in his car and drove home. Only temporarily disconcerted, Maurice decided that matters like this always took a bit of time to iron out.

Charly was making *beurre blanc* when Tommy Glade, the barman, appeared at his elbow in La Fermette's kitchen. It was nearly seven o'clock, Friday evening. Tommy knew better than to interrupt Charly while he was making this tricky sauce, where vinegar was reduced, shallots added, and butter was whisked in bit by bit. Tommy had tried to make *beurre blanc* (white butter) several times for himself and his roommate, and it sometimes worked. Frequently the sauce broke, but it tasted good anyway. Charly, sensing someone at his elbow, said, *"Oui?"*

"It's Maurice and Barbara, Charly. They didn't reserve, but I gave them table ten, for four. Maurice says he's invited his two partners from Fabulous Foods to meet him here. His two partners? Could that be right?"

Charly shrugged. "I neither know nor care. I have done all that I can for Maurice, Tommy. I can do no more. I am surprise that Barbara is here."

"She looks pretty cross, but she's here."

Charly pushed open the doors and went out into the dining room to greet his former partner. Maurice was troweling mushroom spread on bread and saying something to Barbara, who was scowling and looking around the dining room.

111

"Barbara, Maurice. It is a pleasure to welcome you."

Maurice beamed. "Oh, Charly. Martin and Richard are coming. I had such a good time in your kitchen, I wanted them to sample my work."

"What work?" Charly started to say, but turned this into a cough. "Very good, Maurice. And Barbara, it is a pleasure. You dine here almost never."

"Charly," Barbara said, ignoring the remark about dining. Barbara, who was always dieting, hated restaurant food. She knew how Charly cooked: with butter and more butter. "I see what you mean about the apricot, it's looking faded and far too 'ladies boudoir.' I think we're smart to do moss."

"Forests and fields," Charly said. "Mosses and mushrooms."

Maurice interrupted. "Now if I were still a partner, Charly, I'd refuse to go along with that. What you need are reds and yellows, liven the place up."

Charly ignored this. "Would you like to see the menu now, or will your friends appear shortly?"

"We'll want the best of the best, Charly," Maurice said. "So you'd better start cooking now. Lobsters and steaks."

"There are no lobsters, Maurice, and the steaks are cooked as they are ordered. What time will your friends be here?"

"Any minute, now," said Maurice airily.

At eight o'clock, Maurice ordered stuffed pork chops and Barbara ordered grilled salmon.

"Their guests never showed," said Elton Briggs, their waiter.

Maurice, critical of each and every dish he'd ever eaten at La Fermette, praised the pork chops to the skies.

"Why am I not surprise?" said Charly.

112

# THE BACTERIA SURFACES

BARBARA BALEINE SCREAMED WHEN SHE WENT TO THE back room Saturday morning to take her George III armchair down to her upholsterer's . . . and found it missing. The damned chair, she'd paid $7,000 for it—she could charge double, easily—and now it was gone. Her first impulse was to call the police. Her second was to wake Maurice.

"Your what?" Maurice rarely woke before nine.

"My George III mahogany armchair, Maurice. It's disappeared."

Maurice, befuddled by sleep, told the truth. "It's in my car."

"You were stealing it? Or taking it for a ride, to enjoy the scenery?"

"I wanted to see how it would look in my new office at Fabulous Foods."

Barbara slammed the guest-room door and hurried to the garage. Yes, there it was, in the unlocked car. She lifted it out and placed it in her Cadillac. Not for the first time, Barbara wondered what world Maurice lived in.

"If you don't need me," Charly said to Julius, Benny, and Joe Okun after Saturday lunch, "I have to run an errand. Julius, the aspic is made and the chicken breasts are poached, cover them with aspic, please. I leave a cold soup to you. Benny, the *salade* of string bean must be made, also the zucchini. You can both make the coq au vin. I will be back around four."

Benny said to Julius, "You know where he's going, don't you?"

"Snooping around," Julius said. "He wants to find out more about Fabulous Foods. He's nuts. Those guys are nobody to fool around with."

"I think he's going over to Rex's," Benny said. "He told me Rex was going to buy some of that prepared food, and Charly's upset about it. He thinks those guys are going to cheat Rex."

"Of course they're going to cheat Rex," Julius agreed. "Rex, the sucker."

"I like Rex," Benny said. "He's straightforward. Just like Charly. Charly's the great detective, Rex's the great steak man. They both have goals."

Julius rolled his eyes. Every week Benny had a new catchphrase—this week's was goals. Hey, so what? Benny was twenty years old. You had to have goals at that age. "And what's your goal, Benny?"

"To be a great chef, Julius. You know that."

"Yet when Charly offered to send you to restaurant school, you said no."

Benny corrected Julius. "I said, 'not yet.' I figure, if I go there with some experience under my belt, I'll learn more. Maybe I'll go next year. Don't worry, Julius, I've been looking into these things."

"Yeah, I'm sure you have, Benny," Julius agreed. "You're a smart guy. You know how to bide your time. Not acting on the spur of the moment."

"My dad taught me, like, in reverse," Benny said sadly. "He always acted on the spur of the moment. And look where it got him."

Benny's father, alcoholically challenged, died coming home from a bar. He lost control of his vehicle, did combat with a tree. The tree won.

Benny was an infant when his dad died, and Patty was a young mother with no work experience. Except that she loved to bake. She knocked on Charly's back door with samples of her pies and cakes. Charly hired her on the spot. Patty would bake at home, and care for her son, and bring her desserts to the restaurant. When Benny got to high-school age and needed an after-school job, Charly found things for Benny to do. Charly often wondered if Benny and Patty were substitutes for his wife and infant son who had died so many years ago. Why, for instance, did Benny look like a young French boy, with his dark, straight hair and his squat, muscular body? Would Charly's son have looked like that?

Now, in the restaurant kitchen, Benny, on his way to becoming a chef under Charly's tutelage, chopped shallots, chopped parsley, made sauce vinaigrette by combining the shallots and parsley with olive oil, balsamic vinegar, and French mustard. "I don't know why," Benny said to Julius, "but I've got a feeling Maurice is going to try something."

Julius didn't have time to answer because there was a knock on the back door and Maurice Baleine entered, carrying a shopping bag. "Ah-ha," he said. "Where's Charly. I have a shrimp dish I want him to taste." No greeting to either Julius or Benny, so Julius and Benny ignored him.

"I'm going to check the cold room, see what we have to make a cold soup," Julius said to Benny.

"There's plenty of watercress," Benny said.

Maurice planted himself directly in front of Benny. "Do you know where Charly is?"

"Oh, Maurice, I didn't see you," Benny lied. "What do you want?"

Maurice, who saw Benny as a schoolkid emptying the garbage, looked at the solid young man, and said insolently, "Well, what did I ask?"

115

Benny placed his feet firmly on the ground and centered himself. "Look, Maurice, Julius and I are busy preparing dinner. I don't know what you asked. You didn't greet me, so I'd no idea you were talking to me."

Maurice, noticing Benny's stance, hearing menace in his voice, backed away. "I—I'm looking for Charly," he said politely. "Benny," he added.

"He said he had errands to run and would be back at four."

"But this is important. Very important."

Julius came back to the work area lugging a crate of watercress. Deliberately, he banged it down on the counter, sprinkling Maurice with water. "Look at this, a whole crate," Julius said. "I'll make a *Potage Cressonière* for dinner. And we can offer a watercress salad, as well."

"Good idea, Julius," Benny said. "And we can make a watercress sauce for the poached chicken breasts."

Maurice still stood in the center of the kitchen with his shopping bag. "Look, this stuff is defrosting. Zampone gave me a box. Julius, Benny, could you make sure Charly sees it? It's Shrimp Milano from Fabulous Foods; it wasn't presented at the tasting."

"Sure thing, Maurice," Julius said. "You tried it, yet? Is it delicious?"

"No, no, I haven't tried it yet, I may have some tonight."

Benny said, "Why don't I heat some up right now? Charly may want to try some, and I'm sure you're anxious to try it. Here, let me have the box."

"No, no, don't bother, I'll try some later," Maurice hedged.

"What's wrong, you afraid it'll poison you? That it's

116

made with inferior ingredients?" Julius made it sound like a taunt, a challenge.

"Of course not. Fabulous Foods uses the finest ingredients."

Meanwhile Julius had broken open the box and was heating the shrimp.

"It'll just take a moment," Julius assured Maurice. A few minutes later, Julius dipped in his finger, then ladled a portion of Shrimp Milano into a soup bowl. "Here, Maurice, tell us what you think of it."

Cautiously Maurice dipped in a spoon. "It smells delicious," he said. Indeed, the brandy-scented tomato sauce sent up pleasing aromas of garlic, oregano, and wine. "The sauce is great," he said. "The shrimp? Just a trifle rubbery. But you'd never notice over pasta."

"Have some more, Maurice," Julius urged. "You brought far too much. Charly will just want a spoonful."

"And what about you two gentlemen?"

"I'm allergic to shrimp," Benny lied.

"Tomato sauces give me hives," Julius lied.

"Well, you're missing a great dish," Maurice said, helping himself to some more. "Maybe I'll take some home, let Barbara try it."

Dr. Hy Bingham said to Stark, "I always have stomach contents analyzed in cases like this, and Billy Herman's insides showed the definite presence of *Clostridium perfringens*. Guy was poisoned. Something he ate."

"Did you notify the Health Department?"

"Sure did. I said it was an emergency. This bacterium rarely kills except in the very young and the very old, but in Billy's case it was the last straw. He was a smoker, and grossly overweight, he had all the ailments that accompany obesity."

"Where do you think he got it? His lunch place? Food's garbage."

"I think I know where it came from. Mary Herman tells me Billy just put some money in a company up in Sharpsville. They make frozen prepared food for restaurants. Mary thinks the bacteria was in the sauce."

"Any of the others sick?" Stark asked.

"Bud Maris vomited right away, but felt so bad with stomach cramps and diarrhea he stayed home the next day. Susie felt fine. Joe and Teresa Scapece both felt queasy, Mary Herman felt fine. But that's how those bacteria act. They affect some people, and others not at all. I'll get the Health Department to get some samples, we'll close 'em down if necessary."

Richard Zampone, eating Bernice's garlicky meatball sandwiches for lunch in New Jersey, was horrified when he got a call from the Health Department in Albany. They'd traced him through the application forms for Fabulous Foods.

"And the guy died?" Little Richie said, horrified. "Where did he get the food? It's packed for the food-service industry. We don't sell to consumers."

The man from the Health Department said he understood that a Mr. Joseph Scapece had gotten some samples from the chef, and he'd invited Mr. and Mrs. Herman and Mr. and Mrs. Maris for dinner. In any event, they had to obtain samples, to analyze it for the bacterium *Clostridium perfringens*.

"I'll call the head chef, Arthur Arpati, he lives near Sharpsville," Zampone told the health inspector. "I'll get him to bring a box up to your labs in Albany. There may not be any of the old batch left. But if there isn't,

118

I'll have chef Arpati give you some samples from our current production."

The man from the Health Department said what the hell, he'd take whatever he could get. After they had hung up, Zampone telephoned Arpati.

"Thank Jesus you're home, Arthur," said Ricky Zampone. "You know that batch of Shrimp Milano you gave one of those guys against my orders?"

"Yeah," Arthur said uncertainly. "The same stuff you gave to that Morrie guy. And to Rex Cingale."

"Oh, Christ, I forgot about them. Well the fat guy, Billy Herman, snuffed it. The Health Department traced it to our shrimp. So listen, Arthur, what you gotta do is, you gotta get rid of every last box of that shit. I don't care where it goes or what you do with it, but it can't be found on the premises. Then you gotta get in touch with this guy at the Health Department, here's the name and number, and bring him up some fresh Shrimp Milano you made for the party and froze."

# MEDITERRANEAN SHRIMP

## Yield: 4 servings

1 pound large shrimp
3 tablespoons olive oil
3 large garlic cloves, finely chopped
3 large tomatoes, peeled, seeded and chopped
½ cup flat leaf parsley, chopped
Salt and pepper to taste

Peel and devein shrimp. Heat olive oil and saute garlic for 30 seconds. Add tomatoes and parsley. Cook another 30 seconds. Add shrimp and cook until shrimp turn pink—1–2 minutes. Season to taste with salt and pepper.

# POISON LOVES POISON

CHARLY AVOIDED REX'S PLACE SINCE HE DIDN'T WANT to discuss the Fabulous Foods shipment Rex had ordered. Instead of a coffee break Saturday morning, he drove out to visit Doc Ross. Doc was slowing down. Charly didn't know his exact age, he'd been claiming eighty-eight for some years. *When I grow old,* Charly often thought, *I want to be like old Doc.*

Doc was weeding out the flower bed beyond his lawn. Charly could barely see the old man amongst the peonies, wild rosebushes, clumps of budding sage, ruffled tansy, primroses, and wild garlic.

"I call you, Doc, but you do not answer. I take a chance, drive over, I figure you are out in your garden."

"Damn right, Charly. These wild roses'll choke everything out. But look, I just made a discovery. See this?" Doc pointed to a small yellow flower with deep green shiny foliage.

Charly nodded. "It is the *bouton d'or,* very poisonous."

"That's right. Buttercup. Member of the aconite family. *Ranunculus septentrionale.* Well, look at what's flourishing nearby: that's rue with the little grey-green leaves, and this is curly tansy. All three can be toxic. Poisonous plants like the proximity of other poisonous plants. That's my great new discovery. And look, next to the tansy: mayapple, or *Podophyllum peltatum,* a member of the barberry family. Another poison."

"Ah, *Podophyllum peltatum,*" Charly said knowingly. "In homeopathy, is given to small children for *la colique.* Is very beautiful plant, but I cannot get it to

121

grow. Is difficult to get wild plants to grow in your garden."

"Difficult, but there's a secret," Doc said. "A secret that I'm just beginning to discover. It's companion planting. The wild plants won't grow on their own, but they'll grow and flourish next to another wild plant whose proximity they enjoy. Plants like company, but they're very selective. It's up to us to figure out what plants like and what they hate."

"Just like people," Charly said. "I seat the Browns next to the Morrisons, they like each other, they chat across the tables and always order far more, plus brandy and dessert. I seat the Browns next to Peter and Dinah Vann, so *nouveau riche* and *vulgaire* and loud, and Monsieur and Madame Brown leave before ordering dessert."

"That's right, Charly. We're allergic to certain people, and certain plants are allergic to other plants. Look over there." Old Doc gestured to the far end of the bed. "The peonies are magnificent this year and do you know why? Because of the wild sweet rocket growing nearby, and the comfrey, and the lemon thyme, and the mint. All are particularly fine this year, because they like each other's company. I used to thin 'em out, but now I don't."

"*Exactement,*" Charly said. "This year I do not weed out my garlic mustard, it grow next to my lunaria, you know, the money plant, and this year both lunaria and garlic mustard are so bloomful. Like never before."

"Bloomful's a fine word, Charly," Doc said. "Look over here, it's finished flowering, but look at the leaves. Bloodroot. Sanguinaria."

"Very good for *la sinusite*, used homeopathically," Charly said.

122

"Yes, well, it's a poison, too. It's spread to the stone wall, where it's flourishing next to a low-growing variety of buttercup. I stole it from a marsh, the bloodroot, it's an endangered species, but I took some anyway. I planted some in that wet area at the foot of my property, thinking it would like the marshy environment and—guess what? It never came back the next year. But this, because of the company, the buttercup, the aconite, it's been coming back for years."

"If a man's friends are bad, then he is bad," Charly said sententiously.

Doc made a face. "Look who's talking. You idolized Walter Maxwell, that crook, and now you've got Ugo Buonsarde as your best customer. Another underworld gentleman. Does that mean you're a crook, too?"

"Is possible," Charly said, amused at the thought.

"Well, you have to be careful, Charly," Doc said. "I'll never forget how close you came to death at the hands of Maxwell. And speaking of Walter, two of his buddies are up here, did you know?"

"I know everything," Charly bragged. "Men named Scungilli and Zampone, the name of a fine Italian sausage, they have opened up a company in Sharpsville selling frozen entrées for the restaurant trade. Our Maurice has bought some shares."

Old Doc nodded. "Maurice came to see me, invited me to the open house, tried to get me to buy into the company."

"No. Why did he do that?"

Old Doc drew himself up to his full height, five-foot-six, the same as Charly, and patted down his bushy white hair, which made him look like an aging Mark Twain. "Maurice thinks I'm rich." Doc chuckled.

"Where did he get that idea?" Charly said, affecting

innocence. Both Doc and Alma, his late wife, had inherited family money, but they lived without ostentation. Doc lived simply, in a three-hundred-year-old house that an ancestor had built. It was a small and unassuming house with carved moldings and hand-hewn beams.

"Well, I neither know nor care," Doc replied. "Anyway, Charly, I found out a few things about those men, I've got their names inside. Come on in, I opened up a file on them."

After years of being best friends with Jameson's Irish Whiskey, old Doc had gone on the wagon, and now he drank only water, and tea so strong it would rot shoe leather.

"Care for a cup of tea?" Doc asked.

"Not today, Doc, but thank you." After a cup of Doc's tea Charly had to take *Nux vomica* pills, and sometimes he got sick anyway.

Doc told Charly all he'd learned about Zampone and Scungilli, New Jersey hoodlums who had hired chef Arpati, formerly of the Food and Drug Administration until he was caught accepting bribes and reselling condemned seafood. "Oh, they're an outfit, all right. I told Maurice, and he just laughed at me."

"How do you know all this, Doc?"

"Being a doctor, I always filed away stories about medical matters, in this case, food poisoning. Zampone and Scungilli and Arpati used to be associated with a company called Splendid Shrimp down in New Jersey. It's all down in faded newsprint. Splendid Shrimp sold rotten fish for years."

"Maurice laugh at me, too, when I tell him they are not good people," Charly admitted. "He have this *idée fixe* that through this company he will make his fortune."

"Well, they'll get caught sooner or later," Doc said. "Maybe sooner than we think. You know the owner of that awful luncheonette up the road, Billy Herman? He and two of his friends . . ." Old Doc repeated the story of the three partners, their fateful dinner, and Herman's death. Doc Bingham had told him.

"I tell ya, Charly, those men are bad, and their company's rotten through and through. Now, Hy tells me, he's sicked the Health Department onto 'em. They'll get caught, Health Department'll close 'em down, and that will be the end of your Fancy Foods."

"Fabulous Foods," Charly corrected.

"Whatever they're called."

Charly leaned toward the old man and said in a low voice, "Tell me truthfully, Doc, did you really get all of these stories from newspaper articles? You have quite the dossier on these gentlemen, you are like FBI and CIA."

Old Doc Ross laughed aloud. "I got a lot of the stories about Scungilli and Zampone and Splendid Shrimp from my files. Then I called a good customer of yours. Your friend Ugo."

"You call Ugo Buonsarde?"

"The very same," Doc said. "I told you, I've known him for years, I used to treat his parents. And I'll tell you this. Ugo doesn't like those men at all. There's no loyalty among thieves."

# PILCHARD THE GARDENER

EVERSTON PILCHARD WAS ENJOYING THE BEAUTIFUL Saturday afternoon. He sat in a deck chair on the little stone patio he'd flanked with peonies and old-fashioned roses. Neither was out yet, but the white and pink tulips were lovely. He had a pad of paper in front of him and was doing sums. The Arpati man had slipped him a hundred dollars, very good pay for an hour and a half. Dangerous work, though: What would he do if he got caught?

Arthur hinted that this delivery work would probably work out at a job every ten days—maybe a thousand dollars per summer. Teaching school wasn't lucrative, especially at Brooke, where they pinched every penny. And what remained of his trust fund barely bought groceries. So Everston had to find work. Now, if he could get five landscaping jobs at a thousand dollars each, plus the Fabulous Foods deliveries, he could live better. Ah—here was a thought. That Fabulous Foods factory looked pretty naked. Should he ask Arthur about approaching the principals to do some landscaping? He'd wait until he got to know Arthur better. Everston was just the tiniest bit frightened of Arthur. He knew Scungilli and Zampone were far worse.

Win and Morty loved his garden ideas, said they'd mention him if anyone asked, but no one had. The telephone rang.

"Ah, Monsieur Pilchard," said a heavily accented voice, "you do the work of the landscape gardener, do you not?"

"Yes, I do landscaping."

"This is Charles Poisson. I own La Fermette restaurant, you took lunch there last Saturday with Win Crozier and Morty Cohen."

"Yes, Monsieur Poisson, I remember perfectly. You have a charming restaurant. Beautifully landscaped, too."

"Done twenty years ago. But I do not call you about my restaurant. I call about my house. I would like to have some plants in the front of my house. Perhaps we could talk about it and I could show you what I want?"

"Excellent, monsieur. When would you like to meet?" Everston did not subscribe to the theory that you attracted more customers by playing hard to get, overloaded with work, and so on. Win Crozier had told him—when Evvie had tried this ploy on Win—"it's cheapjackery and anyone with a grain of sense sees through it, Evvie. Don't do it." And after that, Evvie never had.

"I cannot do it now," Poisson said, "because I must be in my restaurant kitchen at four o'clock. And tomorrow, Sunday, is our most busy day. Monday the restaurant is closed, but Monday you must be at school, yes?"

"I could be at your house on Monday afternoon at four, Monsieur Poisson. How would that suit you?"

The appointment was made. It was only when Everston was sitting in his deck chair again that he wondered just what Charly Poisson's tastes were. You never knew with the bourgeois French. Daisies and asters and chrysanthemums all bunched together, Everston decided. Or maybe dahlias. Everston loathed dahlias.

Would you believe it? The telephone rang again. Everston hoped this time it would be rich snobs requesting his services. Everston loved snobs. He always knew how to deal with people like that. You prefaced every suggestion with an endorsement from a big society name: "Those asters? I got the idea from Bunny Mellon. Those delphinium massed with thalictrum? Cece De Vries does that. Moss roses with white peonies? Practically a trademark of Taffy Crawford." Never failed. Everston knew all about high society.

But it wasn't another landscaping job, unfortunately. It was the chef at Fabulous Foods, Arthur Arpati.

"Hey, Everston, can you get over here right away? Something's come up, and I need help. Don't worry, I'll make it worth your while."

"Well yes, I can come, I've nothing on this afternoon," said Everston. "But maybe you could tell me more about the job. What's it worth?"

"I gotta get rid of some stuff," Arthur said. "Hundred-seventy boxes of frozen product. It's gotta go bye-bye. I'll pay you a couple hundred."

"Well . . ."

"Three hundred."

"How long will it take?"

"Three hours at the most. Probably much less. We've got to load up some spoiled product, dump it in the Hudson River."

Everston and Arthur loaded the spoiled shrimp in tomato sauce into Everston's old Volvo. Seventeen garbage bags. Plus two crates, as they'd run out of bags. The food filled the trunk ("the boot" Everston called it, being, like all good English teachers, an Anglophile) and the backseat was crammed to the roof. Scrupulously observing the speed limits, they drove west.

"You learn not to ask questions in this business," Arthur said conversationally. "But, I just wondered. You ever do, uh, stuff like this before? What I really mean is, why'd a schoolteacher, a man with a respectable job, take on a job with Fabulous Foods?" Arthur wondered if Everston had been forced by Scungilli or Zampone to apply for this job because they had something on him. That's how they'd gotten Harry Clark, he'd heard, but that was before his time.

"I took this job to make money, being a school teacher doesn't pay much and my summer landscaping business doesn't pay much either."

Arthur continued. "I did a few deals, selling fish— ah—past its prime, which is nothing new, of course, only it wasn't my fish to sell."

Everston concentrated on his driving. Arthur directed him up a little hill to Fisherman's Landing where stood an old, disused dock.

"I live around here," Arthur said. "I told the real-estate lady I liked to fish, and she showed me a place near this little dock. Park over there."

As they carried the bags to the dock and dumped them in the river, Everston said, "You think your bosses would like to landscape the front building?"

"I wouldn't approach them this summer," Arthur said. "They're just getting started, and they have a lot on their minds. I don't think landscaping's at the top of the list."

"That's what I figured," Everston said. "They seem pretty tough."

"They're not men you want to cozy up to," Arthur admitted.

As he drove home two hours later with three hundred dollars in his pocket, Everston was relieved that he'd sounded Arthur Arpati out first about the landscaping.

He'd gotten the impression that the only holes dug around the property would be to bury bodies.

What was he getting into? Then Everston had another horrible thought. Did all those bags really contain spoiled shrimp? Arthur had already packed some up by the time Everston arrived. He thought darkly about dismembered bodies, but dismissed the thought. He'd filled a lot of bags himself, and they all weighed the same. And, the main point: Where else could you make $300 for two hours' work?

# DIPLOMATIC MANEUVERS

RESERVATIONS FOR SATURDAY DINNER WERE POURING into La Fermette.

"Look, Charly," said Patty Perkins. "Peter and Dinah Vann, and Maurice called, he's bringing Barbara and Barbara's mother, and Ugo Buonsarde called at the last minute, party of five, and a Mr. Scungilli and a guest. Isn't he the man Maurice is mixed up with?"

"Yes," said Charly shortly. "The seatings will be difficult. You must pay strict attention, Patty. Signor Buonsarde must not, I repeat, *not* be seated anywhere near Scungilli. And the mother of Barbara, Madame De Groot, does not like Dinah Vann, so must not be seated near."

"Why doesn't Martha De Groot like Dinah Vann?" Patty asked.

"Madame De Groot," Charly lectured, "consider herself Hudson River aristocracy, and Madame Vann, she does not worship at the throne. Also, when Madame Vann was looking for a decorator a few years ago, she first chose Barbara, and then they had a *petite difference,* how you call, spat."

130

"I'm surprised," Patty said. "Barbara's such a diplomat."

"Madame Vann, she want Barbara to fake all sort of paper and get her into the Daughters of the American Revolution, ladies who trace their lineage back three hundred years, which as we French know is nothing at all. Barbara refuse to do it. So Madame Vann fire Barbara."

"Good for Barbara," Patty said. "Be sure to alert all the waiters when you have your floor meeting at half past five, in case I'm seating someone else."

"Good idea," Charly said, and went to the kitchen to check his racks of lamb. The racks were coated with parsley and garlic, mustard and olive oil, then, at point of service, cooked to the customer's specifications. Buonsarde would order a rack for sure, and Martha De Groot would, too.

"Heavens, there's that dreadful Vann woman," said Martha De Groot, sipping champagne. "I'm glad they're on the other side of the room." Unlike Barbara, who was Junoesque, Martha De Groot was tiny, an elfin woman with an acid tongue. Very few people measured up to her standards.

"Good Lord," Barbara said, ignoring her mother's comment. "Look who's here. Two men who look like killers straight out of central casting."

"Where?" Maurice asked, peering across the room. "But, *ma chérie,* one is the co-owner at Fabulous Foods, Martin Scungilli. He's coming over. I'll introduce you."

Martin Scungilli was delighted to meet Maurice's wife and mother-in-law. Eyeing Martha De Groot's diamonds, he immediately began talking about Fabulous Foods and its enormous potential.

"It's the most important prepared-foods company in the United States, Mrs. De Groot, and Maurice is lucky, getting in on the ground floor. We still have places for a few more investors—like my guest tonight, a very important seafood broker. It's a select group."

"Oh, we're going to do great things with Fabulous Foods," Maurice quacked nervously. He knew Barbara's mother didn't approve of him, so he always made matters worse by trying to impress her. "I'm advising the chef; I'll be in my office up there every day. Having been a restaurateur for over twenty years, I feel that my input will be invaluable."

Ugo Buonsarde and his party, two well-dressed couples, arrived, and Charly came out to greet them, to fuss over table arrangements, and to offer Shrimps Charly and aperitifs on the house. Out of the corner of his eye Charly could see Scungilli and his guest craning their necks, trying to hear what Charly was saying to Ugo's party. On his way back to his kitchen Charly stopped at Scungilli's table. He greeted the two men politely and again commented on the good food at the Fabulous Foods tasting. This time, out of the corner of his eye, he could see Ugo glancing over in Scungilli's direction. Ah, ah, this would be a delicate evening.

An hour and a half later Charly, dressed in a fresh white jacket from Dupont & Malgat (on the rue Coquillière in Paris, the Cartier's and the Tiffany's of chefs' gear), with a high white toque on his head, hurried into the dining room to officially visit with his customers.

He went to Maurice's table first, out of deference to his former partner. Charly was curious why Maurice, who usually ordered a lavish meal, had contented himself with a clear bouillon, poached chicken breast with rice. Indeed, as he approached them, he noticed that Maurice was looking decidedly uncomfortable.

"Ah, my good friends. You enjoy your meal?"

"Divine, Charly, as usual," Martha De Groot beamed. As she told her chums, Charly Poisson was the most adorable man.

"Lovely, Charly dear," Barbara said.

"Very nice, very nice," Maurice said mechanically.

Charly, who knew about Maurice's sampling of the Fabulous Foods shrimp dish that afternoon, said chattily, "Did the shrimp you eat this afternoon harm your digestion? A delicious dish, I am told, but one of your co-investors, Billy Herman, died in the hospital after eating it, the poor man. It contain the terrible clostridium bacteria. Of course, it does not kill most people. Only make them very sick."

He leaped back as Maurice sprang from the table, gagging, and bolted from the restaurant. Charly smiled urbanely, bowed to the ladies, and moved on.

Peter Vann motioned Charly over with the grandiose wavings of the inebriated. He'd had four martinis. Charly knew exactly what Peter would say. He bent forward, widening his eyes, and enunciated loudly,

"Not Tanqueray in my martini, Charly."

Charly played his part in the charade, which had been going on for years. "Not Tanqueray? Not what monsieur ask for? I will ask the barman to make you another, on the house, if madame is driving."

"I always drive, Charly," said Dinah Vann wearily. Tonight Dinah was a lilac bush: amethyst rings, necklace, bracelet, earrings, lilac-sprigged silk dress, violet shoes and handbag. Her lavender eye shadow had been generously applied. Still, she and Peter were good and loyal customers.

"An *infusion de menthe,* madame?"

133

"Yes, Charly," Dinah said listlessly, "that would be very nice."

Dinah and Peter had lived in New York City for years, where Peter had some kind of clothing business. Dinah had been the head buyer of Chez Mimi, on Park Avenue. She knew where a lot of bodies were buried. Now, suddenly excited, she whispered to Charly, "You see those two men? Mrs. Scungilli used to patronize my couture shop, and she had a bad habit. She'd try on a dress and walk out with it, leaving her old dress in the fitting room. She only did it once at Chez Mimi, I assure you. She's divorced now."

"Small world," echoed Charly, wondering how much of this was true.

Charly advanced toward his favorite customer, Ugo Buonsarde. Ugo, his bald head shining, his mustache gleaming, smiled as Charly approached.

"Here is the finest restaurateur in the world," Ugo cried, clasping Charly's hand. He introduced his tablemates, the two well-dressed older couples, and told them, "This chef serves the best food in the United States." Everyone smiled. Their plates were empty, Charly was pleased to note. Several bottles of Charly's very special Barolo stood on the serving table nearby. Charly modestly received everyone's compliments, and offered digestifs on the house.

"I noticed one of those Fabulous Foods people here tonight," Ugo said, lowering his voice.

Charly noted Ugo's severe tone. "Not my favorite customer, signor. My former partner, Maurice, has invested in their company, as I told you." Charly gave Ugo a serious look. "People who make plastic food do not interest me. It is a pity they have moved to Van Buren County."

"I understand, monsieur," said Ugo heartily. In a code language which they both understood, Ugo had told Charly he didn't want him to do business with Fabulous Foods and Charly had told Ugo that he had no intention of doing so. Both men smiled at each other, messages received.

"I will see to your digestifs," Charly said. After placing the drinks order with Tommy Glade Charly went to the kitchen to retrieve a treasure from his refrigerator, *Truffes au Moka* from his favorite candy shop in Lons le Saunier, Maison Pelen. Charly had them flown in once a month. Ugo Buonsarde adored them. Charly felt honored to share this delicacy with such a discerning man and his guests.

# MAURICE THE MONEY MAN

ARTHUR ARPATI HAD CALLED RICHARD ZAMPONE down in New Jersey Saturday afternoon when he got home from the Hudson River adventure.

"Every last box is gone," Arthur told Zampone. "I got that deliveryman Pilchard to help me. They sank without a trace."

"I don't want to know," Richard said. "What I don't know, no one can force me to say." An old dictum of his father's.

"Okay. I had to pay the deliveryman three C's, by the way."

"Cheap at the price," Richard said. "We'll take it out of the promotion budget. You call the man from the Health Department?"

"Right after you and me talked. I called the guy, took a sample right up. I told him the old batch was all thrown away, but this was the same stuff."

"Listen, I got to go. I'll see you in the office Monday morning, okay? We got to whitewash this guy's death. I'm not sure how to do that."

"That's no problem at all, Richard. A lotta people ate that stuff and didn't get sick. What it amounts to is simply this, the guy's heart stopped. He had a lot of medical problems, you saw him, coughing and wheezing, the man was seriously overweight."

"Yeah, yeah, still, we gotta talk about it. Dying, that's serious."

When he got off the phone Richard said to his wife, "I think I'll drive up tomorrow afternoon, early. We don't have anything on, do we?"

"It's Linda's baby shower, just girls," Bernice said. "So that's perfect."

"I just got a feeling I should be there, not tell anyone. If Marty calls here, tell him I'm heading up early, but tell him to keep it quiet."

"You got one of your funny feelings again?"

"You better believe it," Richard said. "That guy's death could cause a whole lot of trouble. And I want to keep an eye on Arthur. I got a funny feeling he might start to panic, and then there's this Morrie character, wants to come up every day, give us advice. He could be a real pain in the butt."

"Just like your dad," Bernice said. "You get these funny feelings about people, and you're usually right. I hope you're going to the funeral, pay your respects, maybe send a few mass cards. They Catholic?"

"Yeah, they are. Good idea, mass cards. I'll give Father Evangelista a ring. Him and me get along real good. Funeral's Tuesday afternoon. Marty and I are going. I already sent a wreath, Marty got all the details for me."

136

"Send two wreaths, one personal, one from the company, and get a whole bunch of mass cards," Bernice said. "People appreciate these little touches so much." She was accustomed to dealing with the bereaved. There were so many in her husband's line of work.

Maurice, after rushing from the restaurant Saturday night, had driven to the emergency room of the Van Buren County Hospital in Hogton even though he felt okay, just a touch of nausea and diarrhea. He'd convinced the personnel that he'd eaten poison and must have his stomach pumped.

Considering the money the emergency room charged, the hospital was only too happy to oblige. They called Dr. Bingham, who also thought it was a good idea, after what had happened to Billy Herman. Maurice, with his cirrhosis in remission, would always have an enlarged liver, and he was overweight: Why take chances?

Maurice left the hospital early Sunday morning, gratified that after dinner last night, Barbara had come to the hospital to hold his hand. Now, he drove home to find a note from his wife, "Spending the day with Mummy." He fell into bed and slept until three.

After coffee and toast he decided to take a little drive. No one would be at Fabulous Foods this afternoon, so it would be a good time to look the place over. Maurice had made many false starts in life, but ever the optimist, he felt that this investment in Fabulous Foods was the best thing he'd ever done. The spoiled batch of Shrimp Milano was just an accident, it would never occur again. Things happened . . . remember that round of gorgonzola that Charly had to return to his distributor last year? Bacteria were everywhere.

137

There were no cars in the parking lot. Maurice got out of his car and checked the front door. Locked. He tried the back door: locked too. He walked over to the small building that housed the kitchen: locked. Maurice drove around to the back buildings. The big overhead doors were tightly shut. Maurice spied a small door on the side. He turned the knob and, to his surprise, the door swung open.

Maurice stepped into the warehouse, a cavernous space containing several walk-in freezer rooms, four upright freezers and six low, rectangular freezers that looked like coffins for giants. There was a low hum from electricity and the weak fluorescent lighting indicated that the room also contained machines for weighing, boxing, sealing, and labeling the containers of product.

The corrugated tin hangarlike structure was flimsily built, and Maurice could hear something rattling as the breeze flowed through the building. It was not a cozy place, but it was reasonably clean and looked efficient.

Maurice's chest swelled with pride as he considered that he was now part owner of this place. True, it was small enough now. But Maurice, looking toward the future, saw Fabulous Foods factories all across America. Together, he and Fabulous Foods would revolutionize restaurant food. No more arrogant chefs with their autocratic ways and petty grievances, dictating to restaurant owners. No more pilfering in the kitchen as chefs and cooks walked off with a third of the day's deliveries. No more payola from the meat and fish, dairy and vegetable purveyors to the chefs, who, in accordance with this time-honored practice, would then accept inferior merchandise from these same purveyors. Why, even the great Auguste Escoffier himself had been

138

fired from the Savoy for accepting money under the table from tradesmen. But Maurice would change all that.

As Maurice walked around he found himself becoming more and more enthusiastic. This was the future. Delicious food prepared under sanitary conditions by master chefs, packaged, frozen, delivered in small boxes to hundreds of thousands of restaurant kitchens, and served to patrons who never got food like this at home. All the restaurant had to do was open the box, heat up the food, and plate it. From Arkansas to Alaska, customers would eat a consistent product. This was, truly, a food revolution. Maurice considered himself the Cesar Chavez of the restaurant industry.

In his enthusiasm Maurice, humming and smiling to himself as he strolled around the vast space, tried various freezer handles. All locked. He jiggled the last freezer's door, and was dismayed when the door handle came off in his hand. Oh, well, they were just starting up. Things happened.

He peered inside the freezer. The bottom was stacked with suitcases. Odd. Were the shrimp packed in suitcases? Even Maurice, whose experience in the food-service industry was fairly limited, found this strange. He knelt on one knee and pried up the canvas lid of one of the suitcases. There, in serried ranks, were packs of hundred-dollar bills.

*Brilliant!* Maurice thought sarcastically. *Instead of putting all their payroll and petty cash money in the bank, where it could earn interest, they hide it here.* Oh, these food people. They had so much to learn from him.

Maurice was no mathematician, so he didn't realize that what he was looking at was probably several years' payroll and petty cash money, probably half a million dollars in just this one big suitcase. *This cash should be in the stock market,* Maurice thought. *I must speak to Richard. They're losing so much money, just keeping it here.*

Maurice let the lid of the suitcase snap back. He was about to lean in and pull out another suitcase, just to check, when he sensed someone standing by his side and turned around.

"Ah, Richard," Maurice said in a friendly voice. "This is a coincidence, I was just thinking about you."

"Hello, Morrie," Richard said quietly. He'd recognized Maurice's car outside and immediately removed his pistol, a Beretta 9 mm Parabellum, from his shoulder holster and slipped it into his right-hand pocket. Morrie the menace. Supersnoop. This was the last straw. "How did you get in?"

"The side door was unlocked," Maurice said, "Which is dangerous, with all your petty cash hidden here." Maurice pointed to the bulging canvas cases. Think of the interest you could be making on that cash in a bank, or preferably in the stock market. Really, you food people. Geniuses in gastronomy, but not very practical. It's a good thing I came on board."

"How did you open the freezer?"

Maurice shrugged. "I'm sorry about that. The door handle came off in my hand." Maurice showed Richard the broken handle.

"The money was stored in another freezer, since this one has to be repaired. Why did you move the money?" Richard still spoke quietly, the way his father had taught him. Don't alarm them, especially if you're going to whack 'em. Keep everything very quiet.

"Well," Maurice shrugged again, seeming not to have heard Zampone's question, "I just opened this freezer and saw the suitcases. I opened one and noticed the

140

money. That's a lot of money, Richard, to be hiding in a warehouse. It's not earning any interest."

"Why did you move the money, Morrie?"

"What are you talking about? I didn't move any money," Maurice said indignantly. "It was right here."

Richard sighed, and said, "Okay, Morrie, you didn't move any money. It don't matter. Let's go to my office and talk, huh? I want to hear your ideas on how to improve production."

Richard had a little system. First, he'd engage the guy's attention, ("Let's go out to the parking lot, there's something I want to show you,") and then, walking behind the victim, he'd pull out his piece and give the guy one slug, just behind his right ear. Tidy. You avoided a lot of mess that way.

"An excellent idea, Richard. There's so much I have to teach you about finances." Maurice smiled, and started walking toward the side door. Richard reached into his pocket and was about to withdraw his weapon when the side door opened and Arthur Arpati stuck his head in.

"Hi, Richard, Mr. Uh, I saw your cars and wondered what was up. Richard, I had to do a little moving job in here, wanted to explain."

Richard sighed. "Let's go to the office, okay, Arthur?" He could do Morrie another time. There wasn't any particular rush.

# CHARLY'S KITCHEN

SUNDAY MORNING FOUND CHARLY, BENNY, JULIUS, and Joe Okun preparing for the busiest mealtime of the week. La Fermette served Sunday dinner from noon to 6 P.M. and the kitchen closed at five. Those in the know

141

(practically everybody) knew that most of the food was gone by four. Benny chopped parsley and garlic and heated chicken stock; Julius made salmon roses and mixed crabmeat with sautéed shallots and chopped parsley and made a light béchamel for the crabmeat coquillés. The aroma of roasting meat, hot butter, wine, garlic, and fresh herbs was seductive.

Charly cut the celeriac into matchsticks for the celeri remoulade, claiming that the slicing machine cut the celeriac too thin and that it subsequently turned to mush.

"You see," Charly said, ever eager to give a cooking lesson, "it must be just so." He held up a celeriac matchstick.

"Yeah," Julius said, "but it takes you an hour, Charly."

"*Tant pis*, too bad," Charly replied. He plunged the celeriac into boiling water and drained it. Then he dressed it with mustard and mayonnaise. This was the way Charly's father had made celeri remoulade for his *charcuterie*, in Lons le Saunier. Naturally, it was the only way to do it.

"While I chop and slice," Charly explained, "I think. And I think that Harry Clark committed many sins. He was a bad man, and also a stupid man. He think he will not be caught, because he was so smart."

"That's true of most criminals," Julius said. "They think they're smarter than anyone else. Harry Clark was a big, macho prick hound. Ladies loved him. My aunt wanted to take care of him, baby him, buy him things. He flattered the hell out of her, told her how young she looked, and she rewarded Harry by giving him money. But he really wasn't a killer."

"If he wasn't a killer," Benny snorted, "what was he?"

"A whore, Benny, running after old women. He hit my aunt on the head, then he dumped her in that little pool. He just threw her in and assumed that she'd drown. Not the way a pro would do it. He never thought ahead: that if she survived, she'd put him in the slammer."

"So," Charly asked, "what does this demonstrate about his killer?"

"He did something equally stupid to someone else," Julius said. "He thought the person would be too scared to fight back, and Harry was wrong. So, who has something to hide?"

"Just about everyone," Joe Okun called from over by the sink.

"My theory, *précisément,*" Charly said. "But who?"

The telephone rang. "For you, Charly," Julius said. "Rex Cingale."

"Oh, Rex," Charly said. "You sound *très malade,* sick."

"I feel like shit," Rex said, "and it's that fuckin' garbage from Fabulous Foods. They delivered a case of that frozen Shrimp Milano last week, and I had some. So did Angelo and Sal, other people. So now I got only one broilerman and I'm out a couple waiters as well. We all got the runs, and I'm throwing up, stomach cramps, the whole ball of wax."

"Telephone Dr. Bingham," Charly advised. "It is the same bacteria that killed Billy Herman, the owner of that lunch place near Sharpsville."

"Christ," Rex said, "I didn't know that. He eat the stuff, too?"

"He eat the stuff, too," Charly said. "And call John Stark as well. It may be a criminal matter. Who deliver the sauce to you?"

"Some guy in an old Volvo," Rex said. "I never seen him before. But, uh, Charly, don't say nothing, huh?"

"Why not, Rex?"

"Listen, Charly, you were right. Those are not people you want to fool around with. I got funny vibes up at their plant, but I didn't say nothing."

"Have you signed the contract?" asked ever-practical Charly.

"No, and that's one good thing."

"What will you tell the owners when they call?"

Rex said, "Who the hell knows, Charly. I'm scared of that bunch. I'm sorry I ever got involved. Oops, sorry, gotta run. Nature calls."

"He is not near death," Charly mused as he hung up the receiver. "But he is frightened, and that is good." He stroked his little pencil mustache.

Richard Zampone had gotten rid of Maurice with the excuse that he and Arthur had to go over bills. Now, he sat at his desk. Arthur stood.

"Okay, Arthur," Richard said. "We got to know all the people that Shrimp Milano went to. Everyone."

"Joe Scapece," Arthur said, enumerating on his fingers, "that Morrie guy. And we delivered six boxes to Rex Cingale."

"Who delivered it?"

"That new driver, Ev Pilchard. He's a character, all right, every now and then he remembers to put on a fake English accent. And he calls the trunk of a car the boot. I wonder why he applied for a driver's job here?"

"We pay well, and it's easy work. What's to worry about?"

Arthur said, "He doesn't seem like the type. Seems real educated. Hey, here's a thought. Maybe he could

144

double as a salesman, he looks like a professor. He'd impress the shit out of the restaurant chefs, and you haven't got any salesmen yet."

"We was going to train the other driver, Harry Clark. He was a good-lookin' guy. But he was kinda weird. Anyways, he disappeared."

Arthur smiled knowingly. "Disappeared, huh?"

Richard shrugged. "These guys, they're flakes, they come and go. I figure he's in Vegas or somewhere."

"*Or somewhere,* like, he had a little accident. You wouldn't know about that, would you, Richard?"

Richard Zampone was genuinely puzzled. "Why would I whack him?"

"Okay, Richard, if you say so." Arthur still sounded dubious.

"I got to phone Rex, tell him it was a bad batch, not to use it. I'll do that right now," Richard said. "And Arthur, it's all gone, every box?"

"Every box," said Arthur. "You tell Morrie not to use it?"

"No, I forgot. I'll call him right now; he's probably home, by now."

"What," Arthur asked, "are you going to do about Morrie."

"He thinks he's helping. Anyway, we don't have to worry about him for a few days. He told me he's going on a trip," Richard lied. Morrie was going on a trip all right, going to sleep with the fishes.

Richard called Rex and told him to ditch the product, some boxes had defrosted in transit, they were being recalled. Rex didn't mention his gastrointestinal problems. Richard then called Maurice and left a message.

"You know, I wouldn't worry," Arthur reassured

Richard. "These things happen all the time. Just last week some dry cereal was recalled because of salmonella, and beef patties for fast-food joints are always being recalled, two huge batches recently. There's a recall every week, it seems."

"Not like fifty years ago," Richard remembered. "There was a canned vichysoisse that my dad loved. Some people died of botulism, the company went out of business. In those days, things like that didn't happen so often."

"Happens all the time, now," Arthur said. "No one goes out of business. There's too much money to be made. And too many people whose palms are greased. You won't have any trouble with the Health Department."

At four o'clock Sunday afternoon Charly exchanged his working jacket for a clean one and plopped on his white toque. Time to make his rounds. He circled his pretty dining room, thinking that the brown chintz, due to be retired in August, had done noble duty, and that the creamy apricot walls were looking passé. He and Barbara were right: a pale grey-green moss would make the dining room look like an extension of the woodlands and fields outside.

*"Ah, bonjour, mesdames, messieurs,"* Charly beamed at Honoria Wells, who was entertaining Jimmy Houghton (Charly's and Honoria's investment adviser); Evelyn Holmes, Jimmy's office manager; and Father Evangelista, the Catholic priest.

"Divine meal, Charly," Honoria smiled. "We had the rack of lamb. Father says there's a special place in heaven for you, for that crust."

Evelyn smiled. "I can't get enough of Charly's good

roast chicken. That's what I had. It's got the same crust, hasn't it?"

"The same crust." Charly smiled. "Father Evangelista will lead us all into the great French restaurant in the sky, *n'est-ce pas?*"

"Now, that rack of lamb was excellent, Charly, but did you ever think of adding sage and chopped onion? So healthy, sage. . ." Jimmy started in.

"Oh, Jimmy, you and your sage," Honoria scolded. Don't listen, Charly."

Charly always listened to Jimmy's pecuniary advice, for it had made him a great deal of money over the years. However, he generally ignored Jimmy's culinary preoccupations. He said, "Excellent idea, Jimmy."

"We were talking about Everston Pilchard, Charly," Honoria said. "I knew his parents. Now, he tells me you've hired him to do some garden work. Be careful, Charly. He has to be watched."

"I will take care, madame."

"Now, I've been giving a lot of thought to who might have killed Harry, since I understand Stark thinks I might have done it."

"Harry's a type," pronounced Father Evangelista. "I only saw him at the trial. Carrying his Bible. He tried to look hail-fellow-well-met, but had a certain special look in his eye. Like he was planning something he didn't want anyone to know about."

"That's what made Harry attractive to women," Honoria reflected. "He always looked like he was up to no good. A bad boy. Father, you've known a few sinners. So give this some thought."

Patty came over. "Excuse me, but there's a telephone call for Charly."

Charly took the call at the reservation desk. It was

147

Midge Warburton. "I wanted to tell you, Charly, that we started Socrates on your Bach flowers, and he's so much better. Seems to be back to his old self."

"I am so happy for you, madame. And for Socrate too, of course."

"And we found some books on the Bach flowers, we're going to try them ourselves. I think we both need a change, just as Socrates did."

Charly smiled. "It might change your outlook on life entirely."

Charly hurried back to Honoria's table, but they were again engrossed in conversation, so he decided to move on.

Standing at a distance, he looked at Honoria, Father Evangelista, Jimmy Houghton, and Evelyn Holmes, Jimmy's elderly office manager. Could one of them have killed Harry Clark?

Honoria would be the logical suspect. She was desperate for youth—who was fooled by her smooth face when they saw her liver-spotted, wrinkled hands? Harry had demonstrated all too forcefully that to him, she was nothing but a source of cash. Would she—despite Charly's protestations—have had Clark killed?

What about Jimmy Houghton. He'd killed before—true, in order to save Charly's life—but if you kill once . . .

Father Evangelista. Held the cards of his life close to his vest. Charly knew nothing about the man. He was affable, his parishioners loved him, but, but, but . . . Did Father Evangelista have dark secrets? As Joe Okun said, everybody did. Would he kill if threatened with exposure?

Evelyn Holmes. Formerly taught school. Now, Jimmy's office manager. Patrician, well respected, loved cats, baked walnut and white chocolate chip cookies which Charly and Jimmy adored. Patty now baked them, with Evelyn's blessing. If Clark tried to blackmail Jimmy over something he'd found out, would Evelyn kill to protect her beloved boss?

Sure. Any one of them could have done the deed. But which one?

Charly continued his rounds.

# CELERI REMOULADE

**Yield: 6–8 servings**

3 celery knobs (celeriac) peeled and cut into matchsticks (julienne)
1 cup mayonnaise mixed with
1 tablespoon French mustard
Salt and freshly ground white pepper to taste

Blanch celeriac sticks in boiling water for 30 seconds. Drain and while still hot toss with enough mayonnaise mixed with mustard to coat well. You may need more or less mayonnaise, depending on the size of the celery knobs. Add salt and pepper to taste. Serve at room temperature.

# CHARLY GARDENS

WHEN CHARLY OPENED THE BACK DOOR EARLY Monday morning he sniffed approvingly: the air was mild, there was a hint of rain, and the ground was moist with dew. It would be a perfect morning for working in his garden.

Charly raked away the covering of leaves at the far end of his garden and spaded up the soil for a second row of lettuces and radishes. He planted beets, spinach, Oriental greens, French breakfast radish seeds.

Charly would steam the radish greens (filled with minerals) and slice the radishes, using them to top buttered bread. You always served radishes with butter in France. "You will help me eat the lettuce, eh, Bruno?" Bruno had displayed a penchant for Charly's salads. The dog lay up by the bales of hay, in the little lean-to adjacent to the garden, having a morning nap. Gardening didn't interest him, except when it involved burying a bone.

Then Charly planted the cabbage, broccoli, collard, and brussels sprout seedlings. Later on in the season, Charly would transplant the lettuces, placing them around the cabbages, which provided shade that the lettuces needed in deep summer.

As he spaded and planted, Charly fretted about Maurice and his mad investments. What would happen if Maurice and Barbara ever split up? Barbara would carry on with her successful decorating business, but Maurice? Would he try to return to La Fermette? That would be a disaster. But maybe this Fabulous Foods would work out well—you never knew. The nice thing

151

about gardening was that while your hands were busy your mind was free to wander. Charly being Charly, his thoughts strayed toward death.

Who had killed Harry Clark? Charly had never met the man, and the battered thing that he and Bruno had found wasn't even a person: It was a hunk of decomposing flesh. What was it Rex and Bobby and Vinnie thought? That Harry Clark had been killed by an irate husband? Charly figured that the killer would never be caught, first because so much time had elapsed and secondly, because nobody cared. Harry Clark was hardly a leading citizen.

Charly had bought ten pounds of Khatadin seed potatoes and these, quartered, had been drying off. They were planted next to the horseradish at the foot of the little garden: horseradish was meant to keep the potato beetle at bay. There were just enough potatoes for a dozen delicious meals, and for the fun of digging them—like small brown jewels—in early autumn.

"*Et voilà*, Bruno. Everything is planted, for now." He admired his wild plants, the sweet rocket, mallow, buttercups, the wild garlic-mustard now going to seed, the *Prunella vulgaris* (all-heal), the coltsfoot, the borage with its big, hairy leaves. The wild plants were all growing in the various rows along with the chives, oregano, thyme, lemon balm, Oriental garlic chives, and Egyptian bunching onions. Charly was certain that old Doc Ross was right: the wild plants gave companionship to the cultivated ones, so that all grew in harmony. Suddenly Bruno gave a bark, and Charly looked up.

"Benny—I did not hear you approach."

"No, Charly, I parked my motorcycle by the front. Mom said she was sure you were planting your garden this morning, so she sent me over with these seeds she gathered last year: nasturtium, marigold, and, here, these little wild rose plants. She says she's got too many, and you admired them."

"Never can you have too many wild roses," Charly declared, remembering the potpourri his Tante Jeanne made from the petals.

Benny said, "We were talking this morning at the gym about Harry Clark. One of the guys said he once saw Harry talking to Everston Pilchard."

Charly felt flattered: He was turning Benny into a detective. "I did not know they knew each other. Mr. Pilchard will be coming over here this afternoon to suggest plants for the front, and I will ask him."

Benny changed the subject. "Hey, Charly, Bruno says he's hungry."

Charly glanced at his watch, "Time for lunch. I suppose it is Joe Okun who teach you to find out that Bruno is hungry by reading his mind."

"No, Charly, Bruno's stomach is gurgling. I can hear it. Besides, he's always hungry. You don't have to be psychic to figure that one out."

Charly brought chives, parsley, and chervil back to his kitchen, and he made *omelettes fines herbes* for himself and Benny, with plenty of butter and sea salt. With this they ate crusty French bread heated in the oven, and afterward they had a salad. It was one of Charly's favorite lunches.

"Simple food's so good," Benny said, mopping his last piece of bread around the plate. "I'm glad I gave up meat. Who needs it?"

"Is tradition," Charly said. "Once upon a time eating meat prove to the world that you were a rich man. Everyone want to be rich."

153

"Not me," said Benny. "My dad wanted to be rich, always spending money he didn't have."

Benny's father had died leaving a lot of debts as his sole legacy to his wife and son. Benny never forgot that.

"People are strange," Benny continued, "always wanting what they don't have, always wanting to look rich and powerful."

"And at the end of the road," Charly said, "the only thing that matter is kindness. Eh, Bruno?"

"You forgot his salad," Benny said. "Bruno says a little kindness closer to home would be much appreciated."

"And right here, at the corner of the house, I wonder if a rhododendron would look good?" Charly asked. He and Bruno had had an afternoon nap, and now, at four o'clock, Charly, Bruno, and Everston Pilchard were standing at the side of Charly's little farmhouse.

"Masses of English ivy climbing up the stone foundation and spreading over the entire lawn. That's what I see, Mr. Poisson. Nothing but English ivy, and you'd never have to mow it."

Charly was surprised. "And that is it? Nothing more?"

"Less is more, monsieur," said Everston sententiously. "We'd carry the ivy over to the side. Then at the back, where you have those old lilac bushes, we'd plant a few more lilacs. We want to keep it as plain as can be. This is a simple farmhouse, and you want to honor the simplicity."

"Yes, that would be perfect," Charly said. He was surprised. Having been warned that Pilchard sometimes went overboard, he'd imagined the man proposing hundreds of flowers and shrubs.

"Well, then, that's it. I'll get the ivy, get the soil

154

analyzed, add acid if needed, and we're in business. I'll plant the ivy, but it's up to you to water it. Would you like to sign this standard contract?"

Later, as they strolled to Everston's car, Charly remembered what Benny had told him. "To change the subject, I found a body on my property. The police have identified the body as Harry Clark. Did you know Mr. Clark?"

Everston said easily, "Sure, I knew him. Not well, but we'd greet each other. I've got a part-time delivery job now, Harry Clark used to do it. It seems he never showed up one day, never called—nothing. He had a reputation for unreliability. I read about his body in the paper. It was found near your pond, wasn't it?"

"It was. But the paper did not print that."

"You know how it is, word gets around. But why are you bringing him up? Do you want to do some plantings down by your pond?"

"No, I am merely curious," Charly said.

Everston said he would do the job within the month. Charly was impressed by the man's simple approach. No hard sell, no grandiose flower beds. He decided that whatever people said about Pilchard, they were wrong.

"Do you enjoy being a schoolteacher, Monsieur Pilchard?"

"Not really," Everston said. "The boys are frequently insolent, and they don't apply themselves to their work. It's not a very good school, I'm afraid. Their standards are low. As are their salaries. But I live in a beautiful old house, you must come and see it."

"Yes," said Charly, "I would like that."

"And of course I have my gardening in the summer, and a few loyal clients. I've often thought of moving to the Boston area, for instance, where there are a lot more private schools. But I'm a simple person, Mr. Poisson, and my life here suits me. I love Van Buren County."

"Yes," Charly said, "I, too, love it here."

As Pilchard drove away and Charly and Bruno walked toward the house, Charly thought, *This man cannot be a murderer. He is just like me.*

# SHOTS IN THE DARK

CHIEF OF POLICE JOHN STARK STOOD UNEASILY AT THE gay bar, Frantic Feathers. Abe Reynolds was supposed to question the owner, Nick Queechy, about Harry Clark, but Abe was involved in a domestic, so the chief took over. Stark felt uncomfortable in any bar, straight or gay—he wasn't a drinker, and couldn't understand why someone would waste his money that way.

Normally, the chief of police would never trot around like a detective questioning subjects, but a small-town cop did whatever was necessary, never mind your rank. Stark didn't mind. It kept him in touch.

"So, Nick, you say Harry Clark was a regular, here?"

"Pretty regular," said Nick, mopping down the bar. He felt antsy with Chief Stark. Nick was Abe Reynolds's snitch, and over the years they'd developed a comfortable relationship. Stark was The Law, and a stranger.

Frantic Feathers, a bar and casual restaurant that catered mainly to homosexual gentlemen, was located at the end of a dirt road off Route 81, not a place you'd wander into by accident. The business was housed in the downstairs portion of an old farmhouse: purple-painted barroom, egg yolk yellow dining room, white-tile professional kitchen, wallpapered male and female toilets, (STAGS and DOES, the does used mainly by transvestites) and a chartreuse sunporch where you could lounge on the wicker chairs, and read the magazines: *Soldier of Fortune; The Economist; Vogue; Hustler;* and the *Fisherman.* There wasn't a feather in sight, frantic or otherwise. Nick and his companion, Ritchie Naylor, lived upstairs.

Nick said guardedly, "Well, Harry was pretty much of a regular, if you call once every two, three weeks regular. You couldn't set your clock by Harry. What he liked was the innocents. He'd wow 'em with his tales, he was always after rich old women, but he liked the young guys, too, liked to impress 'em. I don't know if he was gay or not, but why come here if you're not gay?" Nick swiped the bar down again with his clean rag. Everything was clean at Nick's, Stark noted. Hideous paint colors, but clean.

"Dif'rent strokes for dif'rent folks," Abe Reynolds had told Stark. "I don't understand the gay scene. Makes me uncomfortable, but a lot of things make me uncomfortable. At least they're not the Ku Klux Klan. But you know, Chief, whatever they do with their private lives, it's their business, as long as they're not breaking any laws." Stark agreed. They rarely had complaints from the sizable gay community, but gays loved to gossip; Abe had sniffed out a number of good leads at Frantic Feathers over the years.

Now, Stark slid an envelope across the bar. "This is from Abe. He says to tell you he's sorry he couldn't make it this afternoon."

The envelope disappeared. Nick Queechy was part Native American, like many in the county, but unlike most of his sad brethren of drunks, welfare recipients, and forgotten people, Nick had gone to college and done the New York ad agency route where, it was rumored, he'd made a packet.

Then Nick quit the big city and returned to the lands of his ancestors. Bought the farmhouse, got himself a liquor license, and opened for business, catering at first to weekend gays, which he himself had been. The place had prospered. The bar had a laid-back ambiance, and Ritchie Naylor, the house chef, served huge platters of well-cooked food. While the bar was never packed, like Rex's place, it was rarely empty, either.

"We're just plain folks, here," Nick would say, well into his folksy routine. "Now, Ritchie's made beef stew. You want a bowl, Chief?"

"No, thanks," Stark said, "but tell Ritchie I'm sorry to miss his good food." Ritchie had worked as a cook in some of New York City's best restaurants. He was a tiny man, shaved-head-bald, who dressed almost entirely in black-and-grey loose-fitting garments from Japanese designers. Stark thought he looked like the Dalai Lama, only thinner.

"So Harry's dead. I saw it in the paper." Nick chewed on a toothpick.

"I'll tell you what wasn't in the papers," Stark said. "He'd been hit on the head, maybe with a hammer, and dumped in that pond between Route 65 and County Route 16. Hy Bingham says he wasn't much fun to work on."

"I'll bet."

They found those hot peppers like Rex Cingale serves in his stomach; we think he had his last meal there. You don't serve them, do you?"

"No, they're too vinegary. Ritchie hates that stuff."

Stark continued. "You probably couldn't recall when

he was in here last. Or who he was talking to. Or who might have disliked him."

"No to all three," Nick said. "The young 'uns thought he was hot stuff, all macho and handsome. Looked like a movie star. Dumb like one, too."

"Who, in particular, did he hang around with?"

"No one, Chief, I just told you." Nick wished he was joking with Abe. This man, all upright and proper, made him feel like he was at church.

"Okay, let me run a name by you."

"Wait a sec. What, Jamie, two more of the same?" To a gentleman who had approached the bar. Nick blended two colossal strawberry daiquiries and gave them to the man. Stark waited until the man left.

"What about a schoolteacher called Everston Pilchard?"

Nick thought for a bit. "Well, there's a tall man with terrible posture, you know, he slouches, I think he's called Ev, he comes in, oh, once in a blue moon. Always drinks Perrier with lime. I always thought he might be a schoolteacher. Never talks much, always leaves alone, though once, he and Harry Clark were talking."

There was a silence. Apart from Stark, the barroom was empty, and the dining room appeared empty, too. Not surprising on a Monday afternoon. Stark could hear the murmur of voices from the sunporch.

"Oh, yeaah," Nick said. "I've remembered something. One time last winter Harry was in, and this Ev comes over to the bar. They're whispering, see, and I'm at the other end, talking to some folks. Then Harry wants a drink. I come over, Harry's saying to Ev in a real nasty voice, "Well, it would be terrible if certain parties found out, wouldn't it?" Then Harry gave a really evil laugh. And this

159

poor guy, Ev, paid for his Perrier and got right out. Don't think I've seen him since."

"That's interesting," Stark said. It wasn't really. Just idle gossip.

Ritchie Naylor appeared from the kitchen, his outfit—something black and loose—covered with a big white apron.

"Hello, Chief," Ritchie said. "We don't often see you here. Nick, we've got about fifteen servings of stew, so push it tonight."

"I'm asking Nick about Harry Clark," Stark said. "And Ev Pilchard."

"Both losers," Ritchie said. "Harry's death is no loss. And Ev, or whatever his name is, is so timid he's pathetic."

Monday night around half past eight Charly and Bruno went out for their customary evening walk. They turned left and walked up Barrett Road to the fork, which branched left to a dead end, and right to Maurice's big white-icing modern house, which looked like it belonged in the Arizona desert, not in the foothills of the Berkshires. It was a foggy evening, and Charly could feel the moisture seeping into his canvas jacket.

They had just turned left, to walk to the dead end, when Charly sensed a car approaching. For no reason that he could determine afterward—except that, perhaps, he thought it might be Maurice and wasn't in the mood for that gentleman's braying—Charly said "Come, Bruno," and ducked behind a tree. In the light of the moon Charly could see that the car was not Maurice's Mercedes, nor was it Barbara's Cadillac. It was a nondescript dark American car. Charly supposed it was an acquaintance of Maurice's. He was unable to notice much about the driver, except that it looked like a man.

As soon as the taillights disappeared around the bend, Charly and Bruno continued their walk. They walked to the end of the road, Bruno sniffing, lifting his leg, and finally squatting. They turned back.

Charly heard the sound of a truck backfiring, not unusual on the road, but otherwise stillness prevailed. You couldn't even hear the cars on Route 65. Suddenly Charly heard a car, driving fast, coming back from Maurice's. He jumped back into the shadows, grabbing Bruno by his collar, and watched the car rush past, going far too fast for a little country road filled with potholes. Some seconds later he heard a squeal of brakes, as the car stopped before turning onto Route 65. "Foolish, foolish," Charly muttered. Everyone was in such a hurry.

Another car turned onto Barrett Road, this one coming slowly. It was Barbara's Cadillac. The car stopped, and the window rolled down.

"Charly?"

"Ah, my dear Barbara."

"I've been dining with a potential client in Albany. Isn't it foggy."

"Good weather for walking," Charly said. "But bad for rheumatism. Still, Bruno enjoy his walk, and so do I."

"I'm tired. I want to lie in a hot bath and soak."

"A good night for sleeping," Charly said. "*Bonne nuit . . .*"

"*Bonne nuit,*" Barbara answered.

Charly and Bruno, home at last, checked the house, closing windows, locking front and back doors, calling cats, and went upstairs to bed.

161

As Charly was just beginning to reread one of his favorite stories from Alphonse Daudet's *Contes du Lundi,* where a little boy from Alsace-Lorraine remembers when the German invaders cruelly decreed, during the First World War, that henceforth all school classes would be conducted in German, the telephone rang.

Charly, annoyed, almost let the machine pick up downstairs. He loved to reread favorite authors, it was like visiting an old friend. The stories didn't change. But every time you discovered something new. Now, an alien voice was intruding into Charly's bedroom, the ugly cawing of the telephone invading his private moments with Alphonse Daudet.

" 'Allo," Charly said rudely.

"Charly, it's Barbara." Her voice sounded strangled and strange. "Maurice has been shot. I've called the police and the ambulance."

"I am on my way," Charly cried, slamming down the receiver.

# CALLS FOR HELP

CHARLY ARRIVED AT THE BALEINE HOUSE JUST AHEAD of two police cars, an ambulance, and another car with MD plates. He drove around to the garage area so he wouldn't impede the ambulance, and ran to the back door.

Maurice was lying on the kitchen floor, eyes closed, head bloody. Barbara was kneeling by his head, gingerly mopping the blood away with a piece of cotton and some hydrogen peroxide.

"I didn't know what else to do, Charly," Barbara said in a choked voice. "I didn't want to move him, he might have internal injuries."

Charly removed a tiny bottle from his pocket. He unscrewed the lid and dribbled several drops onto Maurice's lips. "Rescue Remedy from the great Dr. Bach, for shock and trauma," murmured Charly, just as the door was flung open and several hundred men, or so it seemed, filled the doorway. Charly quickly pocketed his bottle.

"I will wait in the living room, my dear Barbara," he said as he left the room, after nodding to John Stark, Vince Matucci, two more police officers, and another man whom Charly took to be a doctor from his black bag. In the hall, Charly passed two ambulance attendants with a portable stretcher. Charly heard Barbara say, "I just got home and here he was . . ."

He sat in the living room contemplating the beige wall-to-wall carpet, oyster white walls, low-slung leather furniture from Milan, pink marble-block coffee table, hidden lighting, modern paintings of red and yellow lines and squiggles which hung on the walls.

This was not a Barbara room. Maurice's college classmate, the Milanese architect Carlo Penci, had taken charge of the interior as well as the exterior of the house. It had all of the warmth of a mausoleum. Maurice was immensely proud of it.

Charly had once met Signor Penci, and the two had taken an immediate dislike to each other. ("Both he and his food are so bourgeois, my dear Maurice" was Penci's assessment, archly reported by Maurice, who then urged Charly to convert his menu to a minimalist collage of vegetable strips and raw fish. Charly, quite naturally, refused.)

*Ah, what can you expect from an Italian*, Charly thought. The French and the Italians detested each other almost as much as did the French and the English. This

163

was one reason Charly enjoyed torturing himself by reading the very English *Economist* magazine each week. (On the World Cup in Paris a few years ago, *The Economist* had archly reported that "20 extra tonnes of World Cup condoms have, it is said, been imported.")

Charly heard footsteps receding and doors shutting, indicating that Maurice was being taken out the front door and the police were leaving. Barbara appeared in the doorway. "Thank God it's nothing but a scratch," she told Charly. "All that blood, I thought he was dying."

"But what happened?"

"The police doctor said that a bullet grazed the top of Maurice's head. A millimeter lower down, and he'd be dead. Stark found the bullet lodged in the doorway. From a rifle, probably. Stark thinks a car pulled up near the house, the driver got out, saw lights on in the kitchen, and climbed that little hill behind the house, and shot at Maurice from there. Then he drove off."

Charly told Barbara about hearing what he thought was a truck backfiring, and about the unknown car driving up to the house, then driving down very fast. "I will tell John Stark tomorrow," Charly said. "But come, I will drive you to the hospital."

"No need, Charly. I'll run over and make sure he's all right. The doctor said they'll check him over, just to be sure, but he's certain that Maurice is fine. The bullet scraped along his hairline. I'll stay until he's settled in a room, then I'll come home. The doctor said he could probably come home tomorrow. Can you imagine? When you think of what might have been . . ."

"Our Maurice," Charly said, "is a lucky man. He lead the charmed life. First, *la cirrhose du foie,* the liver disease, then this. *Le bon Dieu* is not ready to carry Maurice into heaven, yet."

"Evidently not," Barbara said dryly. "Go on home, Charly, I'll call you tomorrow. Will you be at the restaurant?"

"Tomorrow afternoon I go to funeral of a fellow restaurateur," Charly said. He could have added, "who ate the frozen shrimp from the company that Maurice has invested in," but he did not. Barbara, poor woman, had enough on her plate.

Back home, Charly returned to bed. But he was too excited to sink into the weepy sentimentality of Alphonse Daudet, so he took a double dose of valerian and passiflora and soon was snoring almost as loudly as Bruno.

"And so my good friend, I call you as last resort. I did not want to involve you in my problems, but now, I fear that I must."

The decision to call Ugo Buonsarde had not been taken lightly. Charly knew that business and friendship rarely mix, and his relationship with Ugo was based on mutual admiration: Ugo took pleasure in Charly's food and Charly took pleasure in Ugo's appetite. To bring business into the mix could easily sour the delicate balance. But Maurice's life was at stake. Charly had no illusions about Maurice's attacker. It was someone from Fabulous Foods, without question. (Charly had no illusions about Ugo, either.)

Charly told Ugo about the attempted killing of Maurice, and Ugo told Charly that both Zampone and Scungilli had a bad habit of eliminating people who stood in their way.

"You must convince Maurice to get out of that

165

company. Even if he loses his money, it's nothing compared with his life."

"Difficult, signor. Maurice is convince he will make his fortune."

"Then it is an impossible situation, my friend. There is nothing I can do. Maurice must make the decision himself: to pull out of the association."

"You are right as usual, signor." Charly sighed deeply. "Maurice has come to a crossroads. It is up to him to choose the correct path."

"But perhaps," Ugo continued, "this will be a lesson for Maurice. Out of adversity comes personal growth. Could this not be a time of renewal, where Maurice admits to his past foolishness, moves on to higher things?"

"Anything is possible," said Charly dubiously.

"Here, let me read you something." Charly could hear Buonsarde rustling pages. "My *I Ching,* it is always on my desk. Listen to this, from Hexagram 9, Hsiao Ch'u, The Taming Power of the Small:

*The Wind drives across heaven:*
*The image of The Taming Power of the Small.*
*Thus the superior man*
*Refines the outward aspect of his nature.*

"Doesn't this sound like Maurice? He will become tamed by the small and mean things that are happening to him. He will grow in stature and improve his spiritual life." Ugo chuckled. "We hope."

"Perhaps," Charly said. "But I have very grave doubt that Maurice is a superior man. What do you think an inferior man would do?"

"An inferior man," Ugo lectured, "would continue on

the path he has heretofore chosen, believing that he is all-powerful."

"And then?"

"And then, my dear friend Charly, he would die."

Charly hung up after avowals of friendship had been exchanged. "Buonsarde thinks Maurice might change," he told his crew. "Maurice will never change. He will never admit that Fabulous Foods is wicked."

"Of course he won't, Charly," said Julius. "Stop giving yourself grief. Maurice is Maurice. There's nothing you can do to change him."

"But why kill Maurice?" Benny asked. "He's stupid, but harmless."

"Many reason," Charly answered. "First, he eat the frozen sauce and go to hospital to have his stomach emptied. Fabulous Food is perhaps afraid of the lawsuit. Then, Maurice go up to Sharpsville every day. He give everyone the benefit of his expertise. He is driving them crazy."

"There's reason enough," Julius said. "He told me once my fish salad needed cinnamon. I said 'cinnamon, are you sure?' And he said, well maybe not cinnamon, maybe cardamom. He'll say anything at all, for effect."

"I believe all of this," Charly said. "But I think there is something more. What, it doesn't matter. But because of it, Maurice will be killed."

Father Evangelista stayed well away from the food at the reception following Billy Herman's funeral. It was at the Herman house and catered by Billy's restaurant, the Happy Farmer Luncheonette, not one of the priest's favorite eating spots. He didn't find much to his liking at the bar, but he made do with cheap vodka mixed with tomato juice.

Neither did he at first speak to the two black-suited men who stood on the fringes of the crowd, Zampone and Scungilli. Both had made generous contributions to St. Mary's, but Father Evangelista doubted that their motives were pure. He nodded curtly, then remembered that Mr. Zampone had also paid for several masses for the repose of Mr. Herman's soul. The priest made his way over to the pair.

"Beautiful mass, Father," Zampone said.

"Very sobering," said the other man, Scungilli.

"A sad time," said Father Evangelista. "Bill Herman will be missed. A good and kind man." He turned away as the Scapeces and the Marises beckoned. "Excuse me, gentlemen."

Charly Poisson watched the priest make his way from group to group. He recognized few people. Not many of his customers were patrons of the Happy Farmer Luncheonette. The food didn't tempt him, either. He was wary of the violent pink cold cuts, creamy salads, and gooey orange cheeses.

As soon as he had paid his respects to the widow Charly edged toward the front door, which opened suddenly, nearly hitting him in the face.

A small man with the thin face of a ferret grabbed Charly's arm.

"You're one of 'em, I can tell. Where's Marty? That bum's nosin' around again. He's gotta come."

Suddenly Martin Scungilli was at the man's side. "Why don't we talk outside, Floyd? Excuse us, Mr. Poisson."

168

# KITCHEN TALES

"HOW WAS THE FUNERAL, CHARLY?" JULIUS ASKED Wednesday morning in the kitchen of La Fermette.

"So and so. What you might expect. I had to go. The two men from the company Maurice is investing in were there, and a messenger come, and this man he think I am one of *les gangsters*. 'I can tell you are one of them,' he say. I think it is my mustache." Charly preened a bit.

"You don't look like a gangster at all," Benny said. "Does he, Julius?"

"Well," Julius said, peering at Charly closely. "Perhaps to an outsider."

"He say 'the bum is nosing around again.' Who do you think that bum could be? Is it anyone we know? I have my suspicions."

"Maurice of course," Julius said. "Barbara stopped by here yesterday afternoon while you were at the funeral. Maurice left the hospital with a big bandage around his head, and the moment they got home he drove off. Said he had business to attend to. She's sure he went up to Fabulous Foods."

"I said, maybe he was at that Herman guy's funeral," Benny said. "But Barbara said no, he considers the other Fabulous Foods partners lower-class, and doesn't want to have anything to do with them. Are they lower-class?"

"We are all princes in our domains," Charly said vaguely, "and outside of our domains we are all lower-class. Does that answer your question?"

"So those other Fabulous Foods partners are just ordinary people," Benny said.

169

"They are not customers of La Fermette," Charly admitted.

"Go on, Charly," urged Julius. "What happened after the messenger told whatshisname about 'that bum,' who we think is Maurice, snooping."

"Mr. Scungilli, he drive away," Charly said. "This is all I know." Charly strolled over to the little mirror and smoothed down his pencil mustache. *Oui*, he thought. *Decidedly, I look like le gangster.*

Scungilli was in his office Wednesday morning at Fabulous Foods. Maurice was, too, making lists on a yellow pad: estimated amounts of lobster tails, crabmeat, shrimp, fish fillets, and now he was comparing that list with the list of foodstuffs that Fabulous Foods produced.

"I'm going to save you thousands, Martin," Maurice crowed. "We're going to attack this surplus inventory. You've got far too much frozen seafood for the amount of dishes you produce. What you need is a plan."

Martin didn't bother to explain that the inventory was big because they were selling to distributors. In fact, he didn't explain anything. Maurice was trouble. They never should have welcomed him aboard. Obviously, he must exit as quickly as possible. But the man seemed to have a charmed life. That Richard should miss—he'd tripped on a tree root at the moment of pulling the trigger—simply set the plan back a day or two.

"I already told some people Morrie was going on a trip," Richard told his partner, "to sort of pave the way, in case he should not turn up one day."

"Smart," said Scungilli. "Maybe he should drive down to Jersey where he could—uh—meet with ill fortune."

"Jersey's a good idea," Richard said. "We're just starting up in Sharpsville. We don't need trouble here."

"Billy Herman's croaking sure messed that up."

"Not really," Richard continued. "Arthur told the inspector that those bad shrimp dishes were made from the last shipment of shrimp from Thailand, and we've changed our suppliers, now."

"The inspector tested the stuff Arthur made, and it was fine. Poor Mr. Herman had a lot of medical problems," Scungilli said. "I talked to the doc. On top of everything else, Herman had a big surplus of magnesium in his body, on account of all that Maalox and Mylanta he drank like water, not to mention the laxatives. He was dying long before he ate that shrimp."

"Cops might visit because *somebody* tried to shoot Maurice, which was one stupid idea of mine," Richard said humbly. "I don't do good at long distance. Goddamn tree root."

Scungilli had another idea. "Want me to fix his car so he crashes? You know, loosen the nuts on a wheel, or cut the brake lines?"

"It's something to think about. Meanwhile, how the hell do we get him off the premises?" Richard stared at his partner.

Scungilli said, "He should work in his own kitchen, for starters, creating new dishes. There isn't room up here, and Arthur hates the guy."

Martin agreed. "He's always saying he used to own a restaurant, knows everything there is to know about cooking. Now's his chance to prove it. He'll be so busy in his own kitchen, he won't have time to come up."

Admittedly, this was brilliant. "I'll speak to him now," said Zampone.

"How are you feeling, Maurice? That was a narrow escape you had."

"I feel fine, Richard, except for a slight headache," Maurice said. "The police think it was kids; they're pursuing it."

Zampone shook his head disapprovingly. "Too many guns out there. When citizens start taking the law into their own hands, it means trouble for everybody. They should leave that stuff to the pros. But Morrie, I got a proposition for you. You know how it is with chefs, always creating. They get stuck. All recipeed out. Arthur's in a rut, and we need some new dishes."

Maurice nodded wisely. "Creative juices stop flowing. I know exactly."

"So, my partner and I want you to spend time in your own kitchen. There isn't room up here, of course. You'd buy supermarket product and we'd pay you back. You've had lots of experience in restaurant kitchens, you say, and I'm sure you're very good at it."

Maurice swallowed, then smiled brightly. "Of course."

Richard handed over a list. "Here's the shrimp product we have now. Milano with regular tomato sauce; Romano with brandy and cream; Napoli with spicy tomato sauce; and Veneziano with light tomato sauce and vegetables. Crab's identical. Could you create six new recipes for each?

"Child's play," Maurice blustered.

"Remember, the ingredients can't be too expensive, no saffron, no caviar; and it has to freeze well. Of course we add chemicals to the cream sauces so they won't separate, so that's no problem."

"Consider it done," Maurice said. "When do you want me to start?"

"Immediately. We'll miss you up here, but these financial matters can wait. Why don't you go now, and give us a call in a week?"

"Excellent," said Maurice. "I'll go right home and get started."

Everston Pilchard had switched classes with another teacher so that his Monday and Wednesday mornings were free to make deliveries for Fabulous Foods. Now that he realized how well they paid, he began to take his job seriously. He wore a white chef's jacket, a white cap like Japanese sushi chefs wore, and drove a sleek white van with the Fabulous Foods logo in red.

Everston had gone from shame and anger at the lowly job to an entirely different perspective. Maybe it was the uniform that did it. Also, the attitude of the chefs he delivered to, friendly and casual, helped to bolster his self-esteem. For while one side of Evvie's personality was timid, another side was grandiose, just like the chefs he chatted with. They, too, saw themselves as the masters of the universe. Consequently Everston Pilchard felt right at home in the kitchens of the Albany area's finer restaurants.

Arthur Arpati and his partners knew that the deliveryman, doubling as salesman, could bring in a lot of business. Evvie would add a touch of class. Arthur gave him a list of product. Everston caught on immediately.

"Give 'em a box of one of the other shrimp entrees they didn't order. Say, they order Shrimp alla Napoli? Give 'em a free box of Romano. Tell 'em they can use the sauce for other things, too, not just pasta topping."

"Cooking is my hobby," Everston told Arthur. "They can make a great risotto, they can even use it to top pizza. Seafood salad's a snap, big bowl of lettuce, that's all you need."

"That's great, Ev. I'll make sure you get a commission on your sales."

"Why, Arthur, that's very generous of you." Everston smiled.

"You're an important man to us, Ev," Arthur flattered.

So Everston, looking every inch the professional chef, put on his white jacket and with that garment went a change in personality. He became an authority, a culinary consultant. He grew in stature in his own eyes. Unfortunately, with a man of Everston's temperament, once the growth started, it was hard to check. The mania, inherited from his grandmother, took hold, and Everston was transformed from loyal subject to emperor.

As he drove the smart white van to the potential clients of Fabulous Foods, Everston saw this turning into such an exciting profession that by the end of the summer, he might be able to give up teaching entirely.

The landscaping business was starting off well, too. Everston had been touched by power. He now saw himself as the Le Nôtre of Van Buren County. His plans for Charly's modest farmhouse grew. Why not landscape Charly's fields, too? Today he'd visit Van Meegrin Nurseries.

Everston grinned madly as he contemplated his future. He would eclipse the Sun King. Le Nôtre's Versailles was but a cottage garden next to the plans he had for Charly's property. And as for Fabulous Foods, he'd become the greatest salesman that the food world had ever seen. He didn't have a 168 IQ for nothing. It took ages, sometimes, for geniuses to find the correct path.

# MAURICE THE CHEF;
# PILCHARD THE EMPEROR

MAURICE WAS EXCITED BY HIS NEW JOB. WITH THE self-confidence that only a double Leo can possess, he saw himself as a master chef, combining, stirring, tasting, adding a spice here, an herb there. What an adventure.

He decided to stop at a supermarket and buy shrimp. Then, at least, he'd have the main ingredient on hand. This was his first eye-opener. Ten pounds of 20/25 count shrimp (that is 20/25 to the pound, quite large,) cost over a hundred dollars.

"A hundred and ten dollars?" Maurice squeaked.

"Yes, sir," the man at the fish counter said. "Those are large shrimp, very select. Our premium quality."

"Would a restaurant use them for a pasta topping?"

"Oh yes, sir," the fish man lied. A mistake had been made, and he'd received three hundred pounds instead of a hundred. He was anxious to unload the suckers. A restaurant would naturally use a much smaller size for a sauce. "Tell you what," he said to Maurice, "Since you're buying ten pounds I'll make a special price, $8.95 a pound. How does that sound?"

"All right," Maurice said glumly. Reality was beginning to set in. "How long will they keep in the refrigerator?"

"I'd use them within two days," the fish man said, fearing a lawsuit. "Seafood's very perishable, you know. Better to keep them frozen."

Maurice visualized the small freezer space in Barbara's fridge. The last time he'd looked, it was packed. Oh, Christ. He'd better buy a freezer.

175

His first thought had been to call Charly and ask for freezer space. But Maurice was a proud man. He wanted to do this job on his own. The last thing he wanted was to have Charly, Julius, and Benny (real professionals) peering over his shoulder, giving advice. And laughing at him. In that tiny portion of his brain where reality dwelled, choked by layers of ego, Maurice suspected that Charly and his crew considered him a fool.

It was late afternoon when Maurice got home. The freezer would arrive tomorrow. He poured an iced Perrier and went in search of cookbooks.

After an hour, Maurice had learned many things about the preparation of shrimp: that the shellfish were very perishable; that the black line which contained the shrimp's excrement had to be removed from each shrimp; that they had to be cooked quickly, or they would turn rubbery.

When Barbara opened the door to Maurice's study at six o'clock she found him slumped in his chair, fast asleep. When she went to the kitchen and opened the freezer compartment, a large bundle tumbled out and crashed to the floor, narrowly missing her feet.

*"J'ai deux amou-u-u-rs, mon pays et Paris,"* Charly sang, as he chopped carrots, onions, garlic, parsley together. It was an old song of Josephine Baker's. "La-la-la-la," he continued, words forgotten.

"You doing the duck, Charly?" Julius asked.

"Caneton à l'orange," Charly said, "little ducky with orange sauce."

He scooped up vegetables and shoveled them into a stainless-steel pan with his bench scraper. He added bay leaves and sprigs of thyme. Next, he checked on the four ducklings that were browning in a hot oven. He

176

took out the birds, poured off the fat, and emptied the vegetables into the roasting pan. He replaced the ducks, drizzled on chicken stock and white wine, and returned the pan to the oven. He grated four oranges and reserved the zest, then squeezed the oranges and strained the juice. Later, the pan juices would be heated with orange juice and zest, salt and pepper. Tableside, half a duckling would be flambéed with Cointreau by Elton Briggs or Hubert Dupont or Tommy Glade or perhaps even Charly himself, for an especially favored customer. Flaming the food while customers watched was theater. It more than paid for itself. Suddenly many people in the dining room wanted a flambéed entrée.

With the ducklings roasting, Charly addressed himself to his next special for the evening—Poulet Creole. He cut the firm Southwind Farm chickens into pieces and floured them. These weren't the pathetic little supermarket fowl that fell apart after twenty minutes' cooking; they were robust, range-run birds. Charly gently placed each piece of chicken into a large pan of hot clarified butter, and when each piece was golden he removed it. Next, onions were browned; then, green, red, and yellow bell peppers were added to the fat, then blanched, peeled and sliced tomatoes, chopped garlic, and a bouquet of parsley, thyme, and bay leaf.

Charly combined chicken and vegetables and poured over hot chicken stock and white wine. The dish smelled extremely promising. It would roast in the oven for half an hour, then finished on the stove at point of service.

Benny, watching, said, "You could add smoked andouille sausage and okra, like Paul Prudhomme did on television."

"I could do many thing," Charly said. "But then it

177

would not be the classic Poulet Creole." He cleared his throat, preparatory to a small lecture.

"I cook the *Cuisine Classique,* Benny, as you know. And it is called classic cooking because these are the dishes that chefs have prepared for many years. They are in a tradition. The American chef, they always want to add something new to make it their own: a sliced banana, a few peaches. Pouagh! Horrible. We must stick with the tradition, Benny. This is why *La Cuisine Française* is great. Because we leave the recipe alone."

"Ha," said Julius. "Remember that quote of Jacques Maniere, the French chef? 'They stick a banana up a duck's ass and call themselves geniuses'? I love that. Talking about all the new young chefs who like to create."

"Creation," Charly said somberly, "is the beginning of the end. Look at what happened to this beautiful world after *Le Bon Dieu* created man and woman. Evil."

"And evil is winning the race," called out Joe Okun.

"Really, can't we talk about something cheerful?" Julius pleaded.

"Well, according to some psychics, the world's going to end in 2014, Charly, so maybe we'll be all together again on another planet," Benny said.

"Assuredly, this Tae Kwon Do is changing your life, Benny," Charly said dryly. Benny was moving into the new age with enthusiasm, encouraged by his classmates at the Oriental martial-arts classes that Charly paid for. Already, he was almost totally vegetarian; he was exploring Buddhism; believed in reincarnation, karma, and extrasensory perceptions. And now, the latest thing, he wanted to try leeches for the bruises he sometimes acquired as he perfected the martial arts. Charly said little about all of this. He believed in young people exploring different paths, as he had done.

"Telephone, Charly," said Julius, handing over the receiver.

"Van Meegrin Nurseries?" Charly queried. "I do not order any plants."

"We've got a big shipment for a Mr. Charles Poisson, chosen by your landscape architect Mr. Everston Pilchard," the man said.

"Shipment consisting of what?" Charly asked, mystified.

"Eighteen French hybrid lilac; twenty Canoe Birch trees; fourteen Little-Leaf Linden trees; twelve Blue Column Juniper; twenty astilbe; twenty-four wooly yarrow; sixty Hosta Royal Standard; and twenty coral bells."

"What? I do not understand, sir. We do not discuss any of these thing, Mr. Pilchard and I. What he is going to do at my house is very simple. When did he place this order? It must be canceled *immediatement*."

"Well to tell you the truth," the man lowered his voice confidentially, "this has happened before. He comes here, does Mr. Pilchard, and he, uh, sort of gets carried away. That's why we always call before we deliver, sir."

"I see," Charly said, though he didn't, really. "Tell me sir . . ."

"Emile Van Meegrin at your service, sir. We've been in business since 1937. An old and, if I may say so, well-respected establishment."

"Yes, yes," Charly said. "Mr. Van Meegrin, you say this has happened before with Mr. Pilchard. He make big order, but does not tell his customer?"

"That is correct, sir. With an estate down your way,

179

owned by a lady. That's all I'll say. He has his moments, does Mr. Pilchard, though he's a charming gentleman. A mental aberration, I believe. It comes and goes."

"*La folie des grandeurs,*" Charly said.

"Yes, the folly of grandeur," translated Mr. Van Meegrin. "Mr. Pilchard was in a great state of excitement when he came here this afternoon. Said you had a vast estate, that he was in charge of landscaping many acres."

"There is not even one acre surrounding my little house," Charly protested, neglecting to add that he owned a hundred acres of neighboring fields. "Mr. Pilchard and I, we discuss English ivy, perhaps some more lilac, that is all. Decidedly, it is most strange."

"We'll simply forget about this order, sir. I'll tear up the bill."

"For how much, sir, out of simple curiosity?"

"A tad over five thousand dollars, sir."

As soon as Charly had hung up, he telephoned Honoria Wells, who he suspected was the lady in question. He explained the problem.

"Oh, dear," said Honoria. "He's in another manic phase. Poor Evvie."

"You told me he did landscaping for you, madame. Did he pull the same trick? Order many things from Van Meegrin?"

"I'm afraid so."

"He will come out of this phase soon?"

"Sooner or later," Honoria said vaguely. "He's a nice man otherwise, don't you find, Charly?"

"Delightful," Charly said dubiously.

"Charly," Julius called. "Shall I make some marinated tomatoes?"

"You want me to boil down some chicken stock for *glace de poulet?"* Benny called.

Running his restaurant was a full-time job, Charly told himself sternly. He must stop with his detecting. And now a simple landscaping plan was turning into a madman's folly. He'd pay Mr. Pilchard a generous consulting fee and let him go; he'd mind his own business where Maurice was concerned; and he would leave the discovery of Harry Clark's murderer where it belonged, in the hands of the very able Klover Police Department. Charly, the eternal optimist, really believed that this would happen.

# POULET CREOLE

## Yield: 4 servings

1 3-pound chicken cut into 8 pieces
½ cup flour
2 tablespoons butter
1 tablespoon olive oil
1 medium onion, chopped
2 garlic cloves, chopped
2 tomatoes, peeled, seeded and chopped
1 bell pepper (red, yellow or green)
chopped
½ cup chicken stock, boiling
½ cup dry white wine, boiling
1 bay leaf
1 handful flat-leaf parsley, chopped
1 pinch (⅛ teaspoon) thyme
Salt and pepper to taste

Dust chicken pieces with flour and brown in butter and oil. Remove chicken and reserve. Brown onion and garlic. Add all remaining ingredients including chicken. Bring to a boil and lower heat. Simmer, covered, for 30 minutes. Uncover pot and cook over high heat another 10 minutes until chicken is very tender and sauce slightly reduced.

# Everston Plans a Dinner

Everston Pilchard drove home from Van Meegrin Nurseries abuzz with schemes. He envisioned bulldozers tearing up the fields behind Charly's house, and in his mind he saw copses of stately trees interspersed with fields of wild poppies and bachelors' button, milkweed, St. John's wort, wild lupin. This was a turning point in his life, a Significant Moment. Times such as these must be immortalized, not recollected in tranquillity but kept ablaze in memory with a dramatic event.

By the time Everston had pulled into his driveway he knew exactly what that event must be. He sat down at his kitchen table with a cup of mint tea and planned a magnificent dinner party.

First, the guest list: Honoria Wells, Win Crozier, Morty Cohen, Arthur Arpati, Mr. Van Meegrin, that investment adviser who made so much money for his clients, Jimmy *quelquechose*. He'd ask Honoria. Should he invite the owners of Fabulous Foods? They might throw business his way. That made nine with himself, a good number.

Next, Everston went to his bookcase and pulled out his mother's old Escoffier cookbook. And concocted the following menu:

Beluga caviar and blinis
Turtle consommé
Paupiettes of sole with Sauce Nantua, a sauce of creamy
    crayfish
Saddle of lamb with braised endive and roast new
    potatoes

Jellied Foie Gras
Peaches Melba
Assorted petits fours and cookies, espresso and tea

Everston looked up a telephone number and dialed.

"May I speak with Mr. Charles Poisson? It's his landscape architect."

"Yes, Monsieur Pilchard?" Charly asked cautiously. "I have just been speaking to Mr. Van Meegrin about that large order you placed in my name."

"That can wait, monsieur," Everston said grandly. "I'm calling you about an entirely different matter. I must entertain a few people, and you are the restaurateur to whom I have chosen to give my custom. It is to be a dinner on a Saturday night two weeks from now, and the menu I have devised is as follows . . ."

Charly listened sadly. This was a sickness he'd encountered before: an elderly gentleman in New York used to do precisely the same thing, order fantastic meals he'd no intention of paying for. He'd tried it in many restaurants, and the chefs and owners' grapevine kept track of his movements. Charly knew what he must do, and he did it:

"A beautiful menu, Monsieur Pilchard. Now, let me explain to you how La Fermette deals with dinner parties. We normally ask for a down payment of fifty percent at the time of the signing of the contract. But since we are talking about foods that must be specially ordered, the caviar, foie gras, saddle of lamb, turtle meat, very costly, you know, I must ask for a down payment of approximately ninety percent. And since the cost for such a menu would be three hundred dollars per person, and there are nine people, which make twenty-seven hundred dollars, I would

184

ask for two thousand dollars up front. Is that satisfactory, sir?"

A mere bagatelle to manic Everston. "We will deduct it from my bill to you for the landscaping project, Monsieur Poisson."

Charly cleared his throat. "Unfortunately, this is not the way I do business. My accountants forbid it. Each job must be paid for in advance, and there are no exchanges for other jobs. Therefore, when you come in to sign the contract please make sure that you have a cashier's check, which the bank will make out after you pay them, for two thousand dollars."

Something checked Everston's wild dreams. "Two thousand dollars?"

"That is correct, monsieur."

"But I'm a man of means. I will pay you after the dinner, of course."

Charly glanced at the clock on the wall. He'd spent enough time with this *coco*. "I am *not* a man of means, sir. I am a businessman, and this is the way I do business. I regret if it does not suit you. Besides, as I told you, Mr. Van Meegrin has telephoned me, and I have canceled the order that you gave him. An order out of all proportion to the matters we discussed."

"I see," Everston said coldly to this peasant upstart. "Well then, sir, I'm afraid that I must take my custom elsewhere." Everston banged down the receiver. He was shaking with rage. He, Everston Pilchard, from the highest society, with a great-grandmother who'd been one of New York City's Four Hundred, being told off by a common cook. Mr. Charles Poisson must pay for this insult to Everston's good name. The man would meet his doom.

Big John Stark leaned his six-foot-four-inch frame back in his swivel chair, swung his feet up on his desk, and locked his hands behind his head.

"I got a feeling we're getting there on the Clark thing," he told Vince Matucci and Abe Reynolds. "First of all, what have you found out?"

Abe was covering the local bars and questioning Harry Clark's former employers, Vince was delegated to call New Jersey Vice, New York City's drug-enforcement group, tap into the National Crime Information Center in Washington: cover every base in the search for information about the Fabulous Foods principals whose driver Harry Clark had been a few months before his death.

"Here's what I found out." Stark reported on his conversation with Nick Queechy at Frantic Feathers. "Harry Clark knew that teacher, Everston Pilchard. Clark was a driver for Fabulous Foods and now Pilchard's doing the same job. Maybe I'd better check out Pilchard. Wonder if he's connected."

Abe said, "I've seen the Pilchard guy, he looks harmless. Still, it wouldn't hurt to look. Meanwhile, I've checked on the owners of Fabulous Foods. Both Scungilli and Zampone have sheets going back years. Selling rotten fish, drugs, you name it. I'm sure that place is a laundry. New York City's bragging about how their crime rate's down. Sure it's down. All the crooks have moved upstate."

Vince Matucci said, "Maurice Baleine, you know, Charly Poisson's old partner, has bought into Fabulous Foods. You want me to check into him?"

"We did that last year," Stark reminded him. "Guy's clean."

"What about Charly Poisson?" Vince continued. "Just

186

because my uncle loves him, doesn't mean he's straight."

"Oh, Charly's okay," Stark said. "And, listen, I don't want to go into combat mode with those thugs in Sharpsville. We're not equipped for war. That's a job for the Feds."

"It would be nice," Vince said, "if Harry Clark's murder was something easy, like an i-rate husband."

"Nothing in life is easy," Stark told them. "Look, I'm just asking one thing. Do your best. If that food group killed Harry, and I'm positive that they did, it'll come out. Health Department's keeping a close eye on them."

"Because of Billy Herman's death," Abe said.

"You bet. The health guys did some checking," Stark said, "and found out what you found out: Their parent company's Splendid Shrimp in New Jersey, which was closed down for selling bad fish. The seafood's condemned by customs and supposed to be destroyed. But it isn't destroyed. It's shipped down to Mexico, where it's disinfected in big baths of formaldehyde so when it's shipped back here, the bacteria count's within normal limits. The Health Department thinks Splendid Shrimp ships it all up here. Fab Foods makes gourmet dishes out of condemned fish."

"Hey," Abe said, "I used to have a buddy, worked as a restaurant inspector for the Health Department. Oh, yuck, the stuff he told me."

"Awww," Vince said. "Restaurants ain't so bad. My Uncle Rex serves really good food, and the kitchen's so clean you could eat off the floor."

187

# MAURICE THE CHEF

As soon as Barbara left the house Thursday morning Maurice Baleine started in on his great adventure: creating the world's most fabulous recipes for the soon-to-be world's most famous prepared-foods company.

Now, three hours later, he stood at the sink wondering how so much could go so wrong. He'd just thrown out his third batch of sautéed spicy shrimp, following the recipe from a famous New Orleans chef's cookbook.

Well, true, he'd made a couple of errors: the recipe called for a quarter teaspoon each of dry mustard, cayenne pepper, and white pepper and one teaspoon of Tabasco sauce. He'd put in tablespoon measures of each, figuring that none of these cookbooks made food hot enough for Real Men. That was batch #1 and he was still sucking ice cubes from tasting the fiery mess.

Batch #2 ("cook over high heat 6 minutes, shaking the pan constantly") had burned when he'd run off to pee, and while in the downstairs bathroom had rinsed his burning mouth out with Barbara's strong mint mouthwash. When he got back to the kitchen smoke was rising from a charred mess.

Batch #3 bit the dust when he dropped the entire pan on the tile floor, having burned his face rather badly. The New Orleans chef had suggested that to keep the buttery sauce from separating, "shaking the pan in a back-and-forth motion" was the way to go. Maurice had seen Charly, Julius, and Benny doing this, so with great élan he agitated the pan. The contents flew up in the air and by some mysterious process managed to hit him in

188

the eyes. He screamed, dropped the pan, ran to the sink, and splashed cold water on his face. At this point he decided that New Orleans Sautéed Spicy Shrimp was not a recipe for the folks at Fabulous Foods.

The next recipe Maurice tried was again from the New Orleans cookbook: Shrimp and Crab in Cream Sauce. It sounded delicious and had many uses: as a pasta topping; stirred into a risotto; turned into a bisque with the addition of fish stock; as a topping for omelettes, fish fillets, or vegetables.

Maurice melted a stick of butter and carefully browned a cup of finely chopped onion. He'd nicked his thumb chopping the onion with a dull knife that slipped and skidded across the wooden board, and blood dripped into the butter, causing it to spatter in his face. "Add the flour," the text continued, "and blend with a whisk until smooth." This, Maurice knew, was called a roux. He rummaged around in Barbara's gadget drawer looking for a whisk, neglecting to remove the roux from the fire while he searched, so that when he finally located the utensil and started whisking, the roux was red-hot. Maurice, unaccustomed to using the whisk, flicked some of the burning roux onto his neck. He fell back from the stove screaming in pain. He had neglected to read the chef's description of roux: "Cooked roux is called Cajun napalm because it sticks to your skin and burns; so be *very careful* to avoid splashing . . ."

There was only one thing to do. Forget the recipes. Forget his scorched face, his badly burned neck, his cut finger, and the fire that still raged inside his mouth. Maurice ran to the drinks table in the living room. He poured Beefeater gin into his crystal martini pitcher. In less time than it took to say "Fabulous Foods" Maurice

189

was drinking the perfect dry martini, stirred, not shaken, with a colossal green olive drifting to and fro at the bottom of the largest tumbler Maurice could find.

As the icy, smooth liquid slid down his throat Maurice felt his troubles slide away with equal ease. It was foolish to try to cook a handful of shrimp dishes when he didn't know how to boil a potato. But he had a wonderful eye for spotting good recipes, so he'd simply take a few cookbooks up to Arthur and let him figure them out. Fabulous Foods was a great company. No way they could fail. Millions were lurking. "Not long now," he murmured to himself, as he topped up his tumbler. He'd promised himself just one drink, and that's what he was having. Topping-up didn't count as an extra drink.

In order to prove to himself that he wasn't the least bit affected by the alcohol, Maurice cleaned up the kitchen. He threw the spoiled food in the garbage, loaded the dishwasher, and even washed his pots and saucepans, though the hot water stung his burnt and cut hands. When everything was put away, he went over the counters with a soapy rag and dried them with the dish towel. He even swept up the floor. See, he wasn't drunk at all.

To reward himself, Maurice filled up his pitcher with gin and ice cubes and carried it up to his bedroom. He deserved a small nap.

Every now and then Julius Prendergast breakfasted with his aunt Honoria, and got to his job in Charly's kitchen an hour later than usual.

"*La Señora* is in the solarium," said Estrella, answering Julius's knock.

"Thanks, Estrella," Julius said. "How are you and Juanito?"

"*Muy bien, gracias.*" Estrella smiled. "Juanito prepare your favorite."

"Huevos Rancheros," Julius smiled. "Terrific."

Once, Julius had told Juanito that his huevos rancheros were the best he'd ever eaten—fried eggs atop toasted tortillas with a zippy tomato-onion-garlic-jalapeno sauce, with refried beans and avocado slices on the side—and this, henceforth, was his breakfast at his aunt's.

"Darling," Honoria said, and held up her cheek to be kissed. She was dressed in a baggy beige cashmere tunic with white tights. The round table in the solarium had been set with Porthault linen place mats and napkins, and a centerpiece of yellow and white roses nestled in a green pottery frog vase. The old girl always did things in style, Julius thought.

"You smell divine, Aunt Honny, and you look younger every day."

"That's my boy," Honoria said. "Now sit down, and tell me all the gossip. How's everything going at Charly's?"

"Everything's in constant turmoil, that's why I love it," Julius said. "Benny's got his black belt and keeps us all up on New Age stuff; Joe Okun talks to Bruno, says he can get into the dog's mind, and Charly's seeking justice and being chummy with Stark and thugs like Ugo Buonsarde."

Honoria chuckled. "I'll bet Ugo's had two hundred men killed in his day. Stark would love to put him away."

Julius said, "One day Ugo and Stark'll meet in Charly's kitchen. What d'you think would happen?"

"I know exactly what would happen," Honoria said. "They'd both be horribly uncomfortable, and blame

191

Charly for it. Stark would never drop into Charly's again, and neither would Ugo. Stark's not amused by killers. And the next time Charly stuck his nose into police business, Stark would find some way to squash him. A little call to the Health Department, or to the IRS—I'm sure Charly has money in some Swiss banks."

"Luxembourg, actually, I saw some papers once . . ."

"And Ugo, if he's anything like Ralph D'Annunzio, is terrified of the law. Correction: terrified of cops who can't be bought. Ugo, like Ralph used to, hides behind an army of crooked lawyers, but it's surprising how often the Starks of this world win. Ugo knows this. He wouldn't have a prayer."

Julius smiled at the thought of Honoria's former lover D'Annunzio. "Stark's probably the only unbribable cop in Van Buren County. And you're right. He'd love to bring down Ugo."

"He was very nice to me over the Harry Clark business. A lot of townspeople said I got what I deserved, but John was a sweetie. I think he doesn't quite know what to make of Charly. He certainly doesn't know Charly pals around with Buonsarde. Listen, how's business?"

"Customer counts are up and our food costs are down. I'm glad I'm there. Still if I ever want to go back to the brokerage business, the door's open. Oh, thanks, Estrella." Huevos rancheros for Julius.

"*Y el desayuno Japonés para la señora,*" said Estrella, placing a lacquered tray in front of Honoria. On it were bowls containing, Honoria told Julius, brown rice tossed with scallions and tamari; seaweed marinated in rice wine vinegar; pickled ginger; and a bowl of steamed mustard greens.

Honoria said, "Guess who stopped in to see me a few days ago? Maurice Baleine. Wanted me to invest in Fantastic Foods or whatever it's called. I said no, then I called Jimmy Houghton. He said they're crooks."

"Maurice is going to lose his shirt, yet again. Or his life."

"Now, I have to warn you about Everston Pilchard," Honoria continued. "Or rather, get you to warn Charly. Evvie's in a manic phase, or whatever it's called, and Charly's asked him to do some landscaping. Remember how he ordered all that stuff from Van Meegrin's and we had to refuse it? I didn't tell Charly the whole story. I thought Evvie was cured."

"Evvie's done it again, but Charly canceled the order. Why," asked Julius, "does Van Buren County have so many nutty characters?"

"It doesn't, Julius. No more than anywhere else. But Charly's restaurant is considered an expensive place, and expensive places always attract odd people. They can smell money like a buzzard smells roadkill."

"Do you really enjoy that Japanese food?"

"I love it. Besides, it's madly stylish. Modified macrobiotic. Everything Japanese is in. But to continue about Evvie. Tell Charly to tread carefully."

"Well, sure, Aunt Honny. But I think he knows that by now."

"Charly called yesterday, and I told him again to watch out for Everston, but he doesn't take this seriously."

Julius told about Charly's refusing to cater Everson's dinner.

"Oh, dear," Honoria said. "You know, I think Everston may be dangerous. I mean, murderous."

Julius took a forkful of his delicious huevos

rancheros. "You think he'd try to kill Charly?"

"I do," said Honoria. "If Charly refused to cater that insane-sounding dinner party, and then canceled Van Meegrin's order, then, yes, I think Everston's quite capable. He's a terrific snob, and I'm sure he looks down his nose at a restaurant owner. Charly's refusals are the ultimate insult."

"I thought you were fond of Everston."

"I am—when he's normal. I never told you this, but Everston was very threatening when I canceled Van Meegrin's order. Luckily Harry was here then. He knocked Everston down and told him never to come back. I think, though I never told the police, that Everston killed Harry Clark."

"Why wouldn't you tell the police?"

"What's the point? I have no proof. It's just a suspicion on my part."

"Why wouldn't Evvie kill you?"

"Because"—Honoria grinned—"I'm one of the super-rich. Evvie has a thing about rich people. He thinks they can do no wrong."

# IN THE MIDDLE OF THE NIGHT

FLOYD COOPER, THE NIGHT WATCHMAN AT FABULOUS Foods, did a certain amount of horizontal watchdog work. Sleepy little Sharpsville wasn't a hotbed of mayhem, so there was no need to stand guard, armed to the teeth, during the whole of the long night. When he woke from his nap on the foam-rubber couch in the directors' conference room at midnight Floyd made his customary round of the building. He didn't have keys to the refrigeration units, though he knew where the money was stored. He'd worked for Splendid Shrimp and knew pretty much everything about the operation. He briefly checked the warehouse area; he'd do a more thorough check later on.

If it hadn't been for his flashlight glinting on something metallic way over in the bushes, Floyd would have gone back to his couch, to sleep until five. His hangover was fiercer than usual since he'd found more open bottles of the wine used at the open house. Opened bottles of wine didn't last, which was common knowledge. He was helping, really.

But something was glinting, all right, and as Floyd approached he saw that it was a car, plowed into a space between two big bushes. An old Volvo. Just then the motor started and the car backed slowly out. Floyd shined his flashlight in the car. He'd seen the guy before. The new deliveryman.

"This's kinda late for deliveries, buddy, whatcha doin'?"

"I'd just pulled over to have a nap," Everston lied calmly. "I'd been to a party in Albany. Now I've woken up, so I'll be on my way." Actually, so elated had Everston been at the success of his midnight raid that he'd felt faint and feared he might pass out at the wheel. So he'd stopped the car, done some deep-breathing exercises, and the dizzy spell had passed.

"You feel okay to drive?"

"Oh, sure," said Everston.

Before leaving Fabulous Foods this afternoon he'd inadvertently discovered several suitcases of money hidden in an old freezer. Well, 'inadvertently' wasn't entirely correct. He'd been snooping. The door handle was off one of the freezers, and the four canvas suitcases didn't look like carriers for frozen shrimp.

Near midnight he'd returned to the plant and calmly helped himself to two of the cases. He couldn't believe robbery could be so simple.

Floyd Cooper returned to the main building. One more place to check, and then it was nap time again. He walked over to the warehouses behind the kitchen. A Mercedes was parked there. Again, Floyd shined his flashlight into the car, and this time he recognized that fat asshole he'd heard Marty and Ricky saying they couldn't stand. Guy was snoring. Floyd rapped on the glass with his fist. The window rolled down.

"Hey, come on, buddy, move it," he shouted.

"What?" Maurice shouted, suddenly awakened. "Where am I?"

"You're in the Fabulous Foods parking lot."

"And who are you?" Even half-awake, Maurice managed to sound imperious.

"I'm Cooper, the night watchman. It's the middle of the night. What're you doing here?"

"I don't know," Maurice said, genuinely puzzled. The last thing that he remembered was drinking his excellent martinis when? This morning? In his kitchen, after giving up on his recipes. What had happened after that? Let's see, that must have been around noon. And now it was the middle of the night. An entire afternoon and evening had disappeared. This was what was called a blackout. Maurice had never had a blackout. Could the doctors be right? That he'd die if he had another drink? He started to shake.

"You want a shot?" Floyd asked. He could smell booze, felt sorry for the guy. Probably had a fight with his wife about guzzling too much and escaped to his office. Floyd, divorced years ago, knew all about that kind of thing.

"Hair of the dog. Set you up real good." Floyd produced his hip flask.

Maurice took a gulp, then another. "Thanks."

"You're welcome."

"Guess I'd better get home, my wife will be worried."

Oh, right. Standin' there with her rolling pin. "Think you can drive?"

"I'm as fit as a fiddle. I'm a Princeton man, you know."

It was half past two by Charly's electric digital clock. Bruno had suddenly given a yelp, and now was standing up, alert. Charly, roused from a deep sleep, looked at the clock, looked at Bruno, listened for a bit, heard nothing, and turned over. "Lie down, Bruno," he muttered.

But Bruno refused to lie down. He stayed standing and growling until Charly said, "Hokay, hokay, maybe you have the stomach upset, yes?"

Charly put on his blue-cotton bathrobe, toed into his sheepskin slippers, which he wore winter and summer, grabbed his flashlight, and he and Bruno padded downstairs. Bruno refused to turn toward the kitchen. He stood by the front door, growling, the hair on his back standing straight up.

"Hokay, we go out the front door," said Charly. He unlocked the door and pushed open the screen. Bruno shot into the darkness and Charly followed, shining his flashlight onto the ground.

It was a magnificent night. The sky was dark blue, and thousands of stars were winking. The trees, outlined against the sky, were black, and Charly could hear rustlings, as night animals went about their business.

Suddenly Charly heard the sound of a car. The car was driving very slowly up the road, it had turned in from

Route 65. It was a Mercedes. Charly couldn't see who was at the wheel, but who else had a big dark Mercedes?

*I wonder where Maurice has been,* Charly thought. Nothing surprised him about the man, and this middle-of-the-night sighting didn't surprise him either. "Come, Bruno," he called.

Bruno loped up, and Charly was just about to turn around when he heard the sound of another car. This time he shined his flashlight at the car, an old Volvo. It looked like Everston Pilchard's car, and it was coming from the left, that is to say, from the road by Charly's fields. Charly kept his flashlight on the car, which stopped. Charly crossed the road in front of the Volvo and the window on the driver's side rolled down.

"Monsieur Pilchard? Is that you?"

"Why, hello, Monsieur Poisson," Everston said in a strange voice.

"May I help you with something?"

"No, I'm just taking a drive. I've always wondered where this road leads to. I often drive in the middle of the night. Insomnia, you know."

"It continues for about half a mile. Left is a dead end, right takes you to the house of Mr. Baleine." Charly played his flashlight around the interior of the Volvo. Warned again by Julius, it had occurred to Charly that Everston might try to set fire to his house, as that pathetic arsonist Marion Arnold had, sometime ago. But he saw nothing suspicious, though he guessed that a jerrican of gasoline would probably be transported in the trunk.

"Well then, I guess I'll be on my way," Everston said, still talking in a nervous voice. There used to be an old barn at the end of Barrett Road, the perfect place to hide his suitcases. But it wasn't there. "Whatever happened to that old barn at the end of the road?"

198

"There has never been an old barn since I live here, over twenty year." Charly wondered if Pilchard was drunk, or on drugs. He and Bruno watched as the car continued down the road. A few seconds later it stopped, then turned onto Route 65. Charly waited until the sounds of the car died away, then he and Bruno went into the house. Charly, suddenly horrified, stood rooted to the floor. *If Monsieur Pilchard wants to harm me, it was foolish to cross right in front of his car so that he could knock me down.* Sherlock Holmes wouldn't have done such a foolish thing. Charly reflected, humbly, that he still had a lot to learn in the field of detection.

They climbed the stairs, and Bruno lay down. Before Charly fell asleep, he considered various possibilities: Maybe Everston Pilchard was the shooter who'd returned for another shot at Maurice. Why would Everston shoot Maurice? Or maybe Everston had driven up this road to harm Charly, but seeing Maurice's car had disconcerted him. Or maybe Everston needed Maurice's help in doing something up at Fabulous Foods. Too many possibilities. Charly yawned. Bruno yawned. Soon they were both asleep.

# JULIUS DROPS A DIME

EVERSTON HAD DRIVEN AROUND FOR A HALF HOUR more, looking for the old barn, but in the end he'd returned to his house and hid the suitcases in the garage under some quilts. When he woke the next morning he ran out to the garage. The cases were still there. They made him even more nervous than he'd been before. In fact, he couldn't stop shaking. As soon as he avenged his good name, that is, killed Poisson, he'd escape.

Julius warned Charly again, Friday morning. "You're watching out for Everston, aren't you? He's in a state, Charly. No telling what he'll do. My aunt thinks he killed Harry Clark because Harry beat him up, once."

"Good reason to kill a person," Charly said. Should he tell Julius, Benny, and Joe about his encounter last night? Perhaps he should wait for a bit. "Try this chicken salad. Does it need more white pepper?"

"Try to take this seriously, Charly." Julius said, tasting. "No, it doesn't need anything else. I mean, the man is not himself."

"*Mais voyons,* what would you have me do? Hide in the closet?"

"I'll sleep at your house tonight," Joe decided. "Bruno and me downstairs, I'll lie on your sofa."

"I'll sleep at the restaurant," Benny volunteered. "In case he tries to break in, poison some food."

"I'll drive over to his house tonight," Julius decided. "I got his address from Win Crozier. If he drives off, I'll call on my car phone."

"All will resolve itself," Charly said placidly. "This Mr. Pilchard, he teaches at school during the day. Perhaps, after school is out, he will drive over here and try to kill me and we can catch him." No, he definitely wouldn't mention talking to Everston late last night and crossing in front of his car. How could he have been so foolish?

It was half past two Friday afternoon, and Charly, Benny, Julius and Joe Okun had finished cleaning the kitchen from a busy lunch. Charly was going to work in his garden for an hour; Julius would drive over to the Hudson River fisherman, to collect some smoked shad, which would be boned, mixed with butter and shallots and chives, and serve as an appetizer; Benny was going to his gym, and Joe Okun said he'd catch a nap.

The telephone rang. Charly said loudly, "Ah, Monsieur Pilchard."

The three other men stopped in their tracks to listen.

"Of course I accept your apology," Charly said. "Yes, I would be glad to discuss another meal with you, on a more modest level."

Charly looked over as Julius shook his head, *no, no.* Charly continued. "You would like to come over this afternoon? You are nearby and can be here in three minutes? Excellent. There will only be me as my crew has already left." He made a face at the three men.

Julius put on the down jacket and watch cap he kept handy and stationed himself in the cold room, door ajar, armed with a veal pounder; Benny hid behind the door of Charly's office, holding a butcher's steel; he didn't want to kill the guy with a knife, just bash him around a little. Joe Okun, claiming that he could feel the presence of his warrior ancestors ready to help him defend his master, stationed himself in the dining room by the swinging doors to the kitchen. First, however, he insisted on Bruno's being taken to Charly's house. Everston might harm the dog.

Five minutes later a car drove up and parked outside the kitchen door. Charly welcomed Everston into the big clean kitchen.

"Come in, Monsieur Pilchard. You had a good day in school?"

"Yes," Everston said. "I leave early on Fridays. I've been reconsidering my party, Monsieur Poisson, and I've decided to be much more modest. Six people for lunch, and I think that a chicken salad with a New

York State champagne would be more within my budget."

Charly looked closely at the man. Every muscle in Everston's body seemed to be clenched tightly. But he appeared quiet enough. Nevertheless, he was up to something.

"As delicious a lunch as one could ask for sir," Charly said smoothly. "A fine chicken salad, with rolls, butter, mushroom spread. Elegant. But let me pour coffee, I have some freshly made. Do you take cream and sugar?"

"Black, with sugar."

"I take mine black, too." Charly said, getting up from the round wooden kitchen table. He poured two cups of coffee and set one down in front of Everston. "It is hot," he cautioned. "Ah, I forget the sugar, just a moment."

Julius, Benny, and Joe Okun were not surprised to see Everston remove a small bottle from his pocket and pour what appeared to be brown liquid into a coffee cup, while Charly was getting the sugar. But what surprised them was that he poured the liquid into his own cup.

Everston, made wily by his mania, knew that Charly would suspect him of poisoning his coffee. Therefore, he put the liquid into his own cup. He deduced that Charly, being suspicious, would, when the occasion presented itself, change the cups around. Anyone who read murder mysteries knew the way things worked. The intended victim always switched cups.

"What a wonderful kitchen," Everston said, getting up from the table to stroll around, and give Charly a chance to move the cups. Out of the corner of his eye Everston saw Charly execute what looked like a quick cup-turn.

"I haven't quite decided on the date, but I'll give you plenty of notice," Everston said, returning to the table. "And I'll sign a contract and give you a down payment in cash. Is a Saturday lunchtime a good time?"

"Usually not too busy," Charly said. "If the weather is fine, you could entertain on the porch. If the weather is not fine, we could open up the dining room." The coffee had cooled. Everston and Charly sipped.

"Delicious," Charly said, smacking his lips. He looked over at Everston's cup. "The coffee is too strong for you, monsieur?"

For Everston had shot up so quickly that his chair had overturned. He ran from the kitchen, leaving the door open in his haste. Charly hurried after him as Julius, Benny, and Joe Okun rushed for the back door.

Everston lay on the ground, writhing, his head surrounded by frothy vomit. He moaned and retched some more, and then he began to scream.

"Calm yourself, Monsieur Pilchard," Charly said placidly. "You could not have poisoned yourself on one sip of coffee from your cup, into which you have poured the natural fertilizer, fish emulsion, which smell so strong that even I, with my *sinusite,* can smell it all over the kitchen."

"I thought you'd change cups," Everston gasped. "That's what they do in the murder mysteries."

"Not in all of the mysteries," Charly said. "I have been reading the Judge Dee murder mysteries set in Fifth Dynasty China, written by Van Gulik, the Dutch ambassador. In one of the stories Judge Dee precisely does not change cups, knowing that his antagonist expects him to do so. Or rather, he does a sleight of hand so that his antagonist thinks he has changed cups. All very roundabout." Charly smiled triumphantly.

"This poisoning business is much too *compliqué* for you, Monsieur Pilchard. Stick to planting ivy."

Charly heard a car start up in the parking lot, but ignored it.

"It is not pleasant," Charly continued, "to drink a puree of rotted fish, but it cannot kill you. It is fear which has made you so ill. You have been poisoned by your mind, Monsieur Pilchard."

Everston stood up. "I wasn't trying to kill you, I just wanted to make you sick, Monsieur Poisson." He stumbled to his car, and drove away.

Joe Okun carried a bucket to the back path and threw water on Everston's mess. He said, "Where's Julius?"

Benny said, "Charly, how did you know which cup was yours?"

"As you know, I always drink from a chipped cup," Charly said. "It pains me to throw them away. They are Villeroy & Boch, and cost a lot of money. So I save them for myself. Naturally I give Pilchard a cup *sans* chip."

"Well, I think you took an awful chance," Benny said.

"Decidedly, Monsieur Pilchard is not a follower of Confucius. He does not understand the logic of the well-ordered mind."

Richard Zampone was furious. The side door to the warehouse had been left open all night, and the suitcases were now in the freezer with the broken door. As a watchman, Floyd was a disaster. He'd started to drink. All those years in Jersey, he'd never touched a drop. Now, he'd become a lush. And, oh, Christ, two of the canvas cases were gone.

Zampone drove over to Floyd's apartment. Woke him

up. Floyd was groggy and forgot that he'd seen two intruders last night.

"Yeah, musta been that Morrie guy, he was up here last night."

"Jesus, why didn't you call me?" Zampone shouted.

Julius, leaving Everston writhing on the pavement outside La Fermette's kitchen, had driven over to the man's house, parked on a side road, and was hiding in the bushes behind the house when he heard a car pull up. As he stood in the greenery he thought with amusement of all the nineteenth- and twentieth-century English novels where people hid behind clumps of foliage. He decided that writing would be much impoverished without bushes. Did Sophocles know about bushes? He thought not. You didn't need bushes when gods could float down from the heavens to alert the actors. And he couldn't remember one bush in Herodotus. Boulders, yes, but no bushes. Julius chuckled to himself. He must reread Pym. Lots of bushes, and people hiding behind them, in Barbara Pym.

Julius heard a car door slam, then he saw Everston stumble toward his back door, keys in hand. But at the door Everston turned and walked to his garage. The doors swung open, and Everston disappeared inside. He came out a few minutes later and proceeded to his back door.

Julius entered the garage. He saw something bulky hidden under old quilts. Naturally, he looked: two canvas suitcases. He pried one of the hasps open and saw that the case was filled with hundred-dollar bills.

Julius had no idea what was going on, but it was easy to assume certain things: Everston was working as a driver for Fabulous Foods, Charly had told him this.

205

Fabulous Foods was a money laundry, Julius would bet on it. And when a place is a money laundry, there has to be money to launder, right?

Back in his car, Julius got the number of Fabulous Foods and called the factory on his car phone. He asked to speak to one of the owners.

"Yeah?" said Richard Zampone, forgetting his genteel façade.

"Your new driver Everston Pilchard stole two suitcases of your money," Julius said, enunciating clearly. "They're in the garage of his house, so you'd better send someone to get them, before he moves them out."

"No shit," Ricky said. "I thought it was old Morrie. And you say it's the driver? To whom do I have the pleasure, sir?"

"Just call me a friend," Julius said. "You have his address? No? I'll give it to you. Got a pencil?"

"My Mont Blanc pen is poised, sir," Little Ricky said, his cultured accent back in place. "I look forward to having a conversation with Mr. Pilchard."

Late tonight, Richard decided, he'd drive over to Everston's house, catch the guy in bed, and make sure he never left it. Then he'd haul the suitcases out of the garage and drive back to the factory. Real simple.

Julius hung up. *Oh, good,* he thought, *tonight I can sleep in my own bed.* He drove back to La Fermette. He had no illusions about Everston Pilchard's future. But he had to drop the dime. Charly's life was at stake. Everston Pilchard was a madman, and he'd try, again, to kill Charly. Eventually Charly would die, because everyone did. But not just yet.

206

# A Busy Saturday

"I'm a genius," Maurice smiled to himself. "I'll find the recipes, really great ones, and Arthur can whip them up in no time."

After finding himself at Fabulous Foods in the middle of the night, he'd driven cautiously home and slept like a baby most of the morning. His little excursion into martini country had ended. When he woke up, he felt no desire for a drink. Blackouts were serious. He'd had his last drop of booze.

Now Maurice was sitting at his desk, late Saturday morning, sipping a creamy cup of coffee and listing the ingredients for Curried Shrimp Trinidadian Style, which he'd found in an old cookbook of Barbara's. It contained twenty-seven ingredients. *The more ingredients, the more professional the recipe,* thought Maurice.

His ideas on cooking, food, and restaurants were oddly skewed. All his life, Maurice had looked down on his father's profession, that of a common restaurateur. But now that socialites and yuppies had become foodies, and being a chef was a stylish profession, Maurice, desperate to be fashionable, was suddenly the expert: the Plato of pots, the Rimbaud of recipes.

Maurice sipped his coffee. It would be nothing but coffee from now on. He couldn't drink anymore, the docs were right. The blackout had frightened him very much. He didn't want to die. Especially now, on the verge of making millions. He decided to run up to Fabulous Foods and show some recipes to Arthur Arpati.

Maurice knocked on the door to the Fabulous Foods test kitchen. Arthur was standing at the stove, stirring his pots as usual. When he looked up and saw Maurice standing in the doorway he said, "Oh, it's you."

"Yes, Arthur, it is I, with a lot of wonderful recipes to discuss with you."

"You know what day it is?"

Maurice glanced at the wall calendar. "I don't mind working on Saturday, not on a project as important as this one."

"You're only a day late. Now, I'm busy. Mr. Zampone's having a tasting with some important people, then I'm out of here. You want to come back Monday, that's fine with me."

"I'll come on Monday, what's a few more hours?" Maurice said jovially, prepared to be affable to the hired help. He opened the door to leave and nearly collided with Richard Zampone. "Oops," said Maurice.

"Listen, the shit has hit the fan," Ricky said to Arthur. Arthur made shushing motions with his hands, indicating the presence of Maurice.

"Yeah, him, too," Ricky said. "You want to work here every day, fine, Morrie, you got to take the rough with the smooth. I had to cancel that tasting, Arthur. I just got a call from the Health Department, a lot of shrimp, pounds and pounds of it, are floating on the Hudson River. There's a box with our logo on it floating there, too; they want to know what happened. I said I knew nothing about it, that I'd talk to you."

"Evvie Pilchard and I dumped all that diseased shrimp, the stuff that killed one of your investors." Arthur spoke indignantly.

"Holy shit," Richard said. "What'll I tell the guy?"

"Easy," interrupted Maurice the expert. "You tell him you told your driver to take the boxes to the dump, and that he didn't do it. He dumped it in the river instead.

Then tell your driver to disappear."

"The driver's already disappeared," Richard said. He didn't explain how he knew: that he'd driven down to Everston's house last night and nobody was home. Everston the paranoid genius had taken the money with him, and slept in the nurse's office at The Brooke School. With commendable foresight, he'd had duplicates made of the school keys.

"I'll get back to the Health Department guy now. I'll say the driver's gone for a few days, and I don't know where to reach him."

Richard went to his office thinking, *This has to be fate.* The fates were laying Everston's life in his lap. You can't question a dead man, right? The trouble was, he had to find Everston first, and where in hell was the guy?

After calling the Health Department Richard went back to Arthur and Maurice. "Listen, I don't want anyone here tonight except the night watchman; I want everything locked up tight. I don't want us to be at home, either, where the cops can get us. We'll meet at Charly Poisson's for dinner. That's one place neither the cops nor the Health Department will think of looking."

Everston was back at home. He figured that the Fabulous Foods people had discovered their loss by now and would come looking for him, but they wouldn't come during the day. And if they did come, his car, with the suitcases in the boot, was parked at his back door with the keys in the ignition. The moment a car drove up to the front and stopped, he was out the back. In a few more hours he'd really be out of there. He had one more job to do.

Tonight, he would kill Charly Poisson. At the height of the meal service when everyone in the kitchen would be distracted. Charly was at the root of all his problems. Everston would rush into the kitchen, unregistered pistol drawn, shoot Charly, and run out before anyone could catch him. Drive down to Kennedy, get on the first plane to London. He'd return in a few years when things had cooled down. With the money in those two suitcases, he'd live like a king.

Now, what could he wear as a disguise? Oh, perfect. He remembered that pig mask he'd confiscated from one of the boys at school.

Everston ran out to his car and checked the suitcases in the boot. Still there, still filled with cash. How long it would take for Zampone and Scungilli to track him down Everston didn't know, but he figured it wouldn't be long, now. There was no time to lose.

He spent the rest of the afternoon at his computer, lining up airplane tickets and hotel reservations, finding his passport, packing an overnight case. He'd buy clothing when he arrived in London. *Turnbull & Asser, Bond Street, here I come.* Finally, he'd have the money to live as a gentleman should. In his superior frame of mind, Everston wasn't too worried about Scungilli and Zampone: they were boors. Why, they couldn't even speak correctly. To outwit such stupid men was child's play.

He'd ordered a suite at the Hilton Hotel (the Connaught was booked solid), and he'd reserved a table for dinner in two days at the Savoy. He guessed that he'd need a day to get over his jet lag.

# CHAOS AT LA FERMETTE

"OH, MAURICE, GOOD TO SEE YOU," SAID PATTY Perkins, standing behind the reservation desk of La Fermette at half past six Saturday night. "And—uh—gentlemen, good to see you, too." She smiled at Arthur Arpati and Richard Zampone. "You didn't reserve, did you? Never mind."

Patty led the three men to a table in the back dining room. She felt they weren't a good advertisement for La Fermette. "Your waiter will be with you shortly." She smiled. "May I get you something from the bar?"

"You certainly may," Maurice said, thinking, what the hell. His morning resolution had dissolved. He craved a drink. Couldn't have a blackout on just one drink. "I'd like one of Tommy's big Beefeater martinis."

"Certainly, Maurice." Patty was too well schooled to show surprise.

Arthur Arpati wanted a Dubonnet; Richard Zampone ordered a Coke.

"You gotta taste the Shrimps Charly," Richard told Arthur. "I wish to hell we could do that, but we can't because they'd turn soggy in the freezer."

"Yes, there are limitations," Arthur agreed. He looked around. This was a pretty fancy place—exactly what his restaurant would look like. He loved the pink walls, the flowered carpet, the big bouquets of flowers in the tin urns. This joint had class. He knew the food would be excellent.

"Gentlemen," said Elton Briggs, presenting menus. "We have several specials I'd like to tell you about. Oh,

211

excuse me for a moment, will you?" Elton looked up as he heard a muffled bang from the kitchen, followed by shouting. Tommy Glade, the barman, was running through the swinging doors to the kitchen, motioning that Elton should follow, and quickly.

Charly, Benny, and Julius had been chopping and sautéeing, and Joe Okun was cleaning pots in La Fermette's kitchen when the back door opened and a man in a pig's head mask sidled in.

"Who the hell are you?" Joe Okun said, lifting an enormous cast-iron frying pan to use as a shield, since the man was holding a pistol. It was a 9 mm Glock, but Joe didn't know this. It looked lethal, that he did know.

Charly, preoccupied, glanced at the piggy face from across the room and said, "Oh, Maurice, what are you . . ." then did a double take as he realized that the face was a Halloween mask. From the man's slouching posture and his thin frame, Charly guessed he was looking at Everston Pilchard.

The man advanced into the kitchen. Joe Okun, short, stocky, and muscular, was on his right, pan raised menacingly. Benny grabbed the handle of the frying pan in which he was sautéeing, shrimp, and Julius raised the #12 knife that he was using to chop shallots.

The man turned his head from side to side. He seemed to hesitate. The hand holding the Glock wavered, just as Joe Okun raised the big pan. The pistol fired with an enormous bang.

There was a cacophony of sounds—screams, a thud as the side of Julius's knife landed on the pig-man's head, metal clanging as the bullet glanced off the side of Joe's cast-iron pan and ricocheted. There was only one shot, but it went wild.

A fraction of a second after the shot, Benny threw the

hot saucepan of Shrimps Charly at the masked man and caught him in the stomach. The red-hot pan seared through Everston's shirt into his flesh, and he screamed and fell. Julius lunged at the shooter, now on the floor, retrieved his big knife, and caught the mask's snout with its tip, ripping it off.

"*Tiens*, Monsieur Pilchard, you visit us again," said Charly, the only one in the kitchen who hadn't done anything but stand and stare. At this point Tommy Glade and Elton Briggs rushed into the kitchen through the swinging doors and behind them came Richard Zampone, Arthur Arpati, and Maurice Baleine. Behind them clustered other customers. In the doorway to Charly's office, Bruno sat on his haunches and howled.

Benny Perkins calmly walked over to Everston and retrieved his pan. The Shrimps Charly lay on Everston's chest, covered in blood.

Julius walked over to Charly's office. The doorway was blocked by Joe Okun squatting beside Bruno, trying to calm him. Julius squeezed past them and reached the telephone, where he dialed 911.

"Patty's already phoned from the dining room, Julius, they're on their way," Tommy Glade called. Already sirens could be heard, and flashing lights seen, as police cars skidded to a stop in both front and rear of the restaurant.

"Is all right, Bruno, everything is fine," Charly said, patting the crouching Joe Okun's black hair by mistake as he headed for his desk. He found Dr. Bach's Rescue Remedy and dropped some onto his tongue.

Now Charly walked to the swinging doors and addressed his customers. "You may return to your seats, ladies and gentlemen. A poor deranged man came into our kitchen and tried to shoot us. But I am hokay, and so

213

are Julius Prendergast and Benny Perkins and Joseph Okun. The police have arrived, as you can see. I offer you all a drink to calm the nerves. And your dinners are, of course, on the house. I am sorry for the disturbance to your digestions."

Encouraged by Charly's largesse, the customers flocked back to their seats, gabbling like geese, to order more free food, though who was in the frame of mind to cook it was a good guess. Bruno, calm now, watched the commotion with interest. The bloody Shrimps Charly that had been lying on Pilchard's chest had disappeared—into his stomach.

Everston had been carried off on a stretcher, with an oxygen mask over his face. The bullet, glancing off Joe's heavy cast-iron frying pan at an angle, had ricocheted and spun back toward the shooter, hitting Everston in the chest. He'd been turning blue, gasping for breath.

*First the pig mask, then the oxygen mask,* Julius thought wryly, watching the ambulance attendants readying Everston, who was breathing but unconscious, for his trip to the hospital.

In the turmoil one of La Fermette's customers calmly walked out the back door, spied Everston's car with the keys in the ignition, and opened the trunk. The man took out the two canvas cases and carried them to his own car. Then he quietly returned to the dining room.

Matters quieted down after Everston's departure. Benny showed Vince Matucci Everston's car. Later, Vince drove it to the police station.

"Is long story," Charly told John Stark, Abe Reynolds, and Will Hackett. "But the short story is, that Mr.

214

Pilchard came to kill me. He thought I had insulted him. He was the only man with a gun. And I only hear one shot."

"Those Glocks can ricochet, the State Troopers carry them, and they complain," John said. He'd been examining the kitchen, noting that the crime scene was already so contaminated by extraneous people, dog hair, by too many factors to mention, that it would be useless to examine it closely.

"It looks like Pilchard fired at you, Charly, missed, the bullet hit something heavy, ricocheted, and got him in the chest," John Stark said.

"Poor Mr. Pilchard," Charly said. "He will live?"

"Doc says it looks bad, but probably not fatal."

"Ah, la la," Charly said, mopping his face with a towel. "A restaurant kitchen is a dangerous place." Suddenly he turned as white as his jacket from Dupont & Malgat. He crumpled. And though Julius and Benny, one on each side, caught their employer, he had lost consciousness. They laid him very gently on the floor. Bruno hurried over and licked his face.

In the dining room Richard Zampone said, "Hey, who wants another order of Shrimps Charly?" It didn't matter if Pilchard lived or died. He was in the hands of the law. The money? Win some, lose some. He'd call Bernice, meet her in Chicago tomorrow, then they'd fly on to Vegas. Martin was already in Florida. Ricky wouldn't be sorry to leave Van Buren County.

The waiters were bustling about the dining room, taking drinks orders and refilling bread baskets and plates of butter and crocks of mushroom spread. Elton said to Maurice, Arpati, and Zampone, "You can wait an hour or two for more food, gentlemen, or you can

215

order dessert. The kitchen hasn't gotten back to normal, yet."

Arthur and Richard ordered the very rich chocolate cake with mango-almond sorbet. Maurice said he'd make do with a fourth martini.

# A FINANCIER'S ASSETS ARE FROZEN

IT WAS LATE SATURDAY NIGHT. THE CUSTOMERS HAD departed. The food had been put away, but Charly had one last task.

Using the small-sized Hobart mixer, Charly poured into its bowl whole wheat flour, powdered kelp, olive oil, water, oatmeal.

"Bruno's biscuits?" Benny called. He, Julius and Joe were ready to leave.

"Yes," Charly said. "I will refrigerate the mixture and tomorrow morning I will roll the dough into balls and bake them."

"You feel okay?"

After he'd been revived, Charly had insisted on carrying on until the last digestif had been served. "John Stark tell me that Fabulous Food dump poisoned shrimp in the river. They will be analyzed. Stark believes that the owners may go to jail for killing Mr. Herman."

Benny said, "Arthur says he loves Van Buren County and may buy a restaurant here when things quiet down. He says Fabulous Foods was doomed from the start, with those crooks for owners and it being a money laundry, and all. He also says you're the best chef he's ever come across."

"He present the good appearance, but I do not think

216

Monsieur Arpati is an honest man," Charly said. "And Chief Stark, he tell me that the Department of Health will probably close down Fabulous Food next week."

"Fabulous Foods is all but gone," Julius agreed. "But it'll reopen under another name, in another state. Scungilli and Zampone are slippery customers; they've been in the business for a long time."

"Indeed," Charly agreed.

Julius continued. "Richard Zampone asked me if I thought Everston Pilchard would go to jail. I said, more likely a mental institution." Julius didn't mention his phone call to Richard about the two canvas suitcases. He assumed the cops would find them in Everston's garage.

"Monsieur Pilchard, if he lives, will probably sue his doctor, who does not give him the proper medication," Charly said. "And he may even avoid being punished, if a clever and expensive lawyer can prove he is crazy. Such men are freed by costly lawyers while poor men rot in jail."

"What happened to Maurice?" Julius asked.

"Tommy Glade tell me Maurice is drinking again. In all of the excitement I forget entirely about Maurice."

Nobody knew what had happened to Maurice.

Maurice, quite dazed after his four martinis, had left La Fermette during all of the excitement and trudged home to bed. It was a half mile walk, but it didn't clear his head. He was numb with gin, and in his confused mind he imagined that he alone could save Fabulous Foods. Richard Zampone was glum; Arthur Arpati was grim; Martin Scungilli was in Florida. Therefore, Maurice figured, it was up to him to save the company that he had invested so heavily in. He didn't realize that the

Health Department would probably shut the factory down, that Fabulous Foods was already dead.

As he lay in bed half-awake at half past one Sunday morning, still inebriated, Maurice figured that the only way to save Fabulous Foods was to turn out some really fabulous food—and despite his kitchen disasters, he knew that he could do it. He slept for a bit, then woke again.

Maurice squinted at his watch and pressed the little knob that made it glow in the dark: half past four. *If I were in Paris, Les Halles would be busy, now,* he thought of the huge French wholesale market where Parisian restaurateurs and chefs used to go for their food before the decidedly unromantic Rungis market took over on the outskirts of Paris. After stocking up in Les Halles, the men would stop in a bar for a *coup de blanc,* a shot of white wine, and then continue to their respective restaurants.

"That's what I need," Maurice thought, "A *coup de blanc.*" He tiptoed down to the kitchen and found, in the refrigerator, a very nice Pouilly Fumé. After two *coups de blanc* Maurice decided to get dressed and drive up to Fabulous Foods. He left a cryptic note for Barbara in the kitchen, "Gone to New York to do research"—he didn't want to be bothered while he created.

It was still dark out as Maurice drove up Route 33 to Sharpsville. Fabulous Foods, too, was dark, early Sunday morning. Maurice parked in a disused tractor shed—didn't want anyone to see his car. He went to the test kitchen door. Locked. He kicked at the flimsy door. It flew open.

Maurice felt on top of the world. He turned on the lights and went through the doorway to the big

218

preparation area where Arthur's test recipes were combined and cooked in huge vats, packaged, and flash-frozen. The vast room had white-tiled walls, a cement floor that sloped toward a central drain. The stainless-steel work areas all had sinks and hoses, with duckboards underfoot. There was a colossal tub filled with colorless liquid, three large tilting frying pans suitable for cooking several dozen gallons of sauce, and two steam jacketed kettles.

Toward the back of the room were the long machines used for boxing, sealing, and labeling the product. A conveyor belt led directly from the machines into a freezing room, now closed, where, Richard had told Maurice, the product cooled to below zero in a matter of minutes. Maurice poked around, opening a broom closet (filled with mops and brooms and buckets, not surprisingly) and glancing in the drawers of a desk—order and requisition forms, quantity recipe cards, two chef's knives, a dirty apron wadded up.

Maurice felt awed in this huge room with its institutional equipment. He returned to Arthur's small test kitchen. In the refrigerator he found a bowl of shrimp, already peeled and deveined, but still raw. There were bowls of chopped garlic, chopped parsley, chopped pimentos. Maurice found the olive oil, and the small saucepans. There was no stopping him now.

He envisioned himself at the stove, stirring a sauce, when Arpati would walk in. Maurice would invite him to taste, and Arthur would cry, "Oh, this is sensational, Maurice. You make the best food I've ever tasted."

Start small. Maurice heated olive oil in a saucepan and when it was hot he spooned in chopped garlic and parsley. Then he added a two-cup measure of shrimp. He stirred the mixture until the shrimp turned pink, then he took it off the stove. When it had cooled, Maurice tasted.

It was wonderful. How could this be? He'd followed those complicated recipes and created inedible junk. But this was a really fine dish. Maurice couldn't believe his good fortune. Was this just beginner's luck?

Jubilantly, he sat in the comfortable swivel chair at the desk and began reading the recipe cards. Ten gallons of Crab Bisque, for instance, called for ten pounds of crabmeat, thirty pounds of crab carcasses, one quart each of onions and celery, three quarts of roux . . . Seafood Alla Portofino, ten gallons, two hundred portions, called for twenty pounds each of sea scallops, shrimp, king crabmeat, langostinos, and so on. It boggled the mind. And, Arthur had stressed, this was a small operation. Tiny, compared to the behemoth food factories, rife in the American food-service industry, that turn out millions of pounds of value-added product hourly.

"Ah-ha, and what is this?" Maurice murmured, glancing in another drawer. He couldn't believe his good fortune: a bottle of Boodles gin, almost full. Chilled, it would be splendid. He'd pour the tiniest sip as a celebration. He was beginning his culinary odyssey. Surely this called for a toast. Arthur would have ice cubes in the test kitchen fridge.

But the refrigerator freezer was filled with containers of sauce and bags of shrimp. Not an ice cube in sight, though Maurice did find a heavy crystal tumbler, nicely frosted. He poured a finger of gin into the glass. Tasted. Made a face. The gin was warm. No, no, he must have ice. Maurice felt the perspiration trickling down his back. Hot work, this cooking biz.

What about the subzero freezing room? He could

220

leave the bottle of gin in there for a few minutes; it would chill nicely. He carried the bottle and his tumbler to the freezer room. The door wasn't locked. It opened onto a world of frost and winter.

Maurice found the light switch, turned it on, then he went inside. The pneumatic door whooshed softly behind him, and for a moment he felt panic. Had he locked himself in? He pushed at the door and it opened immediately, which reassured him.

The freezer room was filled with enormous plastic bags and wooden crates. The cool felt blissful after the stuffy test kitchen. Maurice placed the gin bottle on the floor, strolled around the room, and sipped at his warm gin. It tasted much better in the cold room. He finished the contents of the tumbler, and poured out another measure.

Now, Maurice visualized himself sitting in his Fabulous Foods office. Pin-striped suit, Hermès tie, his cheeks tingling with Givenchy's Monsieur cologne, talking on the telephone, issuing commands, receiving orders, planning trips to Brittany for French seafood, to Marseille for Mediterranean crustaceans, calling the concierge in Paris to make sure his pied à terre was aired and cleaned for a forthcoming visit.

He sat on the floor with his tumbler and poured some more. "Maurice, you're brilliant," Arthur would exclaim, as Maurice (modestly) would divulge a culinary tip. "Morrie, you're a fuckin' genius," Richard Zampone would cry, as Maurice concluded a four-million-dollar deal with a huge chain of Italian restaurants. He could do it. He knew he could. And think how proud Barbara would be. She'd introduce him as "my husband the financier," ever a dream of his. He'd been calling himself a financier for years, less than accurately. This time, it would be true.

The freezing cold felt warm to Maurice as he sat on the floor, the nearly empty bottle of Boodles beside him. And though his plump body had started to turn blue, his mind was racing and his tumbler was always full. He sipped and dreamed . . . and dozed. The cold crept down to his toes, his fingertips, it spread through his internal organs which, well below 95° Fahrenheit, were shutting down, paralyzed by the extreme temperature. He was in the last stages of hypothermia.

Finally, Maurice's heart stopped. He had been dreaming of freezer rooms filled with gold coins, and golden shrimp, and golden cars and riches beyond measure.

# BRUNO'S DOG BISCUITS

## Yield: about 3 dozen

2 pounds whole wheat flour
2 tablespoons powdered kelp
1 cup raw oatmeal (rolled oats)
½ cup olive oil
2 cups water or more

Preheat oven to 300°. Dump all ingredients into large electric mixer (or mix by hand) adding 2 cups water, then, if needed, more water, just enough to make a stiff dough. When well mixed form into balls and place on ungreased cookie sheets. Bake 1½–2 hours, until they are very hard.

# AFTERMATH

ARTHUR ARPATI FOUND MAURICE'S BODY MONDAY morning. He'd arrived in his test kitchen at eight, in sheets of rain, noted the broken lock but decided not to call the cops. Kids, no doubt. Richard could handle it.

He immediately started cooking. After the sauce was made to his satisfaction he sat down with the recipe and multiplied it by two hundred. Richard had a tasting at noon, then Arthur was driving to New York City. Things were closing down up here, and Arthur didn't plan on being around.

By chance, Arthur went into the big processing room to get a box of order forms. He glanced across the room and noticed that the red light above the sub-zero freezer-room door was lit, indicating that the lights were on inside. He opened the door. And saw Maurice's body, rigid with frost.

"Oh, shit," Arthur said.

He ran back to the test kitchen, picked up his telephone, and dialed 911. If his bosses had done Maurice, tough nuts. He wouldn't be here to answer for it. Little change of plans. He next dialed 011-33, the international code for France, then an eight-digit number.

"Hello, Antoine? Yeah, you had a good lunch? Terrific. It's raining here, too. Listen, could you put me up for a few days? I'll phone later with an arrival time. I'm leaving as soon as I put down the phone. And listen, bring the *camionette*. I'll have quite a bit of luggage. Yeah, all my clothes. Plus two heavy canvas suitcases . . ."

❊❊❊

224

Charly knew exactly what to do on a chilly, rainy Monday morning. You made vegetable soup. He cleaned and chopped leeks, carrots, parsnips, onions, garlic and sautéed the vegetables in olive oil and butter. There was a knock on the kitchen door, and Charly called, "Who is it?"

"It's me, Benny. I'm on my way to the gym, but I wondered if there'd been any word on Maurice."

"No word. Barbara says he is drinking again, and he left a note saying he was going to New York City. The police have been alerted, both here and there. She thinks he may be in jail, somewhere. Here, try this soup."

"Salt and butter, that's all it needs," Benny said. "It's yummy."

"And also, little fresh dill," Charly said. "The French rarely use dill, but it grows well in my garden. The Americans, they love dill." Charly added a big pinch of sea salt and an "egg" of butter. While the soup was being brought to the boil, Charly chopped a handful of dill, and when the soup was steaming he turned off the heat and threw in the dill. Again they tasted and pronounced the soup excellent. Charly felt that it was time for a lecture.

"Dill, which in French is called *aneth*, is not much used as a culinary herb, at least not in my region of the Franche-Comté. I have seen it growing wild on the sides of the roads in Provence, great fields of *aneth,* but Provençal cooking does not use it either. They call it 'false anise.' Provençal cooking does use anise and fennel, but not dill. I find that strange because to my mind dill marries much better with other ingredients than do anise and fennel, which are harsh and can be bitter. Dill has a gentle taste."

Benny felt he should make a remark of a culinary

225

nature. "A big handful of dill folded into cannelini beans with garlic and parsley makes it taste rich. Mom makes dill pickle at the end of the summer—they're great."

Charly said, "Joe Okun tells me his grandmother used wild dill seeds for upset stomachs. He says they did not get many upset stomachs because they were always hungry, never had enough in their stomachs to upset it."

The telephone rang. John Stark. He spoke for a few minutes, and Benny watched Charly's shoulders slump and his face drain of color. He said, "Yes" and "I will" and "I see." When Charly hung up the phone, Benny grabbed his shoulders and steered him to a chair. The news was clearly bad.

"What is it, Charly?"

"The body of Maurice has been found at Fabulous Food, and I must go down to the hospital and identify the body. Barbara is too upset."

Charly felt a sense of déjà vu. Maurice's father came to mind. Another ending. There seemed to be more and more of them.

Benny thought, *The hell with the gym.* "Come on, Charly, I'll drive your van. You're in no state to go alone."

Silently, Benny got behind the wheel, and Charly got into the passenger seat. Silently, they drove to the morgue, in the basement of the Van Buren County Hospital.

In the hospital parking lot Benny spoke. "I'll wait here, Charly. You won't be long." Benny laid his hand on Charly's arm, and Charly, eyes straight ahead, clasped the hand. "You are like a son to me," he said.

"And you're like a dad to me," Benny said. They smiled.

Charly felt that he was moving underwater, blindly

226

swimming down the hospital corridor. He felt without weight, without substance. Stark met Charly and took his arm, leading the little man to the basement. "I know this is tough for you, Charly."

Charly nodded, but said nothing. Years later, he would remember nothing of the long walk down a hospital corridor with its stench of formalin and Lysol. But he'd always remember the look on Maurice's face. Maurice was smiling, yet his forehead was furrowed, as though death had caught him in the middle of a weighty thought. Charly sniffed. He could smell alcohol. Even in death Maurice, starting to defrost, smelled like a drunk. Just like—God rest his soul—his father Maurice Senior.

"*Au revoir, Maurice*," Charly said to the corpse. The attendant gently replaced the sheet. Again Stark took Charly's arm.

"We'll go now, Charly."

"Yes, John."

Stark propelled Charly to his van. "I went over and told Barbara. She said she couldn't face identifying the body. I hope you don't mind."

"Of course not, John. I have known Maurice since he was a little boy."

"And I said you'd go straight to her house. Was that right?"

Charly nodded. "Benny will drive me now. Do you think Maurice was murdered by Arpati and Scungilli and Zampone?"

"I doubt it. They wouldn't kill him and just leave him there. They'd dump him in the river. But they must be questioned. We've got an APB out on them now, but they seem to have skipped town. Never mind, sooner or later, we'll find 'em."

Barbara said, "John doesn't think Maurice was murdered. Those thugs are so upset over Billy Herman's death, they'd never kill Maurice and leave him at their factory. They're dumb, but too smart for that."

Charly nodded. "I agree. What was in Maurice's mind?"

"He was trying to kill himself, wasn't he, Charly?"

"I do not think so. I believe it was an accident. The State Police told John Stark there were no locks on the walk-in freezer, that Maurice could have walked out at any time. But do not forget, he was paralyzed by alcohol."

"Mummy said she'd be right over. I hadn't even seen Maurice for almost two days," Barbara said. "He'd left a note saying he was going to New York. Which was a lie. He'd become totally involved with that company."

"I did not like Maurice, I make no secret," Charly said, "but I am sorry that he is dead. You and Maurice had been together for how many year?"

"Seventeen. Oh, Charly, I was bowled over by Maurice, at first. He'd been to a smart university, he was French, and he talked about Paris as if it were just around the corner: somewhere to pop over to. He told me he owned a restaurant, that he had a fortune in stocks. All lies."

"There was no malice in Maurice," Charly said. "Always, filled with good cheer. Always, he make his fortune tomorrow."

"Of course," Barbara said bitterly. "He was a double Leo."

There was a screeching of brakes outside and soon the doorknob rattled. Martha De Groot, Barbara's mother, whirled in like a tiny tornado, nearly bent double by the freight she carried. Charly could see the necks of several champagne bottles sticking out of a black shopping bag. Suddenly, the living room was filled with the scent of Guelain's L'Heure Bleu.

"Barbara," Martha said. Barbara got up, went to her tiny mother, and folded her into her arms. Only then did Barbara begin to weep. Charly tiptoed from the room. Martha De Groot had organized a successful antiques business, she'd organized antiques shows and decorator-showcases and the funerals of several husbands. Now she could organize the funeral of her son-in-law. It would be, Charly knew, a grand occasion.

# A SPLENDID FUNERAL LUNCH

CHARLY CLOSED LA FERMETTE TO THE PUBLIC MIDDAY Thursday, when the funeral lunch for Maurice would take place. Julius and Benny and Joe Okun would be in the kitchen as usual, and he had an abundance of waitstaff.

"Since it is a catered event, Max and Fred could come in and we could get a dishwasher," Charly told them. "You do not want to work two full shifts." But Benny, Julius, and Joe insisted. So did Charly's waiters. Even though Maurice had insulted and belittled every one of them, they still wanted to give him a grand send-off.

"Who's Martha De Groot inviting?" Benny asked Julius.

"*Le tout* Van Buren County." Julius grinned. "All the blue bloods, plus friends and relatives. Barbara's letting her organize everything."

Barbara's mother, who had loathed the live Maurice, now transformed Maurice, defunct, into a social icon whose passing must be honored with the greatest of fanfare.

Charly smiled bleakly. "One time Brad Greenpeace, the undertaker, say to me, 'when they truly hate the deceased, they spend the most money on his funeral.' I see now that is true."

Charly had suggested a subdued, tasteful menu: celeri remoulade, shrimp and scallop *vol-au-vent,* roast duckling, but Martha De Groot said, "I don't get to bury a son-in-law every day, now, do I?"

The menu was revised: every pretentious dish in the French gastronomic repertoire would be represented: fresh foie gras *en gelée* with chilled *vin de paille* from the Franche-Comté; lobster and sweetbread ragout in champagne sauce with Veuve Clicquot; roast pheasant served at room temperature with a salad of baby greens, irrigated by Vosne Romanee Les Suchots; and Patty Perkins's celebrated almond cake, served with hot chocolate sauce, fresh raspberries, and more champagne.

"She should invite the thugs from Fabulous Foods, it's their kind of grub," said Julius. "But I'm sure they're far, far away."

Indeed, Charly heard via the grapevine at Steak Heaven that the police were luckless in their hunt for Arpati, Scungilli, and Zampone.

As Honoria said later, it was a lunch to remember, as you staggered home and swigged down your Alka-Seltzer.

Who were the guests? Win Crozier and Morty Cohen; Billy and Midge Warburton; Honoria Wells and Tiger Cavett; an army of Martha's relations and friends; Barbara's lawyer Jonathan Murray and his wife; Barbara's investment adviser Jimmy Houghton and

Evelyn Holmes; Father Evangelista, who had conducted a beautiful high funeral mass with a ton of incense; and, as Benny said, a hell of a lot of snooty people.

Charly, surveying the festive scene from the swinging doors to the kitchen, felt that it was time to put in an appearance. The main course had been cleared away and desserts were about to be served. Barbara, or rather Martha, had specified "no speeches," and the conversation was general—what Win and Morty would do on their trip to France; the best places to go for leather goods in Rome; what the Crisps should bring back from their round-the-world cruise . . . the talk of moneyed people who know how to indulge themselves. No one liked Maurice, but he had been one of them. Fears of their own deaths, always a common denominator at funerals, receded in a swirl of chitchat, good food, and rivers of champagne.

Charly exchanged his soiled jacket for a fresh one and plopped his tall white toque on his head. Examined himself in the mirror, smoothed his pencil mustache, patted down his very black hair. Dropped four drops of Dr. Bach's formula on his tongue. He must look properly solicitous, yet jolly.

As he stared into the cloudy mirror, Charly imagined that he saw Maurice and his father, both smiling. He also thought he could see his long-dead wife Claudine holding their infant son, who may have been reincarnated into the body of Benny Perkins; his father, Papa Jean, and his aunt, Tante Jeanne. The ghosts, if that's what they were, faded away.

"You want me to keep the guests out of the kitchen, Charly?" Julius asked. All afternoon, people had been wandering back and forth from kitchen to dining room, as if this were a casual house party.

231

"No, let them be," Charly said. "It make for the nice atmosphere."

The lobster and sweetbreads were perfect, he wouldn't change an item in the recipe. Or maybe he would: a puree of roasted garlic would add richness, it was something to try. The foie gras was tender, but perhaps next time he should add a tad more madeira and serve the delicacy on a puree of leek whites, instead of the jelly he'd used today. The salad dressing needed more mustard. Ah, matters of such importance to Charly Poisson.

Soon the funeral lunch would be over, the cleaners would come in and ready the dining room for dinner. He and Julius and Benny and Joe would continue cooking. It was a good life, yet it wasn't the life for Maurice. That benighted individual believed he was destined for something grander.

Charly mourned the man Maurice could have been, but was not. Always thinking of money. To impress whom? Whoever was impressed by wealth, Charly sniffed, wasn't worth cultivating.

Father Evangelista had wandered into the kitchen, picked up a piece of almond cake, commented on the grand food, and wandered out again. Charly hoped that Maurice, wherever he was, was finally at peace. He arranged his face into a crooked little smile, meant to convey happiness and sadness at the same time. Then he went out to his dining room.

Charly was back in the kitchen with his crew, putting food away, and most of the guests were still finishing their coffee and brandy, when John Stark knocked on the kitchen door.

"I won't keep you Charly, I know you're busy. But

since you discovered Harry Clark's body, I know you'd be interested in who killed him. Everston Pilchard is out of intensive care, we were able to question him in the hospital. Everston has confessed to Harry Clark's murder."

Charly was thunderstruck. "Pilchard the killer? *Tiens.* It must have been an accident, he is so clumsy. Do you believe him, Chief Stark?"

Stark said, "Well, I don't know what to think. Everston also confessed to killing John Kennedy, Marilyn Monroe, J. Paul Getty, Ngo Dinh Diem, oh, a whole bunch of people, many of whom died before he was born."

Neither Stark nor Charly noticed that the swinging doors had pushed open, and Billy and Midge Warburton were standing just inside the kitchen. They had come in to congratulate Charly on his spectacular lunch, and had overheard the chief of police.

Billy cleared his throat, and Stark and Charly looked over.

"Everston Pilchard didn't kill him, Chief Stark. I killed Harry Clark."

# THE TRUTH, AT LAST

MIDGE WARBURTON INTERRUPTED. "NO, CHIEF STARK, I killed Harry Clark."

Billy said, "We both killed Harry Clark."

There was dead silence in the kitchen. Finally, Stark spoke.

"Why?"

Charly, wisely, said nothing.

Stark looked inscrutable: how many people were now

going to confess to the killing of Harry Clark?

"Why don't we all go down to the station and I'll take your confessions in an orderly manner."

"That's agreeable," said Billy Warburton. "But Charly should know, too, since we dumped the body in his pond. We didn't know it was your pond, Charly. That acreage used to be the old Woodcock farm. We didn't know you'd bought all that land."

Charly, sensing Stark's disapproval, again kept his mouth shut.

It was not a long story. Midge Warburton told the first part.

"We caught Harry Clark late one night last winter at our house. We'd been out to dinner at the house of friends, and returned to see Harry sneaking out our back door. He hadn't noticed us driving up. Harry's pockets were bulging—stuffed with my jewelry, we later discovered. He was carrying the Degas ballerina."

"I don't know exactly what happened," Billy Warburton continued. "I saw the Degas, which we adore, and I went wild. To me, it was like stealing our child. I grabbed the ballerina and hung on for dear life. Midge was screaming. It was icy underfoot, and Harry and I slipped."

Midge took up the story. "They both fell on the ice, and were struggling on the ground. Harry dropped the statue, and it rolled over to me. I grabbed the ballerina and hit Harry on the head. He released Billy, who got up, took the sculpture from me, and hit Harry on the head, too. We thought we'd just stunned him and were going to call the police."

"It was a heavy little sculpture," Charly said, recalling the dent in the ballerina's head.

"But Harry didn't move," Billy went on, "and he looked, well, awful. We dragged him into the kitchen. We couldn't feel a pulse. He'd—uh—soiled his pants, and his eyes were open. He was clearly dead."

"We both panicked," Midge continued. "Our first, our only thought was to get him out of our house. Now, looking back on it, I can see how ill-advised that was. But at that moment, we both felt the same: get him away from the house and have him found elsewhere."

"Why didn't you call me?" Stark asked. "It sounds like self-defense. I'm sure you'd never have gone to jail."

Billy said, "We'd just been reading that story about the intruder shot by the farmer in England. The farmer's house had been broken into before, and the police hadn't given him much protection. This time the farmer shot the thief, and a jury convicted him of murder. He was sent away for life."

Midge said, "In fact, we'd been talking about that very case at dinner that night, since the people we'd dined with live in an isolated area, too. So imagine our absolute terror when, with that story on our minds, we drove up to our house and saw a pickup truck parked by the back door, and Harry Clark coming out of our house. Harry had worked for us years before, and later, we heard about Honoria. We knew what a horrible person he was."

"The only thing we could think of was to get Harry away. We picked him up and dumped him into the back of his truck, which was right by the back door." Billy smiled grimly. "It was too easy. The keys were even in the ignition. He had a tarp in the bed of the truck, so we covered him with that."

Midge continued. "We remembered that old pond,

and Billy drove over there. I followed in our four-wheel drive. We drove across the field, dragged Harry out, and dumped him in the pond, which hadn't frozen over yet. We figured he'd sink to the bottom, the pond would freeze, and by spring he would have sunk into the muddy bottom."

"What happened to his truck?" Stark questioned.

"We knew where he lived, an apartment in a bad part of Hogton," Billy said. "We left the truck parked in front, with the keys in the ignition. We figured one of the Hogton drug dealers would simply steal it."

Midge said, "We've been living with this horrible secret for months, and finally, we decided we couldn't live with it any longer. We were going to tell you, John, but we hadn't gotten up our courage quite yet."

"The Bach flowers," Charly murmured. "The bringers of truth."

"What, Charly?" Stark asked.

"Oh, nothing. *Rien du tout.* I am talking to myself again."

"But then," Billy said, "when we overheard you just now saying that Everston had confessed, we couldn't let him take the blame. He's a foolish young man, perhaps even mildly demented, but he never killed Harry."

Midge said, "We knew Everston's parents. They worried so much about Everston. He was terribly intelligent, but he couldn't deal with normal life. He lived in another world."

"But he wasn't a cold-blooded killer," Billy finished up. "And neither are we. John, we've said our piece. You can take us in, now."

The guests were gone. The dining room had been cleared for tonight's dinner service. Charly and his crew had a fresh batch of food under way. The men and Patty had been working solidly since eight that morning, so Charly made everyone sit down at five for a big dinner. Earlier, he'd hurried to his house to feed Bruno and the cats, but he returned immediately.

"Thank you, Benny, Julius, Joe, Patty, Elton, Sam, Hubert, Tommy, for giving Maurice such a fine farewell."

"He was the kind of person I never want to be," Joe said.

"Hear, hear," said Julius.

"Hear, hear," chorused the staff.

"Is a small group tonight," said Charly. "With luck, we can finish early. Push the meat loaf with mushroom gravy and mashed potatoes."

"There's extra almond cake," Patty said. "Why not offer it as a special?"

"What'll happen to the Warburtons?" Benny asked.

"Not much, in all probability," Charly said. "Their lawyer will plead self-defense. And that is what it was. They are elderly. Harry Clark was a young, strong man. For him to attack two old people was the act of a coward."

"And Fabulous Foods?" asked Tommy Glade.

"Gone," Charly said. "We will never know if Zampone and Scungilli and Arpati had anything to do with Maurice's death. They have disappeared. But like the bad penny, they will turn up again, I am convince."

Benny cleared his throat. "Uh, Charly?"

"*Oui*, Benny?"

"Arthur Arpati called me last night from Paris, said he'd wire money for me to fly over. Said he was opening up a restaurant over there, he needed a good chef, and the French chefs were all too snooty for him."

Charly drew in his breath. "And you said . . ."

Benny laughed. "Well I said thanks but no thanks, of course."

"Benny, we need you here, in La Fermette's kitchen," Julius said. "And Charly, you nearly got yourself killed. That bullet of Everston's went wild, it could have plowed into you just as easy as not."

"Yes," Charly said. "When the bullet is fired, that is to say, when danger is thrown out into the world, many innocent people are hurt."

"Please don't get involved with any more criminals."

"Of course not, Julius. I never involve myself with criminals. They involve themselves with me. There is a difference. Benny, could you please begin slicing the meat loaf? And Julius, could you sauté the spinach with garlic and pine nuts? The dinner service is about to begin."

Dear Reader:

I hope you enjoyed reading this Large Print book. If you are interested in reading other Beeler Large Print titles, ask your librarian or write to me at

Thomas T. Beeler, Publisher
Post Office Box 659
Hampton Falls, New Hampshire 03844

You can also call me at 1-800-818-7574 and I will send you my latest catalogue.

Audrey Lesko and I choose the titles I publish in Large Print. Our aim is to provide good books by outstanding authors—books we both enjoyed reading and liked well enough to want to share. We warmly welcome any suggestions for new titles and authors.

Sincerely,